The Principal

David Abraham

The Principal is fiction. None of the characters, businesses, organizations, places, or names are true and are solely the product of the author's imagination. None of the characters are intended to resemble actual people, either alive or dead. The characters' activities are likewise fictional and solely the product of the author's imagination. All of the circumstances, events, and occurrences mentioned in the book are fiction. Any resemblance between the fictional narrative and reality is purely coincidental.

Second edition
Copyright ©2017 David Abraham
Printed in the United States of America
All rights reserved
Book-broker Publishers of Florida
Port Charlotte, FL 33980
ISBN:-978-1-945690-18-1

ABOUT THE AUTHOR

David Abraham is the author of 12 other novels, two musicals and a comedy. Novels include *Thy Father's Seed, Flight from Alberobello, Love and Promise, The Principal, Bawdy Town, Tainted Justice, Aaron Burr, Adventurer; Black River, Dark Days of Florida, The Womanizer, Papal Sins, Harriet Tubman: A Passion for Freedom,* and *Florida Cowcatchers and Outlaws.*

Bawdy Town the musical has 22 original songs. The comedy version is titled *Sin City.*

In addition to writing, David is an actor and director with the Charlotte Players in Port Charlotte, Florida.

He has a B.A. from Syracuse University and an M.A. from the University of Idaho. He has been an educator for over fifty years and is the CEO of School Evaluators, an educational review company.

David is a resident of Florida and spends most of his time in Lake Suzy, Florida. Summers are spent in New Hartford, New York.

Chapter 1

THE 747 JUMBO JET sliced through the silent time zones on its way from Spokane, Washington to Kennedy International. James Rahin was taking the second step in his quest to become a school superintendent. The first had been when he obtained a master's degree in school administration.

As the plane gobbled up time and distance Mother Nature began painting broad strokes of red, yellow and orange onto a blue-black heavenly canvas. Watching the arrival of a new day had always been one of Jim's favorite things to do, but this was the first time he had witnessed that great wonder from the air.

When the jet reached Kennedy and taxied to the terminal, Jim disembarked onto the hot tarmac. He dashed toward an opened door and quickly entered the lower level of the building. A group of young women waiting inside the customer's lounge smiled as he passed. Jim returned the smile and nodded hello.

Jim looked tan and fit in his light blue suit as he passed the throngs of people waiting in the lounge. While his football days were behind him, at five feet ten inches tall and a hundred and ninety pounds, he could still carry the pigskin if he had to.

Beyond the pretty faces Jim noticed a man holding a sign that read: MR. RAHIMS. The man was dressed in gray coveralls with South Hudson Valley Central School emblazoned in red script over a chest-high pocket.

Jim frowned. That's a hell of a way to start off an interview. They don't even have my name right. He approached the man and asked, "Are you waiting for someone scheduled for a job interview at South Hudson Valley Central High School?"

"Yeah—are you Mr. Rahims?"

In a hesitant voice Jim replied, "No, I'm Mr. Ra-HIN. I'm scheduled for an interview with Ms. Andrews, the school's personnel director."

Jim's brusque reply caught the man unaware. His face colored as his voice cracked, "Excuse me, Mr. Rahin, I thought they said Rahims. I guess I heard wrong."

"That's okay, Mr...."

"Strong—Charlie Strong. I'm the head custodian."

"Well, Charlie, the only bag I have is this carry-on." Jim handed the small duffle bag to the custodian and motioned for him to lead the way.

Outside the terminal the pungent exhaust hit Jim like an angry man' bad breath. He waved his hand in front of his nose in an attempt to dispel the odor. Turning to Strong, he yelled, "Where to?"

Strong set the bag down and coughed. "I'll be back in a minute."

Charlie crossed the pick-up zone and disappeared among the swarms of other people scurrying off in a multitude of directions with and without baggage.

Jim watched as people big and small, short and tall, hailed taxies, hugged relatives, and kissed loved ones. He pulled out his watch and reset the time.

A few minutes later a horn blast directed Jim's attention to a 1963 Ford station wagon with imitation wood siding; it was Charlie.

Jim threw the duffle bag onto the back seat and slid into the passenger's side next to Strong. The leather seat was uncomfortably hot. He rolled down the window and glanced at the dashboard clock.

"How far is it to the school? I'm running a little late."

"I'll radio ahead and ask the garage to notify Ms. Andrews that you're on your way."

"Thanks."

Charlie picked up the hand mic, flipped a switch, and barked, "Car one, calling base; car one, calling base. Do you copy?"

A voice crackled over the radio. "Go ahead, car one."

"George, this is Charlie. I just picked up Mr. Rahin. His plane was late getting to the terminal. Please notify Ms. Andrews' office that he may be a tad late for the interview."

"Ten-four. Base over and out."

"Roger, over and out." Charlie smiled and hung up. "Ms. Andrews will be notified, but I think I can still get you there on time."

"How long have you been with the district?" Jim asked.

Charlie took a moment before answering, as if he were running the years through a calculator. "Ohhh, 'bout twenty years I guess, give or take."

"You must like the job. Twenty years is a long time."

"Yeah, it's been okay. Some years were better than others. It all depends on who's in charge. I've watched superintendents come and go. Some have been real good to work for and others," his voice went to a low murmur, "well, you know how it is." He grinned. "I started as a cleaner in one of the elementary buildings and worked my way up."

Jim studied the man and guessed that he had to be in his fifties. Strong was of medium build, balding with penetrating steel-blue eyes set between a hawk nose. His weathered complexion and hard body served witness that he had spent his working hours out of doors.

"You live around here?" Jim asked.

"Nah, it's too expensive. I have a place about an hour north of the district. Aside from the cost of rent being too high here, I didn't like the idea of my kids going to the same school where I worked."

Jim understood the logic. I wouldn't want my kids going to the same school where I was an administrator, he thought.

The remainder of the trip was made in silence as the landscape blended into a collage of middleclass neighborhood houses, automobiles, trees and people. About forty minutes into the ride the wagon swung left and entered a circular driveway. It stopped in front of a large brick building. Brass letters on the red brick background read: SOUTH HUDSON VALLEY SCHOOL DISTRICT ADMINISTRATION BUILDING.

Jim left the car, grabbed his bag from the back, and barked, "Thanks, Charlie, you're a good man."

Charlie Strong smiled, and pointed toward the entrance. "The office you want is the second door on the left. Good luck." He gave Jim a quick thumbs-up and promptly drove off.

Jim passed some flowering bushes and waved off some bees collecting nectar. He entered the building through a set of glass doors and proceeded down a bright beige hall. He passed a door with no markings and stopped when he saw a door marked, PERSONNEL DIRECTOR. Upon entering the office he noticed a woman seated behind a grey-metal desk. A sign on the desk was printed in bold silver letters etched onto a black background:

JEAN WALLACE, SECRETARY.

When the woman saw Jim, she stood.

"May I help you?" she politely asked. Her dark hair was streaked with strands of grey. The secretary peered through a pair of plastic-rimmed glasses with rhinestone across the top. The rest of her attire was dull and matronly. As she walked toward him the woman brushed a strand of hair away from her face. Jim noticed that there wasn't a wedding ring on her left hand.

School is probably her whole life, he thought. He flashed a wide smile and said, "Would you please inform Ms. Andrews that Mr. Rahin is here."

"Oh yes, Ms. Andrews is expecting you. I'm Jean Wallace, Ms. Andrews's secretary." Jim nodded. Ms. Wallace smiled and disappeared behind a large door with a frosted glass window. When she returned she announced, "You may go in Mr. Rahims." Jim smiled. "Thank you Ms. Wallouse."

"Wallace!" she quickly exclaimed.

Jim snapped his fingers feigning regret. "Oh yes, of course. I'm so sorry. Isn't it annoying when someone mispronounces your name? They do that to me all the time. The name is Rahin—not Rahims"

The secretary's face flushed. "My apology, Mr. Ra-HIN." She made a point of accentuating the second syllable of his name; then vanished into what Jim assumed was an office coffee room.

When he entered the Personnel Director's office Elizabeth Andrews left the comfort of her over-stuffed leather chair and extended a greeting hand.

"Mr. Rahin. How nice to finally meet you. I trust that you had a pleasant flight."

Elizabeth Andrews was not at all what he had expected. He had envisioned an old spinster the size of a walrus with a chronic case of PMS, bad hair, and clothing to match that of her secretary. Instead Ms. Andrews was a very attractive woman in her late twenties—too young he thought to hold such an important position. She was about five feet four with honey-brown hair and eyes the color of melted caramel; her body would make a bulldog chew its chain. Topping off the vivacious vision was an engaging model's smile and an impeccable wardrobe. Ms. Personnel Director seemed to ooze with charm.

Definitely eye candy, Jim thought. I wonder if she has the intelligence to match her looks.

"Have a seat, Mr. Rahin." The director said in a mellifluous voice. After pumping Jim's hand twice she motioned him toward a large, brown chair, one matching her own. "So you're from Idaho?"

When the director sat, Jim relaxed and took a deep breath. The office was bright with white walls adorned with photographs of theatrical shows and the director meeting with various dignitaries—some Jim recognized..

"Well, not exactly" Jim said, readjusting his focus back to his interviewer. "I'm originally from upstate New York. I went to Idaho to attend law school, but after fifteen credits of law I decided being an officer of the court wasn't for me. I switched to graduate school and picked up a master's in school administration."

"Why education?" Andrews asked. She moved forward until her breast gently touched the edge of the desk.

"Well, law school was the goal I started out with, but I ended up teaching three years before applying to law school. In the middle of my third year of teaching I decided that if I didn't go to law school I'd always wonder if I had made the right vocational decision."

"What did you teach before going to Idaho?"

"History."

"Do you think you'll like school administration?"

"I know that I want a career in education. Eventually I'd like to be a superintendent. If I find that I don't like administration, I'll go back into the classroom."

Andrews flashed a patented smile. "This job is for an assistant principal. It is probably the most stressful job in the system, but it will be a step toward your goal and it will certainly be a challenge. The job will let you know whether or not you were cut out to be a superintendent."

The director sat up straight. "Mr. Rahin, we have a school population of twenty-three hundred students. Gang-related problems are the cause of most of our suspensions, but problem students represent less than three percent of the student body. Most of the kids here are good students who just want a chance to amount to something." As an afterthought she added, "We have an excellent faculty."

"Four dozen students can cause an awful lot of disruption to the educational process," Jim interrupted. "How strong has the administration and board been in supporting the decisions of the assistant principal?"

The director's enthusiastic eyes dimmed a little as she fidgeted with a rosary to the right of her desk blotter. There was a significant pause in the conversation before Andrews replied, "I think you should save that question for the high school principal. He is retiring at the end of this school year and, well, I'm sure he will be glad to answer any questions you might have related to student behavior and discipline. Regaining her smile, the director added, "For now, let me show you our school and tell you a little more about the community."

Following a tour of the building Jim was introduced to Albert Reilly, the high school principal. Reilly was a short, ruddy Irishman with white hair, a freckled complexion and a nervous laugh. He hid his eyes behind a pair of dark glasses.

Jim couldn't decide whether he was a boozer, a lobster, or just ill. When the man spoke, there was no doubt. No wonder he's retiring. Jim thought. The guy is a big fan of the bottle.

"I'm pleased to meet you, Mr. Reilly." Jim extended his hand.

Al Reilly rose from the chair with an intended handshake; it never materialized. Only Jim's fingers and those of Reilly's touched as the principal fell unceremoniously back into his chair.

"Nice to meet you, Jim," the man slurred. "Have a seat."

As Jim sat, Elizabeth Andrews handed the principal a folder. Turning to Jim she said, "It's been a pleasure visiting with you, Mr. Rahin. I hope we get to work together in the future." Jim took her hand and squeezed gently.

When Andrews released Jim's hand, she turned to face Reilly; her mood changed.

"Al, let me know about your choice of candidates. I'll have to fill out a recommendation form for the board to act on at their next meeting. It's scheduled for Tuesday." Without further comment Andrews left the room.

Long before the hour with Reilly and the constant odor of cheap booze ended, Jim had made up his mind. He refused to sign the contract in a congenial manner.

Albert Reilly became hot-headed. His went from crimson to purple. He babbled on about Jim wasting the district's time and money. When Jim tried to respond, Reilly ordered him out of his office and off school property. The verbal abuse continued long after Jim had left his office.

Reilly's ranting was still audible as Jim reentered Andrews' office.

Ms. Wallace was on the phone. Upon seeing Jim she pressed the intercom button.

"Ms. Andrews, Mr. Rahin is back."

The door to the personnel director's office opened and Elizabeth Andrews stepped out wearing a broad smile. "Well, are you going to join our team?"

"I don't think so," Jim replied. "I don't believe Mr. Reilly and I got on all that well. He's in a hurry to sign someone and I need a little more time before jumping into a situation that I still have questions about. The long and the short of it is that I need a ride back to the airport."

Andrews's smile faded. "I'm sorry to hear that, Jim. Let me see what I can do for you. Please come in."

7

Jim took a seat as the director dialed a number. "Hello, George, this is Liz. I need someone to drive Mr. Rahin back to the airport." There was a long pause. Andrews' face took on a pinkish glow as her voice became more provocative. "Well how about just taking him to the city?" There was another pause.

Jim sensed that there was a lot more to this attractive blond than sugar and spice. When next she spoke her anger and disdain for Reilly was evident. "Well that's just fine," she scolded. "Mr. Rahin has a right to say no. What kind of message does Reilly think he's sending to other perspective candidates? Well, we'll see about that. I'm going to raise holy hell about this incident. I'm going to write a letter of protest about that drunken son of a bitch and send it to the superintendent with copies to the board."

The director slammed the phone and turned to Jim. She shook her head and forced a fake smile. She loathed Reilly, but her professional integrity would not allow her to express it to a stranger. "I'm sorry Mr. Rahin, but Mr. Reilly has directed that no one is to give you a ride anywhere. You're on your own—I'm truly sorry."

"I guess that about seals the deal," Jim sighed. "I thought Reilly might be an alcoholic. That's why I wanted more time to think about the job. I know now I made the right decision. I'll need to call a cab."

"A taxi will cost you an arm and a leg." Andrews flipped a switch on her intercom. "Jean, what does my schedule look like for the afternoon?" A moment later she shut off the intercom.

"I'll tell you what, Jim," she said. "I'm getting ready to take a lunch break. I need to be back here in a couple of hours for a meeting, but I'll be happy to drive you to the airport or into the city, whichever you prefer. Reilly can't tell me what to do, especially on my own time."

Ms. Andrews, are you sure you don't mind?"

"The only thing I mind is you calling me Ms. Andrews. Please call me Liz.

"Okay, Liz, but I'm buying lunch."

She smiled. "I'll flip you for the bill."

IN THE LITTLE HAMLET OF Mt Ivy Liz stopped at a Ma and Pa diner for lunch. She took out a coin and said, "Heads I buy—tails you buy." She flipped a coin and waited for it to stop spinning after it hit the road. "Heads!" she exclaimed, pointing to the results. "I buy."

Jim shook his head in disapproval. "Okay, but I don't like it. If we ever do this again, I'm buying, no if ands or buts about it."

While consuming an order of chicken salad and black coffee, Liz gave Jim a synopsis of her life extending from high school up to and including her job as personnel director.

After graduating from the University of New York, Liz took the name of Elizabeth Marks and went to New York City where she traveled professionally, playing theaters across the United States. While doing theater she fell in love with a young boxer in New York City and decided to hang up her scripts for more stable employment. She took a job as an English teacher at South Hudson Valley. Within five years she was asked to take the job as the personnel director.

South Hudson Valley had trouble keeping assistant principals because of the principal's alcoholism. The board of education was aware of the problem, but they were unable to dismiss him. Reilly's condition had been classified as "medical" in nature. However, Albert agreed to retire at the end of the school year when he became eligible for his New York State retirement.

When Liz excused herself to attend the ladies room, Jim made a phone call to his brother in New Jersey.

Lisa Rahin, Jim's niece, answered the call. "Hi, Lisa, it's your Uncle Jim. No, I'm in New York. Is your father home?"

There was a long pause.

"Hey bro, what's hap'nin?" Joe Rahin bellowed as he took the phone.

"I flew into New York for an interview," Jim explained. "I thought if you had the time we could drive to Utica together."

"I'd love to go, Jim, but, I need to check with my boss. I'll see if I can get the time off."

Joe was Jim's older brother. Many people took them for twins. Joe had married a girl from New Jersey shortly after leaving the army and was now living in a town south of Philadelphia working as a milkman.

"If you can't get the time off, don't make a big deal about it. I can always rent a car," Jim assured.

"No, I'd like to go. I haven't been back in over a year. Let me call you back."

Jim gave Joe the number listed on the payphone. "I can't wait too long; I have a ride into the city and I don't want to hold her up."

"I'll call you right back."

Jim hung up just as Liz came out of the ladies' room.

"Calling an old flame?" she joked.

"I called my brother to see if he could pick me up."

"He doesn't have to do that," Liz grouched. "I'll take you wherever you want to go."

Jim smiled. If I weren't a married man, he thought, I'd take you up on that.

"I'm planning to go upstate for a couple of days. If my brother can get the time off, he'll go with me."

Liz checked her watch and grinned. "Well, that is a little far for me to go and still get back for my meeting. How long will it be before your brother will know?"

"He said he'd call right ba—" Jim was interrupted by the ring of the phone. "That's probably him now." He picked up the receiver and after a moment uttered, "Uh-huh. Where?" He looked at Liz.

"How far are we from Montebello?"

She thought for a moment. "It's just down the road."

"Good, that's where he'll pick me up. Turning his attention back to Joe, Jim asked, "How long will it take you to get here?" After listening to his brother's response, he added, "Okay, I'll see you then."

Twenty minutes later Liz pulled her Ford Mustang convertible in front of the Montebello Pizza Parlor.

"Well, Jim, I guess this is goodbye. I'm sorry things didn't work out the way they should have. I think you would have been a great addition to our staff."

"Ms. Andry—uh—Liz, I can't tell you how much I appreciate what you have done for me... including lunch. The next time I get to St. Stanislaus for mass I'll light a candle in your honor." They laughed, and shook hands.

Elizabeth Andrews flashed that special smile and flipped Jim a coin. "If you decide to work down-state, give me a call. I might be able to help. With a wave of her hand, she was off.

Jim waved back then looked at the coin. It had George Washington's head on both sides. He smiled and shook his fist in mock anger.

Chapter 2

JOE RAHIN ARRIVED IN MONTEBELLO shortly after four-fifteen in the afternoon. He hadn't changed. He's still a good-looking son of a bitch, Jim thought.

The two brothers had not seen each other in more than three years.

Joe pulled his '62 Plymouth in front of the diner and got out. He took Jim's hand and asked, "You fadda 'ome?"

It was a humorous greeting that the two brothers had shared as boys. They loved to mimic a Lebanese friend who used to visit their father. The man was relatively new to the United States and had some trouble saying, "Is your father home?" They liked the guy and meant him no disrespect, but his stock question became the signature greeting for the two boys whenever they met.

Joe was hungry. After a short conversation about health, work and family the two entered the diner. Joe devoured a meatloaf dinner while Jim enjoyed a piece of apple pie—and two more cups of coffee. Jim knew it would be a five-hour drive to Utica; a little extra caffeine wouldn't hurt.

When the Plymouth rolled into the Rahin family farm driveway it was close to midnight. The house was dark, but the warning bark of Wolf, the family's German shepherd, soon had lights going on everywhere.

Dave Rahin, Jim's father, came to the kitchen door wearing only his boxer shorts. Gina, Jim's mother, was at Dave's side wrapped in a bathrobe. She appeared diminutive next to her husband.

Mrs. Rahin was in her mid-forties. She was still petite and slender with tinted brown hair to color the encroaching grey.

Dave Rahin was six feet tall and brawny. A wild mixture of black and silver hair made him look like he had just stuck his finger into an electric socket.

"Who is it?" Gina asked in a more than curious voice.

"It's Joe and Jim."

"But Jim's in Idaho." Concern shadowed Gina's brow.

"He *was* in Idaho," Dave replied.

By the time the banter between Dave and Gina ended, Jim had taken the stairs two at a time and was standing at their side. He gripped his father's hand and hugged his mother all in one motion.

Joe followed the greeting sequence before the four retired to the kitchen.

Questions flowed quickly with little opportunity for answers.

Finally Jim said, "Mom, make some coffee, and I'll tell you all about it. Suffice it to say I'm coming home. Hope and I plan to go back to teaching."

THE FOLLOWING MORNING Jim borrowed his father's Oldsmobile 98, and drove to Utica to visit his mother-in-law. When he arrived, Mary Goodhines was baking. The kitchen smelled of fresh-baked cookies and boiled coffee.

Mary was wrapped in an apron and covered with flour to her elbows; she looked wide-eyed at her visitor.

"Jim" she blurted, "I thought you were in New York City."

"I was, but I had an opportunity to visit Utica before heading back to Idaho, so here I am."

"It's too bad Hope couldn't come with you," said Mary as she hugged Jim.

"She couldn't get the time off from work," Jim lied. He didn't want to tell his mother-in-law that they couldn't afford the airfare.

"Would you like a cup of coffee?" Mary asked, as she dusted the white from her hands. "I just baked some chocolate chip cookies. I'll send the well-done ones back with you. I know how much Hope likes her cookies a little burnt." Mary took a tray of cookies out of the oven and placed it on top of the stove. She placed the hot pads on the table, picked up a spatula and shuffled some of the hot goodies onto a plate. "How did you make out with the interview?"

"Not very well, the school has some personnel problems. I thought I'd look for work closer to home."

Mary set the spatula down and became pensive. "Father Westin told me there is a school north of Utica that is looking for a social studies teacher and football coach. Maybe you should look into it."

"Do you remember the name of the school?"

Mary thought for a moment, then grinned as if a light had just gone on in her mind. "North Country, North Country Central—I think," she snapped. "I think it's about fifty miles north of here."

Jim took the phone book from the counter drawer and thumbed through the yellow pages. He found the section on schools and scrolled down the page with his finger. "North Country, North Country," he kept reiterating. Finally he folded a book page. "Do you have any paper?"

Mary rummaged through a drawer and withdrew a small white pad with the name Dr. Manning's printed at the top.

"Is this your doctor?" he asked.

Mary nodded.

Jim took a pen from his shirt pocket and jotted down a number. He lifted the phone from its cradle and dialed.

"Good morning," a cheerful voice answered. "This is North Country Central School, Mrs. Lauren speaking."

"Good morning, Mrs. Lauren, my name is James Rahin. I understand North Country Central has an opening for a social studies teacher. Is there someone there with whom I can speak regarding a possible interview?"

There was a long pause before Mrs. Lauren spoke again.

"Mr. Rahin, do you have your master's degree?"

"Yes, in school administration."

There was another pause. "Mr. Rahin, would it be possible for you to meet with Mr. Edwards, our superintendent ,at one-thirty this afternoon?"

"How far from Utica, New York is the school?" Jim asked.

There was another pause. "Mr. Walker, the high school principal, says that the school is about an hour and a half drive—depending on traffic."

"Thank you, Mrs. Lauren, I'll see you at one-thirty." Jim hung up the phone and glanced at his watch. It was ten o'clock. "I have to run," he said. "I have an interview at one-thirty." He stuffed a cookie into his mouth and mumbled, "I'll see you again before I head back to Idaho."

JIM STOOD AROUND IN HIS UNDERWEAR AS Gina Rahin pressed his trousers. "That's an awful long way to go for a job," she scoffed. "Why don't you try to find something closer to Utica?"

"I like the idea of being in the country. I think that I can relate to country kids better than those in the city. Besides I'm sure the hunting and fishing is great."

At twelve-forty-five Jim entered the office of Mr. John H. Walker, principal of the North Country Central High School. He was greeted by a small pleasant woman with raven hair, a summer smile and twinkling eyes. She was an attractive lady in her early fifties, with smooth creamy skin and graceful facial features.

She approached with a mother's warm and caring manner.

"May I help you?" the woman asked.

"Good afternoon. I'm James Rahin. I have an interview with Mr. Edwards at one-thirty. I know I'm a little early, but I wasn't sure how to get here or exactly how long it would take. I'm the type who would rather be early than late."

"I'm Mrs. Lauren," the woman said with a white, even smile. "We spoke on the phone." Mrs. Lauren noticed Jim eyeing the pin on her sweater and she began to fuss with it. "I'll tell Mr. Walker that you are here. Please have a seat." As an after-thought she asked, "Would you like a cup of coffee?"

"No thank you. I'm all coffee'd out. Everywhere I went this morning family and friends gave me a cup. I won't be able to sleep for a week."

The secretary nodded and pushed a button on her phone. "Mr. Walker, Mr. Rahin is here."

Seconds later a man about Jim's height appeared. He had a fair complexion, brown curly hair and piercing dark eyes. His open-collar shirt, brown trousers, and shoes that hadn't seen polish since they were purchased made him look more like a custodian than a principal.

The man extended his hand. "I'm John Walker, Mr. Rahin. Welcome to North Country High."

Jim took the man's hand. "I'm pleased to meet you, sir."

The principal turned to his secretary. "Mrs. Lauren, please notify Mr. Edwards that I'll be down with Mr. Rahin in about ten minutes.

THE SUPERINTENDENT'S COMPLEX was located a short walk from the principal's office. When they arrived, Jim and Walker were met by the superintendent's secretary, Lora Cleary. Cleary was a squeaky-clean, conservatively-dressed woman of fifty-something with shoulder length—colored hair and a sincere smile.

"Welcome to North Country Central School," Cleary said. "Mr. Edwards will be with you in a moment. He's on the phone with a board member."

Jim thanked her and glanced around the office. The surroundings mirrored the newness of the rest of the educational complex.

While they waited, Walker made small talk about the school's history, including how Superintendent Steven Edwards became the school's educational leader. Mrs. Cleary returned to her desk and continued typing. Five minutes into Walker's history lesson two people entered the office. One was a short portly man wearing dark-rimmed glasses, white shirt, red tie, and gray baggy trousers. At his side was a dour woman in a white blouse and black extra-large slacks.

Jim smiled. That momma could play tackle for the Green Bay Packers.

"Ms. Dykson, Mr. Farmer, I'd like you meet Mr. Rahin," said Walker, as the two approached.

Jim turned and smiled. "How do you, do?"

"Fanny teaches physical education, and Jerry does math and science," the principal continued. "Jim is interviewing for a job."

The teachers were less than enthusiastic. Farmer flashed an antiseptic smile while Dykson ignored the introduction and engaged Jean Cleary with questions about the availability of the superintendent. When Mrs. Cleary informed her that Mr. Edwards would be tied up for the next few hours, Dykson grunted some innocuous remarks. She and Farmer left without further comment.

"Good afternoon," Steven Edwards called as he entered the outer office with an extended hand. He took Jim's hand and said, "Come in, come in." Walker and Jim followed Edwards through a conference room and into his private office. Edwards was of medium height and carried himself very erect in a dark blue pin-striped suit. He had been with the district for many years, first as an elementary teacher, and then as a building principal. In a consolidation move that merged several small schools into one, Steven Edwards became the superintendent by virtue of his administrative seniority.

Edwards motioned Jim to sit. "Did you bring your credentials?" he asked.

Jim felt perplexed. "Well—I don't have them with me, Sir. This interview came up so quickly that I didn't have a chance to put one together." Jim's eyes caught a look of suspicion pass between the two administrators. "You see," he continued, "I gave my credentials to the principal at South Hudson Valley Central School where I was interviewing for a position as an assistant principal. When I rejected the position offered, the man became angry and ordered me out of the building. I left without retrieving my portfolio. I drove to Utica to visit family, heard about this job and—well—here I am, minus my credentials."

"Why don't you tell us a little bit about yourself," Edwards suggested. "Give us an understanding of your background and experience." The superintendent settled back into his expensive chair as if settling in for a long dissertation. "If necessary, we can always get your credentials later."

The time that Mrs. Cleary had guesstimated for the completion the interview had long passed when Jim finished answering questions and pontificating about his educational philosophy.

Edwards cleared his throat and shuffled some papers on his otherwise clean desk. "Jim, the social studies position you called about has been filled. I went through with this interview because I think you are the man we've been looking for to replace our assistant principal. Just before you called this morning I was informed that our assistant principal had accepted a job as a

principal in Pennsylvania. Are you interested?"

Jim nodded in the affirmative.

"I would also like to hire your wife as a third-grade teacher— if you think she would like to teach third grade?"

"I think she would like that very much," Jim replied.

"Good," Edwards continued. "I'll have my secretary send you letters of appointment. I look forward to seeing you both in September. We have an orientation for new staff the day after Labor Day."

When Jim left the superintendent's office he met a well-dressed man with dark hair talking to Jean Cleary. Upon seeing Jim, the secretary broke off the conversation.

"Mr. Rahin, I'd like to introduce you to our elementary principal, Mr. Williams."

Albert Williams flashed a toothy grin as he gripped Jim's hand. "I'm pleased to meet you, Jim. Mrs. Cleary has been filling me in. If you have a little time I'd be glad to show you the district and point out some possible lodging." Williams waved his long-stem pipe like a pointer.

"Thanks, but I think I'll wait until my wife can be with me," Jim replied. "Right now we have a place to stay in Utica. I know it's a long commute, but if necessary I can use Utica as a base when I get back from Idaho. By winter my wife and I should have something closer to the school."

Williams winced. "That can get to be one hell of a commute, especially if we have an early winter. It's not unusual for us to have snow in September. In any case, if I can be of help just let me know."

Chapter 3

BY THE END OF AUGUST, THE RAHINS WERE back in New York. They had driven five days with a loaded Chrysler convertible, a small trailer, a cat and two dogs.

Hope was glad to be returning to the east. Her already slender body had lost more weight while Jim was studying in Idaho; she had not been happy. For the first time in almost a year her blue eyes sparkled just as they had when she and Jim first met.

On Labor Day Jim and Hope headed north in search of housing. As usual the business activity in the north country was booming. It was the last time until spring that the lake's seasonal residents would jam the villages looking for mementoes of their summer stay in the Adirondacks.

The couple spent most of the day driving the back road, byways, towns, and villages looking for housing. With the summer residents leaving, Jim hoped to find a house to rent near the school. He knew that it wouldn't be long before the chain of lakes would be deserted and property owners would be anxious to fill vacancies.

Jim, eager to start work, was positive that he was going to like working in the mountain environment. Hope, on the other hand, wasn't so sure. Most of the old houses and camps she and Jim looked at were in need of extensive renovation—none were what she had envisioned for their love nest.

"I don't want to live in the sticks," Hope grumbled as their convertible headed back toward Utica. "For one thing, I haven't seen one place that I would want to live in—let alone own. In the second place, this area is too far from a major city. Where would we shop?"

Jim's mood became somber and he remained silent until the car pulled into the parking lot of the Kayuta Drive-In and turned off the engine.

"I think we need some ice cream and conversation."

The diner was a hot spot for those traveling from Utica to points north. It had an outdoor serving area where customers could order. A cute strawberry blond with cool green eyes and a toothy grin greeted Jim as he stepped up to the counter.

"Good afternoon," the girl said, exploding with personality. "What can I getcha?"

Jim ordered a vanilla cone; Hope chose chocolate. After paying the bill, Jim guided Hope to a picnic table near the parking lot.

"You know I love you, and I have done everything possible to make you happy—and our marriage work." Jim said in a hushed tone. "I gave up two good jobs in Idaho so that you could return home to be near your family. I found work a short drive from Utica so that you could visit your family as often as you wanted. This administrative job will give me the experience and money we need to be able to eventually move closer to the city. Now you are placing conditions on where we will live." His voice rose in volume. "I will try to find a nice place somewhere between Utica and the North Country Central School, but you are going to have to give a little too. You can't expect everything to be what you want. Marriage is a two-way street. There are things that I need in order to be happy."

Hope pouted. "I don't want to live in a shack."

"I don't want to live in a shack either, but we have to be reasonable and stay within our budget. I can always remodel a place to make it better, but you have to give me time and not complain every day."

A short, stout man with a crew-cut, a three-day beard and baggy pants stopped next to the table. "Excuse me folks," he said. "I couldn't help overhearing your conversation."

Hope looked away and whispered, "See, I told you that you always talk too loud."

The man smiled. "I'm George Lexus. I only said something because my wife and I have a place for sale and we're kinda in a hurry to sell. It's a ranch with two acres. We could make you a great deal as long as we don't have to include a realtor."

"Where is your place?" Jim asked.

"It's a short drive north of here."

Jim winced. "My wife doesn't want to be that far from Utica. Besides, we wouldn't be in a position to buy until we are approved by a bank. That might take a little time."

It was the man's turn to grimace. "How long do you think that would take?"

"We both have good jobs and I have a little money for a down payment, so…"

"Excuse me a minute," the man interrupted. He turned and walked to his car a few steps from the picnic table. The man handed a milkshake through the opened car window and conferred with a woman passenger. Jim assumed that the woman was Mrs. Lexus. She looked to be about the same age as the man and had matching frazzled hair. When Lexus returned, he was smiling. "My wife said that if you like the house and we can get together on price, you can rent the house until closing."

"Give us a minute," Jim asked. After the man returned to his car, Jim turned to Hope. "Let's look at the place. What do we have to lose?"

"Okay, but I really would like to be closer to Utica," Hope grumbled.

Jim waved to the man. "My wife and I are interested in looking at your house. When can we see it?"

"Whenever you would like," George Lexus answered. I'll give you my phone number. Give me a call when you are ready.

THE HOUSE WAS EVERYTHING George Lexus said it was. It had three bedrooms, two baths, a two-car garage, and a huge cellar. The house was just what Hope had in mind, with one exception—location. She thought about the things that Jim had said at the diner and decided that he was right. If she wanted the marriage to work she would need to compromise. She prayed that he would think about moving closer to Utica or Syracuse once he had some administrative experience.

"Jim, if this house is what you want, buy it. I'll learn to love it. I'll just have to restrict my trips to Utica to the weekends."

Before the fall snows covered the ground the Rahins were settled in their new home. Jim built a pen for the dogs and started remodeling the den while he and Hope were fully involved in their new positions.

Jim's students were like those he had taught in his first teaching job before he left for Idaho. However, the students at North Country High were not as impoverished as some of the families he had known during his first years as an educator.

The economy in the North Country district was driven by the logging industry and tourism. Lumber fed the paper mills, furniture factories, and a host of other businesses dependent on wood and wood products. The dairy industry also played a role in the economy of the region, but logs and tourism paid the bills. Families not involved in the tourist industry, farming, or logging worked for the school or traveled to the city for jobs in the health care or insurance industry.

Jim was accepted by most of the students, parents and staff, but there were those who saw him as a Jewish interloper. They believed that he was from downstate and were convinced that he should have stayed in the big city. His detractors rejected the truth and continued to believe that James Rahin was Jewish—even though he and Hope attended mass every Sunday. Some parents, feared that he would try to turn the heads of their little darlings away from Christianity. A few staff members went to great lengths to foster the misconception. They knew the truth, but chose to poison the minds of students and parents against him.

From time to time discipline suffered. The lack of respect shown to Jim by students of distrusting parents created a rift in the school and community. Disciplinary action involving such students was often rebuffed as a personality clash.

Jim was unaware that his job had been promised to another staff member's husband prior to his arrival. When Jim was given the job bitter feelings and resentment festered. Jim became aware of the bitterness many months after he had accepted the job. Only then did he understand the cold greeting given to him by the teachers he had met on the day of his interview.

Jerry Farmer's attitude thawed as the year progressed, but Fanny Dykson maintained her soggy cigar personality whenever she and Jim had an occasion to talk. Fanny was a friend of the woman whose husband had hoped to get the position given to Jim. She was a malcontent who disliked Jim and everybody who supported him. Her sour personality was often passed on to students.

In addition to her dislike of Jim, Fanny Dykson disliked attractive girls. She was viewed as a negative woman. Nolan Franskie, the school psychologist, postulated that Fanny as a young girl, had never known the affection of a boyfriend. As an adult, she harbored resentment toward the concept of young love and scoffed her way through life smiling only at the misfortune of others.

Her closest friend, Constance Anders, was a quiet, unassuming, fairly attractive young teacher who worked hard and was an advocate for students. The dichotomy of the relationship between the two women baffled Jim. Franskie, however, theorized that the two women fed off each other's needs. Connie was quiet and reserved while Dykson was brash, overbearing and confrontational.

THE VICE PRINCIPAL'S OFFICE was next to Walker's office, but Jim had his own secretary.

Alison Block, Jim's secretary, was a cute little farmer's daughter who was reliable and highly competent. She had been a top business student while in high school and remained so throughout her business school training. Alison attended the Utica School of Commerce and was hired by North Country Central shortly after graduation. Some in the community believed that she had been given the job because of her relationship through marriage to the superintendent. Jim didn't care how she got the job, he was damn glad to have her. Alison had everything that he wanted in a secretary.

The only drawback with Alison was her love life. She was smitten with her high school sweetheart. Jim feared that sooner or later the young farmer would drag Alison to the altar. She would leave Jim and return to the life of a farmer's wife. The daunting prospect of having to find another secretary with Alison Block's qualifications was not something he wanted to contemplate.

CHAPTER 4

ALBERTO PENNA WAS FROM BUCK TOWNSHIP. It was a small logging community east of the Lake District. The community was in a backwoods area of upstate New York and had remained isolated throughout the first half of the twentieth century. Over the years, incest had become a common occurrence; everyone in the community was related. The residents of Buck Town had a reputation of being hard drinking and pugnacious. They valued a positive work ethic, but saw little value in a formal education.

Alberto was considered handsome by the girls at North Country High and over the four years of high school he had sampled the fruit of many a fair damsel. For the better part of Alberto's senior year Donna Glick had become his fruit of choice.

Donna Glick resided in one of the more affluent areas of the Lake District. Her family considered good grades and a commitment to attend college as important attributes. Attractive, bright, and popular, Donna had reigned as homecoming queen the previous fall. Her nurse mother and engineer father endeavored to ensure that Donna would have the finest of material things. They exposed her to as much culture as possible. She and her parents often took shopping trips to New York City where theater and museums were always on the agenda.

Young Alberto Penna was not the kind of match the Glicks had envisioned for their only daughter.

APRIL IN THE NORTH COUNTRY CAME LATE with trees budding, crocuses peeking through mother earth's soil, and the fields turning green with the promise of a bountiful summer. Shopkeepers began gearing up for another tourist season while the farm animals displayed a renewed interest in propagation.

Among the student body at North Country High hormones were blossoming into what adults referred to as puppy love. Alberto and Donna decided to take their hormones to another level and ran away from home at the start of Easter recess. It was an agreement they had made months earlier. Both had grown weary of parental interference. They pooled their money in preparation for the appointed hour when they would leave the chains of family biases and be together forever.

25

On the Friday of spring break, at the end of the school day, Alberto and Donna secured a ride to Rome. They told everyone they were going to dinner and a movie. Donna assured her friends that her parents knew of her plans and were planning to pick her up after the show.

Once in Rome, however, the couple made their way to the bus station where they boarded a Greyhound for Syracuse. Upon arriving in the Salt City, the couple took a room in a cheap, seedy motel on Erie Boulevard. For three days they made love, watched television, and ate junk food. They left the motel only to eat meager meals at a squalid diner a few blocks away.

DONNA RETRIEVED HER BRA from the foot of the bed.

Her bone-white, tiny breast, were cold. Red marks were visible where Alberto's stubble had raked her during their long hours of passion. She shivered and pulled a pale blue sweater over her head. At first, she had enjoyed feeling Alberto's hard, naked body next to hers and considered his unshaved stubble an extension of his manly appeal. But after three long nights, his scratchy facial hair was something she could do without.

Her weekend debauchery and passion hadn't been her first brush with the beast called lust. Shortly after she and Albert started dating, Donna submitted to Albert's sexual demands in the front seat of his father's 1960 Chevrolet. The act was rushed and ended with satisfaction for Alberto, but nothing but frustration for Donna. She hopped that intimacy would be more satisfying in the comfort of a bed. It wasn't. Something was missing.

Alberto would always reach a climax early and then fall asleep. Rarely were her needs been met. She wanted to make love, but Alberto was only interested in having sex. For Donna, the excitement had waned and her response to his demands were more from a sense of duty than desire. In the cramped squalor of their seven-dollar-a-night love nest, sleep for Donna had become a stranger. Worry plagued her and she obsessed over having to be accountable for her actions. She was racked by remorse and the constant fear of becoming pregnant.

Donna Glick longed for the comfort of her mother's unconditional love. She pulled a blanket around her frail frame and began to weep.

As the flicker of morning forced its way through the unwashed windows Donna broke free of her sorrow and nudged Alberto.

"Alberto, honey," she whispered. "It's after six. I'm hungry. I'd like to leave for breakfast before everyone is up."

Donna felt the eyes of the other residents followed her wherever she went. She was paranoid and felt that everyone was whispering about her sordid tryst.

When Alberto did not respond, she rolled off the bed and felt the cold, worn wood floor against her feet. Dirt ground beneath her as she watched a bug scurry toward a crack in the baseboard. Clutching her clothing, she entered the bathroom. The smell of mold and dried urine gripped her. She put the grungy toilet seat down onto the yellow porcelain and was repulsed by her surroundings. After relieving herself, she pulled back a faded torn shower curtain and entered a water-worn metal stall. A discolored brown ring of rust worked its way along the base of the enclosure. She turned a handle and felt a hot, biting rinse dash her face. In seconds, all remnants of the dried tears were washed away.

If only I could wash away my sins and this feeling of guilt as easily, she thought. What have I done? Why? How will I be able to face my friends and family?

Alberto heard the rhythm of the water as it shot from the shower head. He sat up, rubbed his eyes and looked toward the bathroom. The scent of the evening's lust filled his nostrils and he grinned.

"Why the hurry?" he yelled.

The noise of the shower cut off any hope of a response.

Alberto left the bed and joined Donna in the haze of the steamy enclosure.

BY EIGHT-FIFTEEN ALBERTO AND Donna walked to the diner for breakfast.

"That motel has taken most of our money," Alberto acknowledged.

"How much do you have left?" Donna groaned.

27

"Not much. We may have enough for a couple of eggs and some coffee, but that's about it."

Donna started to sniffle. "Oh, Alberto, what are we going to do? How will we live? We don't even have enough money to get home."

Alberto paused before answering. He and Donna had been gone for three days. He was sure her parents had the authorities out looking for them by now. If we do call them we will end up on the front page of every newspaper in the state, he thought. We'll be the joke of the school. I don't want that.

But then he looked into Donna's worried face and knew what he had to do.

"What about calling your parents? I'm sure that they would come after you. I doubt they would be willing to give me a ride home. I'll be lucky if your father doesn't shoot me."

"What about your parents?" Donna whined.

"If I called my father he'd just laugh. After some very dirty comments about you he'd tell me to find my own way home."

"What if we called Mr. Rahin?" Donna moaned. "I trust him. He has always been very understanding. He will know what to do." There was a sorrowful, frightened pleading in her voice.

JIM RAHIN WAS ON HIS BACK DECK reading the morning paper and sipping his morning coffee when the phone rang; Hope answered.

"Will you accept a collect call?" the operator asked.

Hope smiled. She was sure the call was from Jim's brother Joe. Joe often called in the early morning after he finished his milk route.

"Yes, operator, I'll accept the call." Hope cupped the mouthpiece of the phone and yelled, "Jim, I think it's your brother."

Jim put the paper down, entered the kitchen, and took the receiver. Hope retreated to the kitchen table to finish her breakfast. "Ya fadder 'ome?" said Jim. His good humor quickly changed to embarrassment. The voice he heard was not that of his brother.

"Mr. Rahin, this is Alberto, Alberto Penna. I'm with Donna Glick; we need your help."

"Alberto! Where the hell have you been?" Jim blurted out. "The Glick family has the whole state out looking for you."

Alberto did not respond.

"Where are you? Are you and Donna okay?" Jim could hear sobbing in the background.

"We're in Syracuse," a dejected Alberto replied. "I know we were stupid, but I'm worried about Donna. She's upset and afraid of what her parents might do. Can you help us?"

"I don't know. The important thing right now is that you are both safe. Tell me where you are and I'll pick you up. After that we will decide on the best course of action."

"We're in a little diner on Erie Boulevard in Syracuse. The place is called The Salt City Café."

"Don't leave. I'll be there in about two hours." Jim hung up and hurried into the bedroom to dress.

"Who was that?" Hope asked.

"You know the two kids I told you about? The ones who disappeared right after spring break started? Well, that was Alberto Penna. He and the Glick girl are in Syracuse. I'm driving there to pick them up."

"Syracuse? Then what?"

Jim pulled a North Country Central sweatshirt over his head and grumbled, "I don't know. I'll have to play it by ear. All I know is that those two kids need my help."

"Would you like me to go with you?"

"I think it would be better if I went alone. They may be reluctant to speak openly if you are there. I'm sure they have been sexually active over the last three days; Donna may feel somewhat embarrassed." Jim grabbed his car keys and wallet, kissed Hope, and left.

It was near one o'clock in the afternoon when Jim arrived in Syracuse. He could tell from the condition of the diner that it was a Ma-Pa operation struggling to make ends meet. The building was dirty and in poor repair. He shook his head in disgust as he entered. A little bell above the door jingled. He surveyed the interior of the diner and spotted the two kids seated in the back; both had their heads bowed in silence. Jim made his way past a group of tough-talking, earthy men at the lunch counter and stood at Donna's side.

"Oh, Mr. Rahin, what are we going to do?" Donna cried when she spotted him. "We were so stupid. We love each other, but what we did was wrong. Please help us." She rose from the table and buried her head into Jim's chest.

Jim put his arm around her and patted her shoulder.

"Have you had anything to eat?"

"Just coffee and toast this morning," a stoic Alberto answered.

"Well let's not try to do too much on an empty stomach."

Jim motioned to a waitress wearing an ill-fitting uniform with some of yesterday's menu still on the front. The short, chunky woman looked like she had eaten too many leftovers.

"How about a cheeseburger and some fries?" Jim asked.

Donna forced a smile as the waitress brought pad and pencil together.

"What can I get cha ta drink?"

"Coffee for me," Jim replied.

"I'll have a glass of milk," Donna said in a hushed whisper.

"Could I have a Coke?" Alberto added.

The waitress nodded and scratched the order onto her pad.

Before she could leave, Jim said, "Make my coffee black."

The waitress jammed the pencil into a tuft of hair over her left ear and returned to the kitchen. The three sat in silence until Jim cleared his throat.

"So, what do you think we should do?"

"No matter what we do, we're in a world of trouble," Alberto moaned. He stood and wandered over to the front window. A man on the other side of the glass walked by, sucking on a libation hidden in a brown paper bag. The bum stumbled as he peered into the diner, spilling some of his liquid breakfast.

"Maybe you should take Donna home and leave me here," mumbled Alberto. "I can't believe that I'm responsible for bringing her to this pit."

"That's not the answer I was looking for," Jim growled. He rose and went to the boy's side. "Now that you have involved me in your mess I am complicit in whatever is done from this point forward. What we do may very well affect my job."

Donna started to say something, but was interrupted by the waitress. The woman set the tray down and placed the drinks on the table.

"What would ja like ta eat?"

Jim and Alberto returned to the table. "Make it cheeseburgers and fries all around," Jim said.

The waitress nodded and left.

"What do you think we should do?" Alberto asked, before taking a sip of his Coke.

"Well, I know that your parents must be worried. I think you should go back and face the music. How bad can it be?"

"Mr. Glick will have me arrested," Alberto blurted. "That's if he doesn't kill me first. I'll consider myself lucky if I come out of this alive."

"I'll tell him that it was my idea," Donna interrupted. Tears were clouding her vision.

"The Glicks can't have you arrested," Jim interceded. "You're both over the age of consent. I just hope this little escapade has taught you that there is more to being grown up than having adult feelings. Physically you may be adults, but emotionally and socially you're still kids."

"I'm a man," Alberto challenged as he stood and puffed out his chest. "I can take care of myself."

"Sure you can! You call your actions in this case that of an adult? When the money ran out you panicked. You didn't think beyond your manhood. You're just not ready for the kind of responsibility that comes with the commitment of marriage and family."

"I want to go home," Donna whined. A single tear ran down her right cheek.

When the waitress brought the rest of the order the three ate in silence. Thirty minutes later Jim paid the bill and, with the lovers in tow, he walked a block down Erie Street to where he had parked the car.

The ride back to the north country took a little more than two hours; both Alberto and Donna dozed most of the way. When Jim was a mile from the Glick residence, he stopped.

"Alberto, I want you to wait here until I return. I'm taking Donna home. I don't want her parents to see you. If you are with us tempers are bound to flare. At this stage of the game that's the last thing I want or need."

The two kids embraced and without further comment Alberto left the car.

Five minutes later Jim and Donna climbed the stairs of the Glick front porch and opened the door. A scream echoed through the house as Janet Glick, Donna's mother, rushed to hug her daughter.

"Donna, Donna, oh, Donna, you're safe. Oh my God, if you only knew how your father and I have worried."

Mother and daughter wept.

"They phoned me from Syracuse," Jim offered.

"Did they, ah, were they…?" Janet Glick struggled for words.

Jim could discern worry and frustration in Mrs. Glick's voice. Embarrassment showed in her eyes.

"I think any questions about what your daughter did and with whom should be best answered by her. It's a family matter and it's nobody else's business. I'm just happy that I could have been of help before something more serious happened."

"Yes, Mr. Rahin, you're right. I just don't understand why my daughter chose to call you instead of me."

"Donna didn't call me, Alberto did. He asked for my help."

A dark shadow passed over Janet Glick's face. Her voice took on a hard edge.

"Where is Alberto?" Her fists were so tightly clinched that her knuckles showed white. At the top of her voice she demanded, "Where is that no good son of a bitch?"

Donna moved quickly between Jim and her mother.

"Mom, it wasn't his fault. It was my idea. I love him."

"I took Alberto home," Jim lied, "I think it would be a good idea if you and your husband met with Alberto's parents when things have cooled down. That meeting should include the kids. Good day."

Jim could hear Mrs. Glick as he left the house. She was saying something to Donna, but he could not make out the gist of her conversation.

AFTER PICKING UP ALBERTO, Jim drove to the Penna home. Mr. Penna was working on a large tractor tire when they arrived. Jordon Penna looked up and nodded; Jim nodded back.

Jordon Penna was a short muscular man with a crewcut and grease on his hands. After eyeballing his son he went back to fussing with the tire.

Alberto exited the car and quietly muttered, "Thanks." He left Jim and walked slowly toward the house. As he passed his father Jordan Penna turned and punched his son full in the face. Alberto hit the side of the house and crumpled onto the ground like a heap of wet clothing.

Turning his attention to Jim, the older Penna grunted, "Have a nice day."

Without comment Jim backed the car out of the driveway and headed south. Visions of girls with whom he had bedded as a teenager came flooding back. He recalled the sexual appetite that propelled him toward a quest for satisfaction. As a younger man his carnal desires were ever present. A man's sex drive is a curse that God has placed upon the male species of the earth, he thought. He remembered the male animals on the farm and how they would go without sleep or food for days just to be near a like species in heat.

I don't blame the kid. If we have been created in the image of God, I wonder if God ever gets horny. Was God ever a kid? If we are created in His image, He must have had a purpose for making the male of His creations the sexual aggressors. Oh well, it's too late to change things now, we'll just have to live with it and hope that in His infinite wisdom God understands how the sex drive in the male animal deprives them of reason and common sense. Maybe that is our cross to bear. If we are supposed to shun temptation, when is it all right to fornicate?

What if couple,s like Hope and me, wanted to wait before starting a family? To be celibate in marriage is not a reasonable expectation. I will continue to do what I think is best for me. If God takes issue with that, then I guess He and I will have to talk about that when we meet—if we meet. I just hope that He doesn't rush that conference.

ON MONDAY MORNING, Jim met with the principal and superintendent regarding the events of the weekend.

Stephen Edwards turned to John Walker. "I'm satisfied with Jim's account of the incident. Do you have any questions?"

Walker paced without comment. After reflecting on Jim's story he approached and sputtered, "Jim, the Glicks are angry with you for not calling them when the Penna boy contacted you. They had a right to know. Mr. and Mrs. Glick would have preferred to drive to Syracuse themselves."

"If Mr. Glick had entered that diner and confronted Alberto Penna there would have been an escalation of the problem. Mr. Glick would have, at the very least, struck the boy. Mr. Penna wasn't happy with Alberto's actions, but Daddy would have taken umbrage if Glick had struck his son. There would have been hell to pay. If I had it to do over again I would have handled it in the same way—perhaps with one exception." Jim took a deep breath. "I would have taken another approach when it came to taking Alberto home. Jordon Penna could have injured his son severely."

Walker laughed. "It serves the little bastard right. Besides, that wasn't the first time his old man kicked the shit out of one of his sons. That's how the Pennas have settled their differences for generations."

"Maybe so, but I didn't want to be a part of fueling a feud between the Pennas and the Glicks," Jim replied.

Edwards stood and moved to Walker's side. "Jim's right John, there would have been a war if that situation had been exacerbated because the school acted improperly."

John Walker's face became dark. "Okay," he snapped, in cold anger. "But in the future any and all matters concerning students under my control will be directed to me before a course of action is determined. I will make the decision on the appropriate response. I'm still the principal."

He looked directly at Jim.

"Do I make myself clear?"

Before Jim could answer, Walker turned and left the room.

Stephen Edwards focused his gaze on Jim. "In the future, Jim, notify John when it involves unusual situations like the Penna incident. If he makes the wrong decision it will be his funeral."

Jim nodded, thanked the superintendent for his support, and left

If some kid is in trouble and asks for my help, he thought, I'll be damned if I'm going to call Walker before I extend a helping hand. I know that bastard would have done what he felt was politically correct. He's big on covering his own ass and not necessarily doing what is in the best interest of kids.

When school resumed classes, Donna Glick was not in attendance. Jim was notified by her parents that Donna had been sent to Cleveland, Ohio to live with an aunt and was not expected to return home until after graduation. The Glicks felt that, in view of Donna's indiscretion, it would be better to remove her from Alberto Penna's influence.

By the end of the school year Alberto was involved with a young girl from the small community of Long Lake.

Donna was accepted at Ohio State University and intended to remain in Ohio for the summer.

Charter 5

THE TURBULENT RELATIONSHIP BETWEEN JIM and John Walker continued in a downward spiral. By the following October the rapport between the two men had reached an all-time low.

After Columbus Day, Walker entered Jim's office.

"I have some bad news for you," Walker announced. "Over the weekend, I happened to be in the Elmwood Bar and Grill in Candlewood Lake. While there, I saw Andy Wind drinking beer. Andy's a football player and as such he is in violation of the athletic code. He must be dropped from the team."

The consumption of alcohol was a violation of the school's athletic code.

"Andy!" Jim exclaimed. "I can't believe it. He's a pretty good kid. I didn't even know he drank. Are you sure it was Andy and not one of his brothers?"

"I'm sure; I sat right next to him."

"That's too bad. His dad is really going to be disappointed."

"His dad already knows. He was also at the bar."

Jim's shock was evident as he slumped into his chair. "I'll call Andy in and notify the coach. He is going to be a big loss to the team."

When Walker left, Alison entered. "Mr. Walker said that you wanted to see me."

"Alison, what kind of family does Andy Wind come from?"

Alison lowered her dictation pad. "I don't know them all that well, but from what I do know, they are very close. Mr. Wind is as proud as he can be of Andy. His greatest hope is that Andy will go on to college."

Jim turned away. "I need to see Andy at the end of this period. I am going to drop him from the football team."

"Oh no! What did he do?"

"Mr. Walker said that he saw Andy drinking at the Elmwood Bar and Grill."

"That's hard to believe. Everyone knows that the Elmwood is Mr. Walker's favorite hangout. If a kid is going to drink, he certainly wouldn't go drinking at the Elmwood."

"Nevertheless, Mr. Walker said that he sat next to Andy and witnessed him drinking. Furthermore, according to Walker, Mr. Wind was sitting with his son."

Alison shook her head. "Mr. Rahin, something about this doesn't sound right."

"Well, I will need to speak to Andy, so please notify him to report to my office at the end of the period."

At one-fifteen in the afternoon a relaxed and smiling Andy Wind was ushered into Jim's office. Upon Jim's invitation he sat in the chair across from Jim's desk. Jim stared at the boy. What a waste.

Andy sat upright waiting for his principal to speak.

"Andy, you have been doing a great job as the team's center," Jim said. "Are you enjoying playing ball this year?"

"I love it."

Jim rose and moved slowly to where Andy was sitting. "Did you have a good weekend?"

A puzzled Andrew replied, "Yeah, my Dad and I went fishing."

"At Candlewood Lake?"

"Yeah—how did you know?"

Jim pulled out the athletic contract that Andy had signed in August.

"Andy do you remember signing this agreement?"

Andy looked at the document for a moment. "Sure, so did my Dad."

"Andy, were you and your father in the Elmwood Bar and Grill over the weekend?"

The boy smiled. "It was my father's birthday, so after fishing he had a beer and I ordered a root beer."

"Are you sure that all you had to drink was root beer? Mr. Walker said that he saw you drinking a draft beer."

Andy grew pale. He lowered his head and groaned.

"I'm sorry, I did have a beer."

Jim slapped the table with the palm of his hand.

"Damn it Andy didn't you know what that would mean? Mr. Walker was right there. I don't have a choice. I will have to drop you from the team."

"I don't understand," a bewildered Andrew Wind replied in a loud whisper. "Mr. Walker said that it would be okay."

"Well, apparently he changed his mind. He probably realized that if he turned his back on your violation of the rules that he would have to ignore any other violations that might come to his attention. We are a nation of rules and laws, Andy, to ignore them would encourage anarchy."

"Mr. Rahin, I didn't want the beer. I ordered root beer. Ask my Dad. Mr. Walker is the one who bought me the beer. He said because it was my Dad's birthday one beer wouldn't hurt."

Jim spun on his heels.

"Mr. Walker bought you the beer?"

"Yes, you can ask my Dad or Butch Drake, the bartender. I told him that I didn't want to violate my code of conduct. It wasn't worth getting kicked off the football team. Geez, I wouldn't do that to the team."

Andy paused for a moment, then blurted out, "I think Mr. Walker set me up because I called the sheriff on him last summer."

"What do you mean, you called the sheriff on Mr. Walker?"

"Last summer Mr. Walker got drunk one night and went to see my girlfriend's mother," Andy said. "I guess that in the past he and Mrs. Ashton had some sort of a relationship. Greta's mother broke it off because of Mr. Walker's drinking. Anyway, it was about eleven-thirty at night when Mr. Walker started banging on the front door and cussing. He wanted to come in. Mrs. Ashton asked him to go away several times, but he just kept banging on the door. I tried to talk to him, but he was persistent and threatened to beat me up. Mrs. Ashton and Greta got scared, so I called the sheriff. Mr. Walker said that he would fix my ass."

Andy looked up with a glum expression. "Well it looks like he made good on his threat. Boy, when my dad hears about this the shit is going to hit the fan."

"In light of what you have told me, as preposterous as it sounds, I'm going to hold off on any action until I have spoken with Mr. Walker. You can continue to practice with the team, but you cannot participate in a game until I give your coach the okay."

After Andy left, Jim walked into John Walker's office.

Walker greeted him with a broad grin. "Well, how did it go? Did the Wind boy beg you not to suspend him from the team?"

"No," Jim answered. "I haven't taken any action on the drinking incident yet."

. "What the hell do you mean?" John Walker's smile faded. "I told you I saw him drinking beer. What more do you need? He was in total violation of his athletic code."

"Yes, John, he admitted that he drank a glass of beer on his father's birthday."

"Then what's the problem?"

"The problem is that he claims that his high school principal bought him the drink even after being told that he didn't want a drink."

"That's a lie. Do you believe that I bought him the beer?"

"The kid made a very convincing argument," Jim said, "but I'm not making any judgments until I check out his story."

John Walker became indignant. "Are you taking that kid's word over mine? Do you intend to impugn my veracity?"

"No, but I still want to check his story. I want to talk to Andy's father, Butch Drake, Mrs. Ashton and Sam Bookmore at the sheriff 's office."

John Walker's mood immediately changed at Jim's mention of who would be questioned about the incident.

"Look, Jim, maybe we are making too big a deal out of this. To tell the truth, I could have bought the boy a beer without realizing that I had done so. It was his father's birthday so I told Butch to give everyone at the bar a drink. I didn't mean Andy of course, but apparently Butch gave him a beer and the kid drank it. It was probably as much my fault as Andy's. Why don't we just drop the whole thing?"

"John, you know I can't do that. If Andy has violated his code I have to treat him the same as I would any other student athlete."

"Okay, okay but why do you have to drag the sheriff, the bartender and Mrs. Ashton into all of this? If Andy has admitted to drinking and I have admitted to buying him the beer, why can't we leave everyone else out of this?"

"Because, John, if what the boy told me is true, then you set him up to get even with him for calling the sheriff when you were harassing Mrs. Ashton last summer."

Walker turned red. "Are you trying to ruin my marriage?" he hissed. "All right, I got drunk and went to an old flame's house. Big deal. I was drunk for Christ sake."

"I have no reason to want your wife to know about your indiscretions," Jim said. "But your behavior in this case touched the life of a student. That boy needs to know that no one is beyond reproach."

"Fuck you, Rahin—you bastard," Walker shouted. "You just want my job, that's what this is all about. Well, take your best shot. Now get the hell out of my office."

Andy Wind's story was corroborated by each of the persons Jim interviewed. All felt that the infraction to the code of conduct committed by Andy should be waived. Jim felt that some token of punishment needed to be measured regardless of the role played by John Walker.

For violating the code Andrew Wind was required to miss one football game. He was allowed to practice and dress for the game, but he was not allowed to participate.

Jim wrote a letter to Steve Edwards condemning the actions of John Walker.

The matter ended with a verbal reprimand of Walker for his lack of judgment. Jim was not pleased. Life at North Country High for Jim would become more difficult.

The Principal

Chapter 6

AT THE END OF THAT SCHOOL YEAR JOHN WALKER left North Country High and took a job as the superintendent in a small school district near Buffalo. Jim was appointed to the position of high school principal following a heated debate between board members. Part of the final agreement to hire Jim included the elimination of the vice principal's position. The job was eliminated as a budgetary consideration and many thought Jim would refuse the job under the circumstances. Mrs. Lauren had considered retiring, but agreed to help guide Jim through the transition.

Most of the faculty hailed the move as a positive step and pledged their support for Jim's appointment. Others, like Fanny Dykson, groused that the district should have opened the position to a state-wide search.

One of the first things Jim wanted to do as the educational leader at the high school was do away with labeling students. The students considered to be bluebirds had been selected early in the educational process. They were considered to be the brightest and the best. Bluebirds were placed in classes with other students of equal ability.

Blackbirds, on the other hand, had been pigeon-holed into classes where the subject matter was easier, expectations lower, and the learning process moved at a slower pace.

The bluebirds were considered college material while the blackbirds took what was described as a "local program."

Little or no consideration was given to the fact that children matured intellectually at different rates just as they did physically. Jim wanted to change the labeling tradition to ensure that when a student experienced mental growth, he or she would be best positioned to accept the challenges of a more demanding educational program. He planned to do away with the local study track and require all students to be enrolled in a Regents program. Extra help would be scheduled for those students who were academically challenged.

Jerry Farmer, the president of the teacher's association, and Fanny Dykson came to Jim's office in late August after word of what Jim was proposing was leaked.

"The association objects to this notion that all students are capable of being Regents students," Farmer bellowed.

"And your notion of having all seventh and eighth grade students taking Latin is preposterous," Dykson added. "How do you expect a child who can barely speak English, to learn Latin?"

"I think you are making some erroneous judgments on both counts," Jim said. "I refuse to tell a parent that their child is stupid. Every student should have the same opportunity to learn. Kids who want to learn a technology can take a Board of Cooperative Educational Services program when he or she is age or grade appropriate. Kids learn from other kids. By separating them we take away vital teaching and learning opportunities. In the meantime I want every child to have a shot at a Regent's Diploma. I want every student ready and able to apply to a college should he or she chose to do so."

Her paused and tried to stare down his two enemies. "And as for Latin, it is basis of the two romance languages, French and Spanish, which are being taught at the high school. Latin will increase the reading abilities of all students. Students who read well will do well. We need to stress reading and language at an earlier level—"

Farmer interrupted. "What about the kids who can't pass the Regents? You will be sentencing them to failure. Some may never earn enough credits to graduate. Have you thought about that?

Jim moved to his desk and took a letter from a folder. "I plan to ask the board to approve the formation of a resource center where students can get extra help with subjects they are failing." He waved the paper and added, "Those identified as slow learners will be scheduled for the resource room instead of a study hall. Some of these kids have too much time designated for study hall anyway. If we must, we will limit students to no more than five subjects a semester. We could establish a grade of fifty-five on the Regents to be used only as a passing grade for local credit. Students, who wish to do so may retake the Regents again in January and again in June or until they get the grade they want. In any case it is not the role of this school to limit a child's opportunities or label them failures before their lives have started. I plan to offer students entering ninth grade the opportunity of earning a diploma over five years instead of the traditional four. For some it would remove tension; for others it would afford an opportunity to take a cooperative distcirct program along with the academics required by colleges."

"Your ideas are too radical for this community," Dykson grumbled. "You can't expect all of these kids to give up graduating with their friends by taking a five-year program. Furthermore, every student is not going to be able to learn a foreign language."

"If what you say is true, Fanny, it's a damn good thing these kids weren't born in Mexico."

"Ah, bullshit," an arrogant Fanny huffed. "You twist everything to suit your position." She stormed out of the office.

Jim turned to Farmer. "Jerry, I plan to hold a faculty meeting on the sixth of September. I will present my plan at that time. If the staff feels they need more time to set the plan into motion, I will hold off the implementation of the proposal until the following fall. That will give us a year to set up the program and hire the appropriate staff."

Farmer frowned. "Okay, Jim. I won't be an impediment to your plans, but I sure hope you know what you're doing. It's going to be a tough sell, not only to the staff, but to this community as well."

AT THE SEPTEMBER MEETING, Jim ran into more opposition from a different source.

"I am totally opposed to this idea that all kids can learn the same material, especially in courses like biology," barked Malcolm Lewis, a pretentious science teacher. "My course is for the brightest and the best. I will not lower my standards for a bunch of brainless kids who are incapable of doing Regents work. Mr. Rich agrees with me. I have his son, Anthony, in my class. Anthony's twin Alfred is in Sam Bryant's class. Alfred's father knows that Alfred is not as bright as Anthony. He believes that your plan will merely frustrate Alfred and force him to give up altogether. Mr. Rich plans to speak to the board about this nonsense."

Malcolm Lewis was an egotistical man in his fifties. During the Korean War, Malcolm rose to the rank of captain. He continued to use the title long after leaving the service. Following the war, he attended college on the G.I. Bill. In college Malcolm studied science with the intent of attending medical school. Upon graduating from Albany State, he applied to several medical collages, but was rejected. Financial needs forced him to take a job teaching biology. He intended to reapply to medical school at the end of the school year, but he became trapped in a marriage and the responsibilities of parenting when his wife presented him with a daughter. The frustrated captain gave up his notion of medical school and resigned himself to the life of a teacher. He believed that he was the best of the best and only wanted to teach the intellectually gifted.

"That's very interesting," Jim replied. "Mr. Bryant is in favor of the plan. He has maintained for years that he has had students in his local biology classes who were capable of passing the Regents, given the opportunity."

"Rubbish," Lewis snarled. He threw his hands in the air and left Jim in the middle of his rebuttal.

Most of the teachers were willing to give Jim's plan a try, but they wanted a year to work out the details. Jim agreed that if the change proved not to be in the best interest of the students, the school would return to its old schedule.

DURING THE YEAR A COMMITTEE was formed consisting of staff, students, and parents to work on a strategy for implementing a one-track educational system. The plan caused dissension among the staff and divisiveness within the community. Jim decided to ask the committee to come up with suggestions on how best to address the controversy.

June Fallen was a well-respected member of the community and a solid thinker. Jim asked June for her thoughts on the matter. At first Fallen expressed doubts, but as the winter months melted away she changed her mind.

June was an attractive forty-something woman. She had been raised in the lap of luxury and chose to remain single, a decision she quietly regretted. Nevertheless, she loved children and considered her work on behalf of the school helpful to "her kids." Through June's efforts and influence a viable program took shape and was ultimately adopted. Her leadership proved to be the deciding factor in the enlistment and support of the community. Part of June's suggestions was to allow staff who objected to preparing all students for the Regents' exams to opt for into teaching junior high classes where there were no Regents.

"I will offer that option to the staff," Jim agreed, "but I don't think many of them will want to go to the middle school after teaching the older kids."

Jim was right. Even Malcolm Lewis chose to stay with his tenth-grade students rather than teach general science to eighth graders.

Fanny Dykson threatened to bring a grievance, but after speaking with union representatives and the state education department, she changed her mind. Likewise, some parents threatened to send their children to another school, but few ever did.

Chapter 7

WHEN EXAM TIME ROLLED AROUND THE following year, there was a great deal of speculation about "Rahin's Folly." The opponents of Jim's plan predicted that large number of students would not only fail the Regents, but would also fail the course. It didn't happen. Special class students were not part of the test mix, but the rest of the student body had the opportunity to take the Regents' exams.

Very few students failed to score a fifty-five. Students who earned sixty-five or better were given Regents' credit. Those scoring a fifty-five were granted course credit. Overall, fewer students failed; many were awarded state credit.

Two days after the biology Regents, Harry Rich visited Jim's office. When the secretary announced that Mr. Rich wished to see him, Jim knew it had something to do with the state exam.

Rich entered Jim's office with a broad smile and extended his hand. "Mr. Rahin, I'm here to shake your hand and eat a little crow."

Jim knew what Rich meant. Of Rich's two sons Alfred, the son who had been considered "slow," passed with a seventy-one. The "brighter" son Anthony, failed the Regents with a sixty-two, but passed Mr. Lewis' course with an eighty-five.

"My wife and I want to thank you for giving our son Alfred a new sense of confidence and self-worth," Rich said. "I was wrong about Alfred's abilities. He now is looking forward to taking

Regents classes next year. He's even talking about going to college. Our only regret is that we didn't place him in the same classes with his twin brother from the start. Had they been schooled together from day one there's no telling what Alfred might have accomplished."

"Alfred is a fine young man," Jim offered. "I'm glad everything worked out okay. I try to get parents not to prejudge their children. Kids develop at different rates even when they are twins. All kids need to be ready to advance themselves whenever the opportunity presents itself."

BY FALL A GREATER NUMBER OF teachers fell in line to support Jim's academic changes. Less than ten percent of the staff remained adversarial. That minority of staff had a few parental followers that agreed with the convictions of Fanny Dykson. Even after the academic success students had with the Regents there were still those who were calling for Jim's removal.

One such family had a son who was a school bully. Jim had reprimanded the boy on several occasions, even suspending him for striking a young girl.

Gandy Ferris was a stout young man of fourteen. At five feet eight inches tall and two hundred pounds he was bigger and stronger than most of the other students in his class. He took great delight in forcing his will upon smaller and weaker students. However, despite of his size and strength, Gandy's parents refused to allow him to play football.

On a warm October afternoon Jim stood against a wall halfway between his office and the cafeteria. His presence served as a lighthouse warning students that running in the halls, was a no-no. Violators were forced to wait next to the principal until all other students had passed through the lunch line. Runners were the last to eat.

Like tiny ants scurrying off to some sweet treasure-trove of goodies, students moved quickly past Jim giving a glancing look to see if the principal was watching. Once past the "hall-cop" and at what they thought was a safe distance from authority, some students would break into a slow trot, hoping to reach the lunch line ahead of their schoolmates.

"Johnny," Jim shouted.

A devil-may-care boy who had misjudged his speed came to an abrupt halt. Jim crooked his finger and motioned for the boy to join him. Soon Johnny was standing next to Jim; the boy's head downcast. Other passing students shot a quick glance at Johnny and snickered.

By the time the halls were clear Jim was ushering five racers to the cafeteria, like a mother hen guarding her brood. The chicks all clucked their way to the cafeteria complaining about the unfairness of their plight.

As Jim approached the lunch line a wide-eyed young girl came scampering to meet him.

"Mr. Rahin, Mr. Rahin," the frail girl yelled. Her speech coming with large gulps of air. "Gandy Ferris and Monty Keefer are gonna fight."

"You five guys get in line," Jim ordered. The boys joined the slow lunch line as Jim quickened his steps toward the cafeteria eating room.

As he entered the dining area he saw a gathering of students massing around. Gandy Ferris, who had a firm grip on Monty Keefer's shirt. Keefer was a few inches shorter than Ferris and less than half his weight.

"Get your fuckin' hands off me, fatso," Keefer snarled, "or I'll kick you in the bal—" Monty stopped when he saw the principal. At the same time Gandy released his grip on Monty's shirt.

Jim reached the boy and quickly yanked on Gandy's collar pulling him away from Keefer. An emboldened Keefer shoved Ferris as a final act of bravado.

Gandy fell into Jim knocking him against another student who was carrying a tray of food. The contents of the boy's tray spewed onto Jim and the floor. After regaining his posture, Jim positioned himself between Ferris and Keefer.

"What is it this time?" Jim demanded.

Each boy rapidly sang his version of the events leading up to the altercation. After a moment of bedlam, more students began to gather.

Jim's voice rose to its upper limits. "Quiet! I'm sick and tired of you two guys disrupting the lunch room because of your petty quarrels. Come with me."

Like soldiers marching to the guard house, both boys followed Jim out of the lunch room and into the gym.

They entered the wrestling workout room located away from the basketball court. The room was design for team practices. Red mats hugged the walls and floor; it reminded Jim of Dante's Inferno.

"Take your shoes off," Jim ordered. Moments later the two boys stood in their stocking feet. "Okay," Jim bellowed, "You want to fight—fight!"

When neither boy responded, Jim gave each a shove toward the other.

Gandy looked like a sumo wrestler as he arched his back and stalked his out-weighted opponent.

The freckled-face, sandy hair Keefer circled Ferris, but stayed well beyond the bigger boy's reach.

Suddenly Gandy lunged forward, seizing Monty's shirt and drawing the slight-of-build challenger into his massive chest.

As the two boys grunted and huffed, Ferris jerked Monty from side to side, trying to get added leverage.

Monty finally broke free and shoved the bigger boy back with all the force he could muster.

Ferris slipped on the slick surface of the mat and fell backwards. He landed face up with eyes the size of saucers. Gandy remained perfectly still staring at the ceiling.

Ahh shit, Jim thought, the kid's hurt. My ass is going to be in deep trouble.

"Are you all right?" he asked.

Gandy didn't move but was able to mutter, "Yeah."

Monty stood to one side with a puzzled look on his face.

Jim studied the vanquished bully. He could tell from the boy's expression that something was drastically wrong.

"What's the matter?"

Ferris continued to remain prostrate on the mat as a rivulet of perspiration ran its course. He rolled his eyes and looked at Jim.

"I had an accident." he said in a voice just above a whisper, hoping Monty wouldn't hear.

"What do you mean you had an accident?"

With his ego in shambles and his pride suffering from embarrassment, Gandy mumbled in a voice barely audible, "I just shit my pants."

A broad grin flashed across Monty's face. He looked away and snickered.

Jim forced back a grin of his own. "Keefer, report back to the cafeteria."

When Monty left, Jim helped Gandy to his feet.

"I want you to remain in the locker room," Jim directed. "Take off your clothes and take a shower. I'll have your clothes washed and dried."

Jim left the wrestling room and went to the custodial office. He found Ed Carter, the head custodian, seated at his desk eating a sandwich.

"Hi, Ed," Jim hailed. "I need someone to wash a batch of clothes for me. One of our students had an accident. He apparently has a case of the runs and soiled himself. I sent him to the locker room."

"I'll get one of the cleaning ladies," Carter answered. "Have someone put his clothes in the laundry room."

When Jim returned to the locker room, Gandy was gone. After checking with the office, Jim returned to the lunch room. Gandy was nowhere to be found.

Jim made a quick search of the gym area, but Gandy Farris wasn't there either.

As Jim left the locker room Laura Jones, the school nurse, came to see him. She had tears in her eyes.

"Mr. Rahin," she called. "I need to see you."

"What's the matter, Laura?" Jim went to meet her. "Why are you crying?"

With a burst of laughter Laura said, "Oh, I'm not crying; these are tears of laughter. Gandy Ferris came to my office. He told me what happened. He wants me to take him home so that he can shower and change clothes. Apparently he has human waste everywhere on his body including his socks. I have him wrapped in a blanket. Is it okay for me to take him home?"

"Sure, if that's what he wants. It will give his parents something more to bitch about."

An hour later Alison Block entered Jim's office—she was smiling.

"Excuse me, Mr. Rahin, but Gandy Ferris has just returned to school. He would like to speak to you."

Jim grinned. "Ahhh yes, Mr. Ferris. Please send him in."

Ferris blustered into Jim's office with determination written on his face. "Mr. Rahin! Can we finish that fight tomorrow?"

Jim studied the vanquished bully. He could tell by his demeanor that Gandy was consumed with anger—but clean. He was dressed in a clean pair of jeans, a blue tee shirt and brown shoes. Jim smiled, Hummm...brown, shoes.

"I thought all that nonsense was over," Jim snapped.

Gandy's neck flushed. "I was willin' ta let bygones be bygones, but Monty's going around telling everybody that he knocked the shit outta me."

Jim rose from his desk and put his arm on Gandy's shoulder.

"I'll speak to Monty and get him to stop embellishing his account of the fight. But if you two do decide to fight again you better do it outside of school." Jim took a long pause. "If you fight in school again I'm going to suspend you both. Understood?" Gandy nodded.

As Ferris was leaving the office Jim called to him. "Gandy, if you do choose to fight Monty again, maybe you should think about boxing."

Gandy's cheeks became two ripe apples. He turned and slammed the door on his way out.

Chapter 8

GARY OWEN CAME TO UTICA on a blustery December day. Owen had been one of Jim's professor friends in Idaho. He and Jim had hunted and fished together while Jim was attending law school at the university. Two days after arriving to visit his family, Gary called Jim to ask if he would be interested in doing some rabbit hunting.

"My brother, Ed, has a great rabbit dog," Gary said, after the normal hellos. "He usually hunts somewhere in the town of Ohio, but the word is that white rabbits are even more plentiful where you are. Do you know any good spots up that way?"

"Sure do," Jim replied. "Tell you what, tomorrow is Saturday. Why don't you and Ed meet me at the Moonlight Diner on Route 28 in Otter Lake—say around seven. I know of some state land we can hunt."

The next morning, as planned, Gary and Ed Owen met Jim at the diner. It was a small, intimate eatery with a fireplace and lots of Adirondack charm. Jim had arrived early and was just finishing his second cup of coffee when the brothers entered.

"Hey buddy," Gary called, "how ya doing." Jim rose and shook hands with Gary and his brother as they slid into the booth across from him.

The three men talked briefly about family, friends, and Idaho. Ed broke the chain of chatter by asking, "What's good?"

"Whatever you order will be great," Jim guaranteed.

"I'm hankering for a tall stack of pancakes," Gary announced.

A cute waitress with dancing eyes, dark hair, and a well-filled starched uniform sashayed to the booth.

"Can I get you gentlemen some coffee?" the girl asked.

Jim held up his cup. "I'll have another splash of decaf and an order of eggs over easy with rye toast—burnt and add an order of hash-browns."

"I'd like a large stack of pancakes," Gary interrupted, before the waitress had finished with Jim's order. "Make my coffee regular and give me an order of Italian toast slightly browned." He pointed to Jim. "I don't want mine black. This guy likes to eat charcoal." Everyone laughed.

The waitress smiled and waited as Ed scrolled his finger down the menu. Finally he looked up. "I'll have regular coffee, two eggs—up, an order of biscuits, a slice of ham and a large glass of orange juice."

"What's the matter Ed? Doesn't your wife feed you?" Jim joked.

The waitress extended her smile and headed for the kitchen.

"So, Jim, where are we going to hunt?" Gary asked.

"Well, after I talked with you I called a friend of mine. He has a long-legged hound—I think it's a walker-beagle cross. He told me that he hunted a swamp just north of here last weekend and took home his limit. He'd like to join us and try that spot again."

"It's okay with me as long as his dog and mine get along," Ed said.

"I've hunted with him before. His dog always got along with the other hounds in the pack. Oh, they'll sniff at each other when they first meet, but once they get a rabbit going hounds don't give ah shit about anything else. Now if we were trying to feed them it might be a different story."

By eight-thirty Jim and the Owen boys arrived at a patch of woods near McKeever. The timber was next to a large swamp on the east side of the Moose River. Paul Glenn was sitting in his red 1958 Ford pickup. In the cab with him was a long-eared hound. Upon seeing Jim's car, Paul left the warmth of the pickup and threw his cigarette into the snow bank.

"It's about time," he yelled. "I thought maybe you had changed your mind." Paul stood six feet tall and was built like a lumberjack.

Jim was struggling to put on his orange down vest.

"Nah, we were held up a little at the diner. Paul, meet Ed and Gary Owen. Ed eats like it's his last meal."

There were more snide remarks as Paul shook hands with the two brothers.

"You boys are in for a treat," said Paul. "If the bunnies are running the way they did last week, you'll have a great day. I had a hell of a good time last weekend. I could have filled my limit many times over."

Paul let his dog out of the cab at the same time that Ed released his beagle. Paul's hound was a foot taller than the beagle. The dogs sniffed at each other and then entered the swamp. Soon the hounds were singing their sorrowful tune.

"We better spread out and see if we can cut the rabbit's circle," Paul suggested.

The four men went in different directions in hopes of cutting the path of the hare.

Jim headed for a small patch of evergreens that bordered a section of hardwoods. After a five-minute walk he found a large mound of snow jutting upward. It must be snow over some blowdowns or a large bolder, he thought. He could hear the yap of the dogs as they turned and headed in his direction. That mound would make a great vantage point, he thought. He knew that the rabbit would be two or three minutes ahead of the dogs. That should give me enough time to get in place.

He trudged onward with his bear-paw snowshoes packing nature's fluff beneath him. Snowflakes gathered on his clothing and a chilled wind snapped at his nose. Suddenly out of the corner of his eye Jim saw a flash of white.

"Shit," he mumbled. "The rabbit got by." Continuing his trek toward the mound, Jim's mind raced. If the other guys don't get it first, I'll shoot that sucker the next time around. A few minutes later he heard the muffled sound of a shotgun. Shortly thereafter the dogs stopped their baying.

When Jim reached the mound he noticed a large limb sticking upward. It must be an old maple tree that got blown down in a windstorm, he surmised. After circling a couple of blue spruce he started to make his climb up the snowy rise. He tugged on the appendages of the tree until he reached the top. Jim surveyed the surroundings and began packing the snow beneath him; it would make it easier to move right or left without too much noise. Pleased with his vantage point, Jim set himself into a watchful pose.

Meanwhile, the dogs had picked up the scent of another hare and the woods once again filled with the sound of hound music.

Jim took the safety off the shotgun and fit his finger in front of the trigger housing. Suddenly the snow beneath his perch gave way and he fell in disarray into an open cavity. He threw his shotgun away and groped for a maple bough. After securing a branch, he tried to pull himself upward. In doing, so one snowshoe snagged on a limb while the other landed on something that felt like a gloppy pillow.

Soft snow, he thought. Jim's assessment of his situation was simultaneously shattered when the hole was filled with an angry roar.

The object under his right leg moved. In a flash a black head emerged with a full mouth of menacing ivory.

Jim was face to face with an angry bear. It emerged using Jim's body as a ladder. The animal had been hibernating and was highly agitated by the interruption of its sleep by a human.

Jim could smell the bear's breath as it scrambled to extricate itself from the tangle of branches. Its body shoved hard against his, clawing in an effort to escape.

When the bear was out of the hole it turned to sniff at its human intruder. The bear's ears were flat against its neck and the hair on its back bristled. Lifting its upper lip it growled as saliva drooled from the corners of its mouth.

Jim was nose to nose with the pink and black of the bear's snout. The white of the bear's teeth and the pungent odor of its hot smelly breathe engulfed his senses; hysteria took hold and he almost lost his bowels.

The animal snorted and shook its head as if trying to rid its nostrils of the human scent. Suddenly the bruin became aware of the barking dogs and instinctively leaped from the mound. In two bounds it was into the hardwoods. Upon seeing the bear in flight the hounds left the scent of the hare and took after the larger game. Their barking took on a quicker cadence.

There was no question that the hounds were in pursuit of something larger than a rabbit. The change in tempo and rapidity of their yaps told the other hunters that the dogs had jumped another animal. They hoped that it wasn't a deer, which could lead dogs miles away.

Gary was the first to reach Jim.

"What the hell is going on?" he asked. "It sounds like the dogs jumped a deer."

"Never mind the dogs, they won't go far. I need help getting out of this hole."

Gary started laughing. "That's a hell of a watch you've got there, partner. I wish I could find one like it."

Ed and Paul rounded a clump of small pines and hurried to the foot of the mound.

"What happened?" Ed asked. "Are the dogs on a deer?"

"It ain't deer." Paul yelled.

Paul had circled the mound of snow and was standing where the dogs entered the hardwoods.

"Take a look at these tracks."

While Gary helped Jim out of the hole, Ed went to where Paul was standing.

"Holy shit," Paul mumbled. "It's a fuckin' bear. Where the hell did it come from?"

Jim and Gary joined the other two hunters.

"From there," Jim said, pointing to the mound.

"Are you shitting me?" Paul snapped. "You mean to tell me that you fell in on top of a bear?"

Jim nodded in the affirmative.

"You're damn lucky you're not dead or maimed," Paul continued. "That bear must have been really pissed. It's a good thing the dogs came along."

"Well I'll tell you, I was so scared I thought I was going to wet myself," Jim confessed. "When that son of a bitch stood over me and opened his mouth I thought my ass was grass. Look at my clothes." Jim's hunting attire was torn and in total disarray. The son-of–a-bitch tore the hell out of my pants and jacket."

"Speaking of dogs, we better get after them before they end up in another county," Ed urged.

"Nah, they're okay," Paul interrupted. "Listen. The hounds have already left the bear. They're back running bunnies."

The four men headed in the direction of the baying hounds. About two hundred yards into the hardwoods they saw the bear silhouetted high in the top of a lone pine tree.

"Hell, it's only a cub!" Gary quipped. "Shit, it can't be more than a hundred and fifty pounds. Jim you're bigger than the damn bear. When it saw you it must have shit itself in fear."

"Come to think of it, it did leave some droppings when it got out. The crap damn near landed on my head."

The woods rang with laughter.

Gary placed his hand on Jim's shoulder. "You know, Rahin, you are a dangerous man to be around. This is the second time you've gotten me involved with a black bear. Remember that fishing trip we took to Canada? That mama bear wanted to tear you a new ass. If I hadn't intervened she would have knocked you out of that tree you were in and had you for lunch."

"That wasn't my fault," Jim argued. "You're the one who left the food where the damn bears could get at it. I had to give up all my fish just to get mama and her cubs away from camp."

"Hey," Paul yelled. "Are we hunting white rabbits or rehashing old fishing stories?"

THE LIGHT WAS FADING BY THE TIME each hunter had bagged his limit. The men grabbed the dogs and headed for Forestport. It was near four o'clock and the temperature was dropping fast and it was snowing harder. All four men were ready for some pasta and beer.

Forestport Station owed its existence to Teddy Roosevelt. At the turn of the century Roosevelt had summered on Honnedaga Lake, located about sixteen miles north of Remsen. The lake was situated in Hamilton County in the heart of the Adirondack Mountains. Remsen was the nearest railroad station. From Remsen, it took more than a day for Roosevelt to reach the compound. Through Roosevelt's influence another rail station and hotel were built a mile or so from the village of Forestport. Whenever he came to the Forestport station Roosevelt stayed at the hotel and continued to Honnedaga Lake the following day.

Forestport had been an important part of the Black River Canal system. Farm goods and lumber products were transported down the Black River Canal to the Erie Canal on their way to market in New York City or Buffalo.

After World War II the railroad station closed and the hotel was sold. The hotel was converted into a restaurant. It was called The Buffalo Head because of the large bison head that was displayed prominently in the lobby. The restaurant became a well-known eatery, especially for people with camps on Kayuta Lake, Hinckley, and the lakes and the communities that dotted the area.

Garramone's Restaurant was located a short distance east of the Buffalo Head. For Jim, the Italian cuisine at Garramone's was his favorite.

After pasta and a pitcher or two of beer the men said their goodbyes. Paul chose to linger a bit longer; he was not ready to call it a day. He knew a little honey who worked as a waitress at the Buffalo Head and he decided to try his luck at bagging a two-legged bunny.

Chapter 9

HOPE RAHIN THOUGHT ABOUT the direction her life had taken. She didn't like living so far into the Adirondacks, nor did she enjoy working in the same school district where Jim was an administrator. Whenever she walked into the teachers' room the others would stop talking about union business. The staff feared that what they were talking about would get back to the administration and the board.

Furthermore, Jim's responsibilities often kept him at school late into the night. On weekends he spent most of his days hunting or catching up on school business. Hope rarely had an opportunity to spend time with him and it bothered her. She felt as if she and Jim had become strangers; they shared the same house, but their lives were going in opposite directions.

When Jim returned from rabbit hunting, Hope was sitting in front of the fireplace knitting. Her long blue robe and fuzzy woolen slippers made a comical picture.

"Hi," Jim said as he set his shotgun in the corner next to the brick hearth. He had remodeled the room when they first bought the house. Hope loved an open fire so a fireplace was added against the outside wall in the den. He had chosen brick rather than stone because of brick's ability to retain heat.

"You won't believe what happened to me today," Jim said. "I was almost eaten by a bear."

Hope said nothing.

He went to the fire and asked, "Is something wrong?"

Hope remained silent.

Oh shit, she's in one of her moods, he thought.

"Hope, please tell me what the hell is the matter."

Hope put the knitting down.

"I'm not happy. I want to get a job in a different school. I don't like working at North Country. I don't want to teach in a school where you are an administrator. The other teachers treat me like a leper. They're all afraid that what I hear in the teachers' room will get back to the board through you; I want to move. In the winter this place is like a morgue. When I want to do something or go somewhere I have to travel over an hour. In the winter that is almost impossible. I'm sick of sitting home. I haven't been to Utica in over three weeks."

"Is that all? I thought that I had done something wrong. You can get a job at one of the other school districts closer to Utica if you'd like. As for where we live, I'll start looking for another place in the spring. Maybe a job will open further south."

"There is something else we need to talk about," Hope replied. She rose from her over-sized chair and placed a small log on the fire.

The wood popped as the flames ate away the bark of the fresh log.

"We never do anything together anymore," Hope continued. "You are tied up with school almost every day until late and on weekends all you want to do is hunt. There is no time for us. God help our marriage if you become a superintendent. I'll never see you."

"What do you want to do?" Jim blustered. "You go shopping on weekends or visit your mother. I know that you have been hemmed in by the weather the last few weekends, but I had no idea that you were unhappy. If I weren't hunting I would have taken you to Utica, but you know that I don't like to shop. I agreed to return to New York because of you. You know that I love being in the woods on my days off. It's my time for peace and quiet. Do you want to go hunting with me?"

"No, but why can't we get involved in theater again? We used to enjoy that."

"I don't think you want to drive to Utica every night for rehearsals; that's a hell of a commitment."

"We don't have to go to Utica. There is community theater in Old Forge; we could get involved there. The theater is located in town."

"What are they doing?" Jim asked.

"Auditions are this Friday night at seven o'clock for 'Fiddler on the Roof.' Can we at least attend the auditions together?"

"We have both done theater, but never a musical," Jim reminded her. "I sing in the shower, but that's about it."

"Please, Jim, even if all we do is chorus or help work on sets. At least it's something we can do together."

Jim went into the kitchen and returned with a glass of water. After taking a long drink he looked at Hope and smiled.

"Okay honey, if that's what it will take to make you happy, that's what we'll do."

"I love you James Rahin."

"Actions speak louder than words, lady."

Hope smiled; her cold mood thawed. She took her husband by the hand and guided him toward the bedroom.

Chapter 10

REBECCA FITCH, A TWENTY-FOUR year old brunette, was hired by North Country in August to teach art. Rebecca was a graduate of the University of Florida.

Becky, as she preferred to be called, had first taken a job as an art teacher in Louisiana where she taught high school art for three years. While in Louisiana Becky became caught up in the voodoo culture of a backwater-bayou community. During her third year as a teacher she professed to all that she was a witch. Becky constantly threatened to cast a spell on any student if they didn't behave. Whenever something bad happened to one of Fitch's students in or out of school, Becky was said to have placed a curse on the child. Concerned parents sought to have her dismissed.

The school board searched for an excuse to terminate the art teacher's services without attracting the attention of federal officials. Affirmative action was sweeping the South and Rebecca had the support of the black community.

Becky Fitch's boyfriend was a black man. Dismissing her would be construed as a racist act and a violation of her civil rights by the National Association for the Advancement of Colored People. The members of the board of education eventually sought the help of the Ku Klux Klan. The days of hanging people had been abandoned by the Klan, but there were still hardcore racists that knew how to get their message of hatred and fear across. Action was prescribed in the hope of forcing Becky to resign her position voluntarily and leave the parish. Within weeks the Ku Klux Klan set forth a plan.

One night several men cloaked in white robes and carrying large torches burned a cross in front of Becky's house. A large noose was hung on her front porch along with a note of warning written in what looked to be blood.

The following morning the distraught art teacher called the school and said that she was sick and would not be able to work. Later that same morning Becky contacted the sheriff's office and told them about her late evening visitors. She was given a sympathetic ear and lip service promising protection.

When a brick was thrown through her front window the next evening and a Rebecca Fitch effigy was hung in a tree, Becky decided that it was time to leave Louisiana.

The school superintendent feigned sympathy and regret. He promised to write a letter of condemnation to the local newspaper and granted her a leave of absence. Becky left Louisiana the following day and flew to New York City.

In New York she stayed with a college friend. When she read in the *New York Times* that North Country High was looking for an art teacher, she applied.

The superintendent in Louisiana gave the North Country High officials a glowing recommendation, regarding Rebecca's teaching abilities. According to her former boss, Becky was of the highest moral character and ability.

No mention was made of her association with voodoo or her claims of witchery.

WHEN JIM FIRST MET REBECCA FITCH he was impressed. She was dressed in a green-and-yellow plaid skirt, a yellow blouse, and sandals to match. At five-feet-two inches tall, she looked more like a student than a teacher.

At the interview Becky showed a remarkable understanding of her subject matter, teaching techniques and district expectations. Jim decided to hire her. In his introductory remarks about the school and community, he cautioned Rebecca about being too friendly with her male students.

"This is a very conservative area," Jim stressed. "Most of the kids here have never been out of the county except to go to Utica or maybe Albany. Parents are very protective and suspicious of outsiders who pay too much attention to their children.

Don't put yourself in a position where gossip of teacher impropriety can develop. You know how boys can be. They often make up stories to impress their friends. Rebecca, you're a very attractive young lady. Avoid situations where you might be alone with a young boy, especially behind closed doors."

"After the fatherly advice, Jim added, "I give the same advice to young male teacher concerning their rapport with girl students."

IN THE EARLY FALL Jim observer Rebecca several times, in her classroom to assess her ability as a teacher. His first evaluation in October described her as having promise.

Rebecca became popular with her students and after a football game in the late fall, she was invited to a victory party at the home of the star quarterback, Gerald Frank. He was a handsome, top senior athlete.

Rebecca had not slept with a man since leaving Louisiana. She was attracted to Jerry. He was just what she had been looking for. She justified her infatuation by telling herself that there was only a few years difference in their ages.

The Franks had a successful two-hundred-acre farm located a few miles southwest of the school. At the party Rebecca spent as much time as she could in Jerry's company. She constantly expressed an interest in cows, horses and farming in general.

In the festive confusion of the party—when Jerry's girlfriend was occupied with her other friends, Rebecca took Jerry by the hand and led him out to the back porch. After talking about the game, the weather, the cool October evening, and the predictions of snow, Becky asked Jerry to show her the barn. Jerry was pleased that his teacher was interested in the farm and offered to show her the animals in the barn.

"We milk about a hundred head," Jerry said, his hot breath turning to a white mist as it hit the air. He switched on the light in the barn and cautioned, "Watch your step, this isn't a classroom. There may be some fresh cow pies in the walkway."

"What do you feed them?" Rebecca asked as she began her move. She pretended to be interested in the farmer talk that Jerry was babbling. The teacher was searching for an appropriate nest to consummate her seduction.

"This time of the year they are still grazing during the day," Jerry continued. "We add grain to their diet at night. After milking in the morning, they are released to graze in the pasture."

"What's that up there?" Becky asked, pointing to the loft.

"Oh, that's where we keep the straw for their bedding."

"You mean a hay loft?"

"Well, most people refer to it as a hay loft—and we do store hay there for the winter, but..."

"Can I see it?" she interrupted.

Jerry paused. "Gee, I don't know, Ms. Fitch. I don't think it would be proper, you being a teacher and all."

"Please, Gerald, we're not in school. Outside of school we're just friends. Call me Becky." She reached past him and hit the switch for the lights. The barn became a bottle of ink. "Now show me the loft." She took his hand and pulled him toward a wooden ladder leading to the loft.

"Do you find me attractive?" she whispered.

"We shouldn't be doing this," he groaned. A tremor resonated through Gerald's body.

Rebecca reached down and felt his manhood.

"I want you," she husked. "Please take me to the loft." She took the wooden rung of the ladder with her free hand and lifted herself. She purposely allowed her skirt to ride up, exposing her under garments.

Excitement raced through Gerald as he followed his teacher to what was to be their bed of bliss. His senses became blurred and for the first time since entering the barn he could smell the fresh soap on her body and her perfumed hair.

By the time he reached the top of the loft, Rebecca had already removed her blouse. She took his hand and drew him close.

"Kiss me she whispered. She took his hand and brought it to her breast.

Gerald fumbled with the clasp on the back of her bra while she removed her skirt. She unfastened his belt and allowed his pants to fall.

In less time than it took to undress, it was over. Gerald's senses returned to sanity and he quickly dressed.

"Sally's gonna miss me—I better get back to the party."

Without looking at his teacher, Gerald descended the ladder and returned to the party.

Rebecca frowned. It had all happened so quickly that her ardor had not been quenched. Kids, she thought, all they think about is their own needs. I need a man. She was determined to satisfy her connubial needs before the party ended.

TWO WEEK LATER, RABECCA FITCH entered the main office during her break. "I need to see Mr. Rahin," she announced.

Alison rose from her desk and went to the counter. "Good morning, Ms. Fitch. How have you been?"

"Fine." I wonder if the boys have been bragging to their friends about their little trysts with me, she thought.

"Alison smiled. "I'll see if Mr. Rahin is free." Alison went back to her desk and hit the button on the intercom. "Mr. Rahin, Ms. Fitch would like to see you."

"Please send her in, and would you check on Gerald Frank's schedule. When he has a free period, I'd like to see him." Jim's request did not go unnoticed by Rebecca.

"You can go in," Alison said, as she moved to the student schedule file.

Rebecca's face flushed as she walked toward Jim's office. He knows, she thought. She straightened her black skirt, and took inventory of the buttons on her white blouse. Before opening the door, she ran her hand over her hair. When she entered his office, Jim rose to meet her.

"Good morning, Becky, have a seat."

Becky sat in a chair across from Jim's desk. She fidgeted with the onyx ring on her finger and forced a nervous smile.

"Is something bothering you?" Jim asked. "You seem on edge."

Becky's mind raced for an answer. "Ah—well, I don't know quite how to say this, but some of the students are saying things about me. Some of the older boys are flirting with me in class and I'm not sure just how to handle it."

Jim grinned and jokingly replied, "I'm envious. You're a very attractive lady. I suppose if I had had a teacher that looked like you, when I was in school, I would have flirted too." His demeanor became more serious when he added, "Just maintain a professional posture at all times. If someone crosses the line and it's something you feel needs my attention—let me know."

Becky rose and took a small piece of paper from the pocket of her skirt. Without comment, she placed the paper on Jim's desk and backed her way to the door. She offered a faint smile and said, "Thank you, Mr., ahhh, Jim."

Before Jim could react, she was gone. He reached across the desk and took the paper that Becky had left behind. When he opened the note his brow wrinkled. Her problem is greater than she had indicated, he thought. Jim folded the paper and placed it into his shirt pocket. There was a knock on his door.

"Come in."

Alison opened the door and entered. "Here's Gerald Frank's schedule. He has a study hall eighth period, but if you need to see him sooner, he will be eating lunch in twenty minutes."

"Thanks, Alison. Get word to him that I'd like to see him after he finishes eating."

At twelve-forty-five, Alison announced that Gerald was sitting in the outer office.

Jim rose and moved to the door in anticipation of Gerald's arrival.

"Send him in."

When the boy entered Jim motioned to a chair and asked him to sit. He studied the student for a moment then returned to his desk.

North Country had received a letter of interest from Penn State University. They wanted Gerald to visit the campus in November, after football season was over.

Jim searched for the letter among the other papers on his desk, but couldn't find it.

Gerald Frank's anxiety over being in the principal's office was evident. Normally he oozed with self-confidence. He possessed a nonchalant attitude even with school officials but today he was different. He was quiet and sullen; his eyes remained downcast.

Finally Jim spoke. "Gerald, perhaps this is not the best time to speak with you, but I…"

"It wasn't my fault," Gerald blurted. "I tried to tell her that it wasn't right, but she just kept insisting that we go to the hay loft and before I knew what was happening we did it. I felt so bad that I left her there in the loft. I guess that makes me an adulterer or something. I feel really bad. What's my mother going to think?"

Jim was not shocked by the comments. He knew that some of the kids were sexually active. Apparently Gerald and his girlfriend had sex on the weekend.

"I can see that you are upset," Jim replied. "If you and Sally would like to talk to a counselor, I'm sure something can be arranged. Your parents, needn't know, unless you decide to tell them."

Gerald looked up with a start.

"I don't want Sally to know. Geez that would ruin everything. She'll probably find out sooner or later, but…" his voice trailed off. He looked straight at Jim. "I don't know if Ms. Fitch has told anyone. If she has, it will be all over the school in no time."

Ms. Fitch! Jim came out of his chair and moved to where Gerald was sitting. "I think you had better start from the beginning."

For the next fifteen minutes a despondent Gerald Frank relived his encounter with Rebecca Fitch. "I just left," he concluded. "I saw her with Donny Fusco later, but I didn't talk with her again."

"Do you know if she and Donny were alone? Did she go to the barn with him?"

"They went outside together, but I didn't see where they went." Gerald blustered. "Mr. Rahin, am I going to be suspended?"

"I don't know yet. What happened took place off school property and at an event sponsored by your parents. While there were no laws broken that I know of, there was certainly a breach of professional etiquette. For now, please keep what happened at your party to yourself. I will talk with you and your coach later. There are others I need to speak with. I have to decide how this incident will impact your athletic eligibility."

When Gerald left, Jim took the note that Fitch had given him and read it again. There in bold letters was a message: "I WANT YOU." Jim placed the note back into his shirt pocket.

A few minutes later Jim entered Rebecca's classroom. She was busy helping a student with a portrait. He could understand why an older student would find her alluring, but why she would seek the companionship of a boy was an enigma.

When Becky moved away from her student she caught sight of Jim and quickly went to him. Her hair caught the light and gave a sheen that reminded Jim of the black mink coat that he had purchased for Hope the previous Christmas.

"Is this a professional visit or social?" she asked. The white of her smile contrasted with her hair and emerald eyes.

"Professional," Jim whispered. It wasn't the time to question her about the incident in the Frank's barn, but if there was another boy in her class looking to jump her bones, he wanted to prevent it as quickly as possible. He took out the note and opened it. "Is the boy who gave you this note in this class?"

Becky gently touched his arm and whispered, "No, that note is from me to you."

The sound of her voice hit him like a cold shower. For the first time in a long time he was speechless. He folded the paper and placed it back in his pocket. Without looking at her he hushed, "See me during your free period."

In an erotic voice she whispered, "You are my lord and master. I will do anything you ask of me."

Jim turned and left the room. Thoughts raced through his mind as he walked to his office. When he entered, Alison looked up. She knew when Jim was upset.

"You look like you're mulling over a serious problem," she said.

"Yeah, I've got a fourteen-karat nut on my hands, and I need to deal with her in a hurry. Inform Mr. Edwards that I need to see him. Tell him it's urgent."

Alison smiled. "Does this jewel concern the art teacher?"

Jim spun around to face her. "How did you know?"

Alison's eyes searched the office. When she was sure that they were alone, she answered, "I understand that Miss Fitch took on the entire backfield at the Frank party. I didn't say anything sooner, because I thought you knew. I assumed that was why you called Gerald to the office."

Jim opened his office door. "It's gone beyond kids. Now she's working on staff." He didn't elaborate. "If we don't get her out of here, there's going to be a revolution. I'll have parents, teachers, wives, girlfriends and who knows who all, clamoring for her hide—and maybe mine too. Tell Mr. Edwards that I need to see him as soon as possible. Tell him the matter is urgent."

Steve Edwards was out of the building when Alison called. She left word with his secretary that Mr. Rahin needed to see him as soon as he returned.

Rebecca came to the office at the end of the school day, but Jim was with another teacher. She called to Alison, "Ms. Block, please tell Mr. Rahin that I couldn't wait. I will see him in the morning."

Before Alison could respond, Fitch was gone.

Chapter 11

Rebecca Fitch drove to White Lake for what she hoped would be a passion-filled evening with Eric Manley. It was a dark, damp night, and she longed for the warmth that only a man's arms could offer.

Eric Manley taught industrial arts. The kids called it shop. He was a tall handsome man in his late twenties. He had taken the job with North Country after spending six years with the Adirondack Cheese Company in Watertown. Eric was well liked and assimilated into the North Country educational community with ease. His chiseled facial features, sandy brown hair, and athlete's build was accentuated by a jocular personality.

Becky had flirted with Eric on and off for over a week before she decided to seduce him. During lunch, on the same day that she propositioned Jim, Becky passed him a note similar to the one she had given Jim.

Eric's reaction was much different than the response she had received from Jim. Eric returned the note with an invitation to meet him that evening at his parent's camp on White Lake.

In late fall the lake was secluded. It was unlikely that anyone would see them.

Becky had never met Eric's wife or his two little daughters. She wondered if he would be reluctant to satisfy her intense sexual fervor.

From the age of twelve, after her older brother had taken her virginity, Becky became promiscuous, fornicating when, where and with whom she pleased. She knew that for most men sex was merely a matter of time, place and opportunity. With most married men it wasn't that they needed love or that they didn't love their wives. Extra marital sex was an animalistic drive that, for men, was almost impossible to control.

Before marriage and in the early months of married life, most women were always ready and willing to meet the sexual needs of their man. As connubial malaise set in wives, especially those with children, became less accessible to their husbands. Becky snickered as she thought of how stupid most women were. They were always so eager to rush to a divorce court just because their man strayed from the marriage bed.

Most women equate the sex act with love, she thought. Men seek a little extra-curricular roll in the hay just for the enjoyment. It has nothing to do with love. Perhaps for some, it's a reassurance of their manly prowess, Becky thought. Most wives are reluctant to do the kinky stuff that I enjoy. Most wives are conservative lovers. I guess it goes back to their religious training. If they don't want their husbands to stray, they need to get rid of all that taboo shit about sex that they get from the church and concentrate on satisfying the man's innermost fantasies. Women are always looking for emotion and constant assurance that they are loved. When and if I marry, my husband will never need to find another woman. His needs and mine will be on par.

Becky pulled down a narrow dirt road and saw Eric's white pickup truck parked next to a shabby dark green cottage. The camp was nestled among some tall pine trees where its faded paint blended with its surroundings. She parked next to the truck and got out. As she rounded the south corner of the building she heard his voice.

"Come on in. I'm trying to get a fire going." He had seen the lights of Becky's car when she pulled in. "It's colder than a witch's tit in here," he called

"Hey, watch what you say about witches. My tits are soft and warm."

"Well, I don't consider you a witch, and as for your tits, I'm from Missouri."

Becky smiled. *If all goes well, mister, you'll know much more about me before this night is over.*

She removed her jacket and moved next to him. He was blowing on the flame inside a small, black, potbelly stove.

"Let me do that," she cooed. "I'm a great blower."

Eric stood and looked into her eyes. His body was already showing an eager hunger to touch her.

"As I said," he whispered, "I'm from the show-me state."

Becky crushed her body against his and arched her hips into his erection. "Why are we wasting time?" she moaned. "I'm from the do-me state."

They embraced. Eric lifted her into his arms and entered a small bedroom off the kitchen. He held her lips to his until he was able to set her gently on the bed. As he undressed, Becky threw off her sweater and did a worm dance until she was free of her slacks and underwear. By the time she set her bra on the floor, Eric had already mounted her. He groped at her loins, but she held him off.

"Not yet, big boy," she hissed.

Her sound only served to excite him more.

"I want to make good on my boast." She kissed his hairless chest and slid beneath the covers.

IT WAS ONE O'CLOCK in the morning when Eric rolled away from his paramour and put on his boxers. "I need to check the fire," he mumbled. "It must be almost out."

"Why bother?" Becky cooed. She stretched her arms up and out from under a heavy quilted comforter. "I'm going to have to leave soon or I'll never be able to make my first class in the morning."

"You're probably right. I don't know what kind of story I'm going to tell my wife. She thinks I went into Utica to visit a friend in the hospital."

"Just tell her you met another friend from school that you hadn't seen since college. Say that you went out for a beer and the time just got away from you."

"Yeah, that might work, especially if I kiss her and tell her that I love her when I get into bed."

Rebecca laughed. "Wives are so gullible. If that's your plan, lover boy, you better wash before you get too close to her. My scent is all over you."

Eric sniffed his arm. "You may be right. I hadn't thought of that." He left the cottage, ran to the lake and jumped in.

A few minutes later he returned shivering. He snatched a towel from a nail on the entrance porch and vigorously rubbed himself.

Becky appeared at the door. She had dressed while Eric was splashing around in the dark. Eric moved past her and stood next to the stove; it was barely warm.

"Jesus," he said, "That damn water is like ice. Would you get me my clothes?"

Becky wrapped herself around his nakedness. "Would you like me to warm you up? Your little man has shrunk to nothing."

"My little man has had enough for one night," he said.

Eric moved away from her and entered the bedroom. After dressing, he made the bed and searched the room for evidence that might lead a family member to conclude that someone had been there.

"Will I see you again?" Becky asked.

"Let's discuss that at another time. Right now I need to get my ass home. What happened tonight was good, but I don't want to lose my happy home over it. I'll probably have to deal with issues of guilt for a while, but…"

Eric bent over and kissed her gently on the cheek. "Thanks for a wonderful evening."

He ushered her out of the camp and after assuring himself that the door was locked, he hurried to his truck.

"You know the way out of here, right?" Without waiting for an answer he added, "I'll see you at lunch. We can talk then."

Eric entered the pickup and backed his way up the dirt road. His tires were kicking loose gravel all the way to the top of the hill.

Before Becky could maneuver her car and follow, the lights from Eric's vehicle were no longer visible.

Chapter 12

AT FIVE THIRTY IN THE EVENING, Steve Edwards listened as Jim related the most recent information regarding the misconduct of his waif-like art teacher.

"...and so, she appears to be morally bankrupt. She's a nymphomaniac who believes that she is possessed of demonic powers. In short, she's a nut case. Her goal is to screw every male in the school, regardless of age or marital status."

"How do you want to handle this?" Edwards asked. "We don't want this blown up in the papers."

"I'd like to suspend her with pay pending a hearing. That will get her out of the school and away from kids."

"Yeah, but she's living right in town. How are we going to keep the boys out of her apartment?"

"I'll tell her where we're going with this and give her the option of resigning. If she's willing to resign, I'll place a note in her file stating that she left to take another job—or something like that. The alternative for her would be for me to turn the matter over to the authorities. I'm going to tell her that one of the boys with whom she had sex is only sixteen. He doesn't reach the age of consent for another month. She could be charged with statutory rape."

"Is that true?"

"That one of the boys was under age? No, but she doesn't know that. I'll run a bluff. I think she'll go for it. At the very least we could file a 3020-A with the state and charge her with violating the ethics code. If she's found guilty she would lose her license to teach."

"That would mean that the kids would have to testify. I don't think the parents or the board are going to go for that."

"I don't want that either, but I don't think it will ever come to that."

"Okay, but don't do anything until I talk to the president of the board."

"I'll need some direction soon. This thing could blow up in our faces."

"I'll get back to you within the hour."

It was late when Steve Edwards finally called.

"I'm sorry it took so long, Jim, but I had a hard time getting an answer from the board. All but one member want her suspended with pay and an attempt made to have her resign. If that doesn't work, we'll have to conference with the board to see what steps they want to take next."

"I'm going over to her apartment immediately and confront her with the matter. I'll call a substitute teacher to cover her classes until this matter has been resolved."

The village of Parma was located a few miles from the school. Rebecca occupied a one-bedroom flat above the ground floor antique shop. When Jim arrived at Rebecca's apartment, he noticed that her car was not parked in front as would normally be the case when she was home. A little bell jingled as Jim entered the shop.

"Hello, Mr. Rahin," a little Polish lady in a babushka and shawl said as she entered the shop. She had a room in the back. "Are you interested in some antiques?"

"No thank you, Mrs. Kistowski. I'm looking for your tenant, Ms. Fitch. Would you know where I might be able to find her?"

Mrs. Kistowski's smile faded and she turned away.

"I don't keep track of her, she mumbled, her friendly demeanor gone. "I haven't seen her since she left for school. With that one you never know. She has boys and men coming and going at all hours of the day and night. It ain't right. She's not a good Christian woman. I hear things when men are up there. Her bedroom is over mine. You should do something about her. It ain't

77

right, it just ain't right. If she wants to be a fallen woman, that's her business, but with young boys—it just ain't right."

"That's why I'm here, Mrs. Kistowski. I just became aware of her actions. I'm here to put a stop to it."

"I'm sorry," she apologized. "I thought you were here for personal reasons. I see some of the other teachers going upstairs with her. It ain't right. I know some of them are married men with families."

"Do you know what time she usually gets home?"

The old woman shook her head. "I don't know. Sometimes it's late. I'm usually already in bed. When she takes a shower it wakes me up."

"Thank you for your time and the information. I guess I'll have to wait until tomorrow to talk with her."

Jim drove back to the school and called Alison at home.

"Alison, would you mind calling one of our subs for tomorrow. I will need someone to cover Ms. Fitch's classes."

Alison agreed.

"And have you heard from Ms. Fitch? I can't seem to locate her."

"I don't know if this means anything, but Ms. Fitch and Eric Manley were talking in the office after school. It sounded like they were going to meet somewhere."

"Did they say where?"

"If they did, I didn't hear. My phone rang and by the time I was finished with the call they were gone."

"Thanks, Alison; I'll see you in the morning."

After hanging up, Jim called Eric Manley's home. On the second ring a young girl answered.

"Hello," Jim said in a soft voice. "Can I speak to your father?"

"My daddy isn't home."

Suddenly there was another voice on the phone; it was Eric's wife.

"Hello, Norma speaking—can I help you?"

"Norma, this is Jim Rahin, is Eric home?"

"No, Mr. Rahin, he went to Utica. He said he probably wouldn't be back ''til late. Is there a message I can give him?"

"No, thanks, it's not that important. It can wait until morning. Have a nice evening." There's nothing more I can do now, he thought, I guess I'll just have to call it a day. I'll catch up with that horny bitch in the morning.

At seven forty-five the following morning Eric Manley entered the office. After signing in he turned to Alison. She was in the process of organizing the morning announcements.

"Excuse me Alison, but Mr. Rahin called my house last night. Is he in?"

"I'll see if he's available."

Alison quickly went to Jim's door, knocked and then opened it before he could respond.

"I'm sorry for interrupting, Mr. Rahin, but Mr. Manley is in the outer office. Would you like to see him before he goes to his homeroom?"

"Yes, ask him to come in."

Eric entered wearing a nervous smile. "Good morning Jim, you wanted to see me?"

"Yes, Eric, have a seat."

Jim left his chair and sat on the edge of the desk.

"Eric, there is an ongoing investigation concerning alleged improprieties and improper conduct of Ms. Fitch—both in and out of school. What is your relationship with her?"

Manley's cheeks became hollow and his eyes took on a sullen look. He stared at Jim trying to gauge how much the principal really knew.

"We are just colleagues and friends, I guess."

Eric decided that Jim was fishing for information and he was not going to admit anything unless it was something that Jim already knew.

"Have you seen each other socially

"The answer to your question is no, but I don't see how that is any of the school's concern. What I do outside of school is my business."

"Normally I would agree with you, but when your activities outside of school have a direct bearing on your students and how they view you in the classroom, it becomes a school matter. Weren't you with Rebecca Fitch last night?"

Eric's complexion changed and he dropped his head just as Alison appeared at the door.

"I'm sorry to interrupt," Alison said, "but Ms. Fitch is here."

"Have her wait and find someone to cover Mr. Manley's homeroom."

When Alison left, Jim reiterated the question. "Did you spend the evening with Ms. Fitch?"

There was a muted whisper. "Yes. She wanted to see my camp on White Lake."

"How long did you stay at the camp?"

Eric shook his head. "I don't remember."

Jim returned to his chair behind the desk.

"Eric, Ms. Fitch has been having sex with a great many individuals, including staff and students."

Eric's head shot up. He looked stunned.

"We are trying to keep this matter as quiet as possible. If a list of her conquests gets out it will mean trouble for men with families and for the school from a hell of a lot of wives and parents"

"Oh shit. Please, Mr. Rahin, keep me out of this. My wife is so trusting. If she thought that I had cheated on her it would mean the end of our marriage. I love Norma and my kids. It would kill me to lose them."

"I don't intend to say anything to anyone outside this room, but we are dealing with a very sick person. I can't predict or be accountable for anything Rebecca might say or do. When I tell her that she is being fired, she may become vindictive."

"Can I talk with her? Maybe I can persuade her to just leave without ruining the lives of others." Eric was shaking. He took a deep breath. "If it's a matter of money, I—"

Jim interrupted. "If you offer to pay her, she'll expose you. She has tried to proposition everyone, including me. Ms. Fitch needs more help than we are equipped to give her here."

When the bell rang ending the homeroom period, Eric stood like a frightened little boy.

"What do I do now?"

"Go to your class and don't say anything to anyone regarding our conversation. I'll keep you posted on the outcome."

"Thanks, Jim. I'll never put myself in this position again. If I get through this without losing my wife and kids I'm going to be the most devoted husband and father anyone ever saw."

When Eric Manley left Jim's office, he passed Rebecca waiting in the outer office. Their eyes met for an instant, but no words were exchanged.

Eric felt odd. *I should have said good morning or something,* he thought. Guilt, shame and fear clung to him like a wet shirt. *How could I have been so stupid?*

Rebecca entered Jim's office in a huff. There was no pretense of being nice, polite or coy.

"What the hell is going on?" she exploded. "Why is there another teacher in my room?"

"Ms. Fitch you are being suspended from your teaching duties with pay, pending a hearing."

"A hearing for what?" she scoffed.

"Well, the list isn't complete yet, but mostly for breaching professional etiquette, and on ethics charges involving illegal conduct with students."

A smirk crossed her lips. "You're just ticked off because of what that sniveling shop teacher told you. What happened, did his conscience get too much for him? And you, did I hurt your pride and ego by my going to bed with Eric instead of you? Ethics! That's a lot of bullshit. What I do outside of school is none of your business. I can sleep with whomever I please. I haven't done anything in school that can be construed as improper."

"What about this?" Jim replied. He held up the note that Rebecca had given him the previous day."

She smiled. "Oh, that. I told you that some student gave me that note. You know how upset I was when I came to see you."

"Ms. Fitch, the note is in your handwriting."

"Before I came to see you I destroyed the original note out of anger. When I thought better of it, I rewrote what was on the note and brought it to you."

"You will have an opportunity to explain your conduct at a hearing. You are banned from school property until then. You will be paid for each day you are out, but if the hearing officer finds cause, you will be terminated and a letter will be placed in your personnel file."

Becky turned her back to Jim.

"Are you telling me that you are going to fire me because I slept with another teacher?" Her eyes now took on a pleading look. "Please Jim, don't do this to me. I really need this job. Come on, we all have fantasies about having sex with people we are attracted to. I'm sorry that Eric is married, but he's a big boy. He could have said 'no thank you, I'm a married man and I love my wife.' He wanted me as much as I wanted him."

"This is not about Eric Manley or any of the other staff members with whom you have coupled; it's about kids," Jim said. "You committed statutory rape upon a sixteen-year-old boy last Saturday night in the barn of the Gerald Frank family party. We know that you had sex with a number of boys who were there. One of those boys will not be seventeen until January. Even with his consent the act constitutes rape of a minor. Furthermore, your actions at that party breached the line of etiquette and ethical conduct between student and teacher. If this goes to a 3020-A hearing, you will lose your certificate to teach school in this state. You will, more than likely, be arrested at that time."

Fitch collapsed into the chair. She was ashen. Her appearance, for the first time since entering Jim's office, was submissive. She folded her hands and looked at the carpet.

"I thought all the boys were old enough," she managed. Her voice was barely audible and her lower lip quivered. "We were just having fun. Nobody got hurt. Christ, kids have sex all the time. It's no big deal."

"I don't think a judge, jury or hearing officer will see it that way."

Becky wrapped her arms around herself and looked up. "Jim, do I have any options?"

"If you resign—effective today, I think I can convince the board that we shouldn't go to a hearing on this. There would be no need to place students, families, Mrs. Kistowski, or staff members in the embarrassing situation of having to testify."

"What about my record?"

"There will be nothing in your file about this. All that will be in your file for others to see will be your letter of resignation and the reasons you stated for resigning." In his mind Jim had other thoughts. *My phone conversation with other administrators looking for a recommendation on you, honey, is another matter.*

Rebecca frowned. "If you will have Ms. Block type something up, I'll sign it."

"I think that is a wise decision. Rebecca, if you choose to remain in education, I would advise you to change the way you deal with students and staff. Find yourself an unmarried man and stay away from schoolboys."

Three weeks after Rebecca Fitch left North Country Central, Jim received a letter.

Dear Mr. Rahin,

This letter is to let you know that I am back in New York City and away from the provincial attitudes of Hicktown, U.S.A. I am teaching art in a private school that appreciates my special talents and sensibilities. I am dating one of my students; he is of age. Nobody is making a big deal out of it. As for North Country and the way I was treated, I have placed a curse on you all. You especially will know the wrath of my power. From this day forth you will never know the warmth of a woman's arms or the fruit of her love. You will wander the earth lusting, but never attaining that which you seek. Only when you have come to me, repent and dip your staff of life into my well of forgiveness, will your loins know the true warmth of a women's passion.

As for your illustrious shop teacher, he too will flounder in a pool of despair. His wife will leave him and his manhood will be damaged beyond repair. Even as I set pen to paper there is a movement within your district to deny him tenure. You know this is true. Then know too that all I have written will come to pass. When you feel remorse and wish to make amends, I can be reached at the School of Gifted Minds, in Manhattan.

Satan's Servant

Rebecca

That evening, after Jim and Hope had made love, Jim remained awake for a while thinking about the letter and its contents. Seems like I didn't have to wander too far to find what I was looking for. The warmth of Hope's love was all the fruit I need. Yeah, poor Becky is a sick bitch. She shouldn't be allowed to be around kids.

He rolled over in bed and waited for sleep, but it wouldn't come. Something about Rebecca's ranting was bothersome. Then it hit him.

How did she know about Steve Edwards' decision to eliminate Eric Manley from the faculty? The decision had not been made public. Even Eric didn't know. The move had nothing to do with the events surrounding Rebecca. The decision had been made to cut the industrial arts program based on cost and numbers in classes. The last hired would be the first terminated. How did she know that? Only the administration and members of the Board had that information. Had she slept with a member of the administration? Perhaps a board member had been compromised. Is she really a witch? It was three o'clock in the morning before sleep found him.

Chapter 13

IN JANUARY, STELLA KISTOWSKI'S antique shop and the apartment that Rebecca Fitch had rented burned to the ground. Poor Stella had allowed her insurance to lapse. As a result she was left with nothing. At seventy-two years old Stella was forced to leave the North Country with only the clothing that neighbors had given her, and went to Rochester to live with her daughter Dolores.

Dolores Kistowski had left Parma shortly after graduating from high school and moved to Rochester, where she took a job with Kodak. While there she met Joseph Kornatowski, a bricklayer. Kornatowski worked on a construction site near the Kodak plant.

Three months after sharing their first kielbasa sandwich and a glass of beer at the Picture Perfect Diner, Dolores announced that she was pregnant. She and Joseph had a quiet wedding that included Joseph's brother, sister and parents. Stella did not attend. Her moral indignation over Dolores' sudden physical predicament left her angry and embarrassed. In Stella eyes Dolores' fall from grace was an offense against God and an abomination to the family.

The Kornatowskis had two more children over the following eight years, but in the summer of their ninth year of marriage Joseph disappeared. The gossip among friends and workers suggested that he had left Rochester with a cute Polish nurse. Six months earlier, Joseph had been forced to seek medical attention for an injury sustained at the work site. Joe apparently bonded with a young nurse ten years his junior and after six months of hiding their affair the two left their lives in New York and ran off together.

Dolores never heard from Joseph again. When she questioned Joe's parents they disavowed any knowledge of his whereabouts. Joe's brother, however, told Dolores that the last time he heard from his brother he was in California. Dolores never sought a divorce. She raised her children on her own, refusing to seek assistance from friends or family.

At the age of fifty-four Dolores accepted a buyout from Kodak, which at the time, was trying to reduce its work force as part of a budgetary cut-back.

With her children grown and gone, Dolores retired. In order to augment her meager retirement dollars she took a job in a tiny Polish bakery on the east side of the city. Life became tolerable and Dolores looked forward to the day when she would be old enough to collect her social security. Supporting Stella was not a burden Dolores had anticipated.

JIM RAHIN STUDIED THE charred ruins of what had once been Stella Kistowski's pride and joy. "Did they ever find out what caused the fire?" he asked Steve Edwards.

"No," Edwards replied. "They say it was a space heater, but it could have been faulty wires. The fire department just doesn't know. It's too bad that Stella didn't have insurance. I feel sorry for her."

The two men walked to the Four Corners in town and entered The Parma Coffee Shack.

"What will it be?" a waitress with gray hair asked.

"Good morning, Frieda," Steve answered. "We'll have a couple of coffees." He turned to Jim. "You want a donut or something?"

Jim shook his head. "Coffee's fine," he replied.

When the waitress returned with the coffee she interrupted the quiet conversation of the men.

"Is there anything more on that fire?" she asked. "I bin lis'nin' to the conversation in here. Some say she did it."

Jim looked up. "Who is she?"

"You know," the waitress continue with a wink of her eye. "That teacher that was boffin the football team—you know, the one you'se guys fired. Stella heard everything. I can't tell ya how many times old Stella would come in here ta complain about the goins on in the middle of the night. Why it was like a friggin' parade ground wit men coming and going all the time. It's a wonder she did any teaching. I'm surprised you'se guys never got wise." She winked at Jim. "Or maybe ya did. I hear she even banged a couple a teachers. If Stella said it once, she said it a million times. That woman's impropriety just wasn't right."

"Tell me, Frieda, just how did Rebecca Fitch, manage to burn the place down? At the time of the fire she was in New York City," Jim asked.

"She told everybody that she was a witch en I for one, believed her. Half the stuff she talked about doin' has come true. She threatened poor old Mrs. Kistowski—said that she wuz gonna make her life miserable. Well it can't get more miserable than it is now."

"Frieda, if you can take a little time away from your speculations, I'd like an order of toast," Edwards interrupted.

Frieda gave Steve a cold eye and left without further comment.

"Do you believe in all that witch bullshit?" Steve asked.

"I didn't used to, but some of the things that have been happening around here since Fitch left have me wondering."

"Ahhh it's all coincidental."

"Like I said, it still gives me cause to wonder." Jim gave a wave of his hand and accidently knocked over his coffee. The brew splashed across the counter and onto his crotch.

Frieda quickly approached with a towel. "You're a little clumsy this morning ain't cha?" She wiped up the brown spill from the counter and looked at the stain on Jim's pants and smiled. "Ya wanna see if I can git that stain outta yur crotch?"

Jim dipped his napkin into a glass of water and applied it to the stain. "No thanks," he replied. "These pants have to go to the cleaners anyway."

Steve Edwards smiled. "Maybe the witch made you spill your coffee."

Jim frowned. "Maybe, but the only witch I see around here is Frieda."

"Youse guys can joke about it if ya want, but that woman ain't done causing havoc around here yet." Frieda snatched up the towel she had used to wipe the table and left.

OVER THE NEXT FIVE MONTHS several things happened to further stimulate Jim's thoughts regarding the veracity of Rebecca Fitch's claims.

Gerald Frank was involved in a snowmobile accident and needed to be hospitalized for the balance of the school year. During his incapacitation Sally Dunn, Gerald's girlfriend, broke up with him and started dating his best friend.

In May the Frank barn burned down. It was the same barn that had served as the passion pit during the football party. Like the Kistowski tragedy the fire department could not determine the cause of the blaze. Unlike Stella the Franks did have the barn insured, but the loss destroyed a prize bull that was not insured.

By the end of June, Eric Manley was out of a job. Due to financial disputes and rumors of infidelity, Eric's wife took the children and moved back with her parents. Another boy rumored to have slept with the self-proclaimed witch was killed in an automobile accident graduation night.

In late July the elementary principal Al Williams had a stroke and was forced to retire on disability. He was only fifty.

During that same month a board member, one who had been the most vociferous about driving Rebecca out of the area, had a heart attack.

Jim was starting to believe in witches.

Chapter 14

STEVEN EDWARDS SERVED IN FRANCE during the Second World War and received the Purple Heart for injuries sustained during fighting outside Rennes. Edwards was only eighteen years old when he joined the army.

Steven was discharged in Washington D.C. after spending six months in the hospital. With an education voucher, compliments of the G.I. Bill, he entered the University of Pittsburgh. Less than four years later he graduated with a degree in elementary education and spent the next five years as a sixth grade teacher. During that time he married Helen Kent, a nurse he met had while recuperating in Washington. The Edwards had one son. Jenner was named after Helen's father.

After seven year of teaching Steve was appointed principal; he was thirty-four years old. Six years later he became the superintendent of a small school in upstate New York. The entire district had less than six hundred students.

In early 1960, New York offered an incentive to small schools making it fiscally advantageous for them to consolidate. Edward's school, Beaver County Union, joined with five other small north-country schools to form one large central school district. The new consolidated district comprised more than four hundred square miles and fourteen hundred students. The new district took the name, North Country Central School.

Steven Edwards, by virtue of his seniority, became the district's first superintendent of schools.

YOUNG JENNER EDWARDS had been spoiled from birth. What his parents didn't give him, his grandparents did. Steve and Helen kept their son safely locked in a protective cocoon and sheltered him from accountability, including discipline exacted by teachers.

Jenner became a verbal bully. Whenever a student or teacher attempted to rebuke him for his inappropriate remarks—or behavior, Papa was always there to intercede. After a while teachers gave up trying to reprimand Jenner and allowed him to do as he pleased.

As an elementary student Jenner browbeat other students on a daily basis. He threatened to tell his father lies about teachers who attempted to discipline him. He often made up tales about teachers whom he did not like. Steve always took Jenner's side.

"My son isn't perfect, but he doesn't lie," Steve would reply when others tried to enlighten the Edwards family about Jenner's behavior. When Jenner came to the high school, John Walker was well aware of the boy's antics but chose to play the game of supporting the Edwards family as a matter of professional courtesy.

When Walker left North Country, Jim was determined not to allow Jenner to continue his inappropriate behavior.

TWO YEARS INTO JIM'S PRINCIPALSHIP the collision happened.

Nelson Andrews, Jenner's English teacher, refused to allow Jenner to leave class before the end of the period. Jenner wanted to get an early start on lunch. He chose to ignore his teacher's directive, and left the class with his index finger held on high.

The rest of the class grumbled. The students knew that nothing would be done. Some excuse would be given about a medical reason for Jenner's need to eat early or that he had permission to leave early to have lunch with his father. It was always some inane excuse, but the result was always the same. There would be no accountability for what Jenner believed to be his prerogative.

When Jim was notified of Jenner's insubordinate actions he immediately went to the cafeteria where he found the boy in the lunch line. Jim picked up Jenner's tray and said, "Young man, come with me. You are going to eat your lunch in my office today."

"Why? I want to eat in the cafeteria with my friends." Jenner showed no anguish.

"I'm not interested in what you want. You left class without permission, so I'm placing you on detention."

Jenner huffed, "We'll see about that. My father will show you who is boss. I'll bet I don't spend one minute in detention."

Students who were in the cafeteria applauded as Jenner followed the principal in verbal protest.

In the office Jim placed Jenner's tray on the conference table.

"You will eat here. When you have finished I'll escort you to the detention hall."

Jenner was fuming and grumbled, "I'm not hungry."

"Not hungry? You told your teacher that you were so hungry you couldn't wait for the period to end. Are you sick?"

"Yeah, sick of you," Jenner mumbled.

Jim heard the remark, but chose to indulge the sarcasmfor the time being.

"I'll have the nurse take a look at you just in case. If you are sick, I'll call your mother and have her pick you up."

"I'm not sick!" Jenner exclaimed.

"Still, if you're not hungry I think I'll have the nurse check you out." Jim hit the intercom. "Ms. Block, would you ask the nurse to come to my office."

"I told you I'm not sick," Jenner reiterated.

A few minutes later Laura Jones entered Jim's office. "Did you want to see me?" she asked.

"Yes Mrs. Jones. Jenner left his English class early because he said he was too hungry to wait until the bell. Now he says that he isn't hungry. I just want to make sure he isn't sick."

"Geeze, I already told you, I ain't sick," Jenner snapped. "How many times do I have to tell you? I just ain't hungry."

The nurse moved to Jenner's side and took his pulse.

"His pulse is a little elevated, but not so that we should worry." She looked into Jenner's eyes and had him stick out his tongue. "I don't think we need to send him home," she said with a smile. "I think he'll be all right for the remainder of the day."

Jim nodded. "Thank you, Mrs. Jones, that will be all."

Laura Jones giggled and left.

After an hour or so, Jim called Alison into his office.

"Ms. Block, ask Jenner if he has finished eating. If he has, have someone take his tray back to the cafeteria."

When Jenner told Alison that he wasn't hungry, she removed his tray.

"Jenner, for insubordination and leaving the classroom without permission, I am placing you on in-school suspension for three days. You will have your class work brought to you each day. You will have your lunch brought to you at noon and should you need to use the boy's room, a teacher will escort you there, and return you to the hall when you have finished. Furthermore, you are barred from attending this weekend's football game and evening dance. Do you have any questions?"

Jenner flashed a smile. "Mister, you just lost your job. When my father finds out about this, you are toast. He has the final say around here, not you. You will be overruled, count on it."

Jim took a deep breath. "You may be right, but until I'm overruled, you are going to the detention hall."

Ten minutes after one Jim left Jenner at the detention hall. By the time he got back to the office, Jenner had already walked out of detention and was on his way to the superintendent's office

"Mr. Rahin," Alison called, "Mr. Limmer called. Jenner walked out of the detention hall as soon as you left. Mr. Limmer thinks that he is on his way to the district office to see his father."

Jim smiled. Well I guess this is the showdown. Maybe you will have a new principal before the day is out. If Edwards overrules me on this I'll walk. The rules are for everyone. If Jenner can do as he pleases then there will be no discipline for anyone else. I will not treat Jenner any differently than I do other students. If I leave, the board of education and the public will know why."

Just as Jim was finishing his declaration the private entrance to his office opened and Steven Edwards entered.

Alison quickly closed the other door.

"Rahin," Edwards bellowed. "What the hell is going on? Are you trying to get yourself fired? I put you in this job, and I can just as easily take you out."

Jim moved to his desk and sat. "Mr. Edwards, your son has been insubordinate to me, his English teacher, and to Mr. Limmer. Jenner is being disciplined in the same manner that any other student would be under similar circumstances. He is your son, but I intend to treat him the same as any other student in the building."

The superintendent leaned over Jim's desk until he and Jim were nose to nose.

"Now you listen to me," he bellowed. "I don't give a damn how you treat the other students, but Jenner Edwards is not going to sit on his ass in some detention hall, be escorted to the john, have someone else deliver his lunch or sit home on the weekend just because he wanted to eat five minutes earlier. Your rules are stupid and my son is not going to abide by them. Do I make myself clear?"

Steven Edwards was white with anger and shaking from rage.

Jim pushed himself away from the desk until the back of his chair struck the wall behind him. He studied his boss for a moment. He wanted to make sure that he did not respond in anger or retaliation even though he was so angry the knuckles on his hands were pale from the grip he held on the arm of the chair.

Jim responded with cool candor. "I'm sorry that you have become frustrated with Jenner's behavior. I understand the anger you feel because of the disciplinary action taken against him. I also understand what you are saying. But before I can respond, I need to know in what capacity you are addressing me?"

Steve Edwards straightened himself and took one step back. The pallor of his cheeks began to gain a more pinkish tone. He looked at Jim in a puzzled manner.

"What do you mean?"

"Are you addressing me as a concerned parent or as my immediate supervisor?"

Edwards studied Jim for a moment. His voice was still shaky as he ran the palms of his hand down the side of his blue blazer.

"I'm speaking to you as a parent."

Jim gave a quiet sigh of relief and stood. He adjusted his tie and spoke in a voice that one would use to assure a sad child that all would be well.

"Mr. Edwards, I thank you for taking the time away from your busy schedule to look into a school problem affecting your son. I'm sure that Jenner is a fine young man, but kids make mistakes. It's part of the maturation process. You know what they say about learning more from our mistakes than we do from our successes. Unfortunately, because Jenner walked out of the detention hall, I'm going to tack on another day to his in-school suspension."

Steven Edward stopped and glared at Jim, but said nothing. He was numbed by Jim's response. He took one step back, turned and left the room. There was a resounding "thud" as the door hit the jamb.

When all was quiet, Alison opened the outer door to Jim's office.

"Are you okay?" she asked. "Man oh man, Mr. Edwards could be heard way out in the outer hall. Teachers were coming in to see what was going on. They were making bets on whether or not you would still be here at the end of the day."

"And how did you vote?" Jim asked.

"My money was on you. Did I win?

"I'm still here, but I would have resigned if he had overruled my decision. Who knows? He still might."

"Is there anything I can do?"

"Yes, I need to send a letter to the Edwards family about Jenner's behavior and the subsequent disciplinary action. I'd like it to go out today. I'll have a draft for you in about fifteen minutes."

As promised, Jim gave Alison the letter explaining everything that had happened during the day and the terms of Jenner's in-school suspension, detention, and exemption from all weekend extra school activities. He ended by writing, *your continued interest in Jenner's educational progress is commendable. Please know that the administration and staff appreciate your steadfast support.*

If you would like to discuss this matter more fully or Jenner's educational progress in general, please let me know.

Sincerely,

James Rahin, High School Principal

When Alison returned with the letter for Jim's signature she also handed him a note.

Jim set the letter on his desk and opened the note. It read:

Arabs 1, English 0.

"Who's this from," he asked.

Alison smiled. "It's from Mrs. Cleary."

Jim nodded and placed the note in his pocket. He signed the letter and leaned back in his chair. Ahhh, life is good.

JENNER EDWARDS BECAME a changed student. From the day his father slammed Jim's door, Jenner's attitude about school, his teachers, and other students changed. He was no longer the school's recalcitrant bully.

A month after the incident with Jenner, Jim found himself riding to a meeting with Steven Edwards. They had not spoken since the incident. Now they were on their way to Albany to attend a meeting sponsored by the Board of Cooperative Educational Services.

The miles passed in relative quiet, with only the fundamental courtesies being exchanged. When the two men reached Albany, Jim could stand it no longer.

"How's Jenner doing?"

Steven Edwards kept his eyes focused on the road.

"I'm glad you asked," Steve replied. His demeanor did not change. "I have been meaning to thank you. Since that embarrassing exchange in your office there has been a remarkable change in my son."

The superintendent seemed to shrink in his seat. "I guess kids aren't the only ones who learn from their mistakes. I realized that I have been making a real ass of myself for a long time. Jim, I want to apologize for my ranting. You were right. All students need to be treated the same regardless of parentage."

Steve smiled. "I guess Jenner should have had his ass kicked a long time ago. That was my fault. Helen and I smothered him with protection. Kids need to have a few hard knocks once in a while. Even Jenner is glad it happened. He has a better rapport with his teachers and he now has friends that aren't afraid to come to the house. He even has girls calling."

The station wagon pulled into the parking lot of the Holiday Inn and stopped.

"Jim, I hope there are no hard feelings."

"There are no hard feelings. As far as I'm concerned it never happened."

Chapter 15

THE NEXT TWO YEARS flew by as if fastened to a time machine. Jim had considered other job openings, but none were any closer to Utica than the one he had.

A new problem for schools—and kids—was on the horizon. It came under the heading of drugs. Marijuana, or "weed" as it was called, and crack cocaine started turning up in many of the city school districts. Jim knew that it was only a matter of time before North Country High would be faced with the new social curse. He was concerned about the handling of student or staff caught with drugs and decided to ask if he could discuss the matter with the board of education in executive session.

"Executive meetings are for matters concerning budget or staff," Steve Edwards said. "I don't think we can talk about drugs."

"What about students or staff suspected of doing or selling drug? Do you want that information discussed in an open session of the board?"

"No!"

"Okay. I suspect that we have a couple of students bringing marijuana to school. I want to know how the board feels about the issue."

At the next board meeting, the president announced that the board was going into executive session to discuss a student problem.

Brandon Flansburg, the president of the board of education, was a former jock who had squandered his youth. As a high school athlete he had received the adoration of his school mates and the community. Shortly after graduation, he married his high school sweetheart; she was in a family way.

The responsibilities of marriage and family life dashed any plans Brandon had for attending college. The once tall, rangy athlete allowed himself to go to seed. Beer and a sedentary life style hurried the onset of middle age. He was no longer the chosen one. Brandon became content to relive his past glory and golden years as an athlete through his athletically gifted sons. To ensure that his sons would receive every advantage the school had to offer, Brandon ran for a position on the board of education. In addition to shepherding the educational future of his two boys, Brandon hoped to regain his popularity in the community. Brandon vowed that his sons would not make the same errors in judgment that had cost him a college career.

"Well, Mr. Rahin, what's this business about drugs in our school?" Brandon questioned with a smile. "I asked my sons if they knew anything about drugs at North Country High and they laughed. This ain't the big city ya know. If our kids get high on anything, they get high on sports."

"Mr. Flansburg, I hope you're right, but marijuana has already made its way into Albany, Watertown, and Utica schools. It won't take long before drugs are here in North Country. I had a phone call last night regarding two sisters from Lumber Falls. They have been bragging about bringing some marijuana to school tomorrow."

"Where would these girls get drugs?" Gary Storms, a quiet shopkeeper, asked. Storms ran for a seat on the board because of the insistence of his wife. The Storms had a daughter in the tenth grade. The last thing he wanted was to have his daughters introduced to drugs.

"The sisters go with a couple of boys from Utica. They met the boys over the summer. All I need to know from the board, is how do you want me to handle cases involving kids and drugs?"

Brandon Flansburg was still wearing a condescending smile. "What do you suggest, Mr. Rahin?"

Jim swallowed hard. He was about to suggest something that his ultraconservative board would not like.

"I would like to suspend all first-time drug offenders for five days, and defer the matter to their parents. Second time offenders would be turned over to the law. Staff members found with drugs in school would be arrested and dismissed. We should have a zero tolerance policy, especially when it comes to adults with drugs."

"I think we should have a zero-tolerance policy for all violators," Flansburg said. "If kids had a proper home supervision they wouldn't be messing around with drugs. When we come out of executive session, I will entertain a motion stating that the North Country Central School District shall maintain a zero-tolerance policy toward any person or persons found with drugs in their possession."

"I will move that motion," another member yelled.

"And I'll second the motion," Storms followed. "I certainly don't want someone giving drugs to my daughter."

I hope you people won't be sorry about your decision, Jim thought.

As Jim had warned, two girls were found to be in possession the following morning. Jim turned the two students over to two officers from the sheriff's department. The board of education was delighted.

Two days later Jim received a tip from Gandy Farrow that three football players had brought a nickel bag of hashish to school and had the contraband secreted in the locker of Rex Collier. Rex was on the football team and had never been a discipline problem.

Jim stationed himself in a room near Rex's second period study hall and waited. Less than ten minutes into the period Rex left the study hall and stopped at his locker. From there he walked to the nearest boys' room. Jim followed undetected. A few minutes later Jim entered the lavatory. He could smell smoke. He determined that it wasn't the normal smell of tobacco; it was the distinct odor of "grass".

Upon seeing the principal, Rex started waving his hand around to dispel the haze. In the urinal Jim notice a cigarette butt.

"I think you better come with me," Jim said. "If that butt is what I think it is, you are in a whole lot of trouble."

"Okay, so I was smoking." Rex quickly hit the flush handle and watched the evidence drain away. "It was just a cigarette."

"I smell pot," Jim exploded. "I know the difference between cigarette smoke and marijuana."

Rex hunched forward and emptied his pockets. "Search me. I don't do drugs."

Jim looked at the glazed eyes of the athlete. "I'm going to have you checked by the nurse, and then I'm going to check your locker."

"You can't open my locker without a warrant or my permission."

"Well, I'll tell you what. I have reason to believe that contraband is secreted in your locker. I am going to have Ms. Block call the sheriff's office and ask that an officer be sent to school. That officer will have the authority to open your locker. If marijuana is found, you will be arrested."

All six feet of Rex's seemed to shrink. He went pale.

"Can we make a deal?" he asked.

"That depends. If you give up the source, I'll look the other way on this bust."

"Geez, you're asking me to give up my friends. I can't do that."

"Then I guess you'll have to get busted for possession and take your chances. In any case, you are no longer on the football team. I will inform your coach about this incident and have him pick up your gear. Smoking is a violation of the code."

Rex became filled with emotion. "Come on, Mr. Rahin, if I get arrested it will kill my parents. Please give me a break. Please!"

"You heard my terms. One way or another, I'm going to find out who is bringing that crap into my school. I'll find out sooner or later. If nothing else, your arrest will let everyone know that North Country High has a zero tolerance when it comes to drug users." Jim took Rex by the arm. "Come with me."

"Wait a minute—wait a minute, please. If I tell you what you want to know, do the other guys need to know who gave you the information?"

"No. I won't say anything, but you know as well as I that things have a way of getting out."

Another student entered the boys' room. Upon seeing Jim, the boy did an about-face and left.

"The longer we stay here the more people there will be who will have seen us together. What will it be?"

"Okay, I'll tell you. I have a bag of hashish in my locker, but it's not mine. I'm just holding it for Lance Bedger."

"Bedger! His father is on the board."

"Yeah, and so is Matt Flansburg's father. He's the board president."

"Are these guys users or sellers?

"Bedger is a user like me, but Matt is buying the stuff from the same guy who gave the Combs sisters their grass."

Rex's glum appearance suddenly changed as if he had been struck with brilliance. "You can say that the information came from one of the sisters. That will get me off the hook."

Jim ignored the suggestion. "When is Matt supposed to pick up the bag?"

"Right after school. He's gonna pick the stuff up before he goes to football practice. He plans on selling some of the grass to guys on the team."

"That's just great. One of the team leaders is providing drugs for the team. That's real nice."

At three-forty-five the bell rang ending the academic school day. Rex was cooling his heels in Jim's conference room, with the shades down.

Jim had hid himself in a room directly across from Rex's locker. He kept the door to the room slightly ajar so that he could observe the locker undetected. Five minutes after the bell, Matt Flansburg approached the locker with Lance Bedger at his side. Matt quickly opened the locker and glanced around. After assuring himself that there were no teachers nearby, he withdrew two plastic bags. One he stuffed into his pocket, the other he handed to Lance. Matt smiled, slapped his buddy on the back and closed the locker door.

Jim left his blind and took both boys by the arm. "Gentlemen please accompany me to my office."

Both boys were shocked by Jim's sudden appearance.

"What's the matter, Mr. Rahin?" Fear resonated in Matt Flansburg's voice. "We were just on our way to practice."

The look on Lance's face showed panic. "Can't we see you after practice?" a pasty-face Lance asked.

"No, I need to see you both right now. Practice can wait." Jim spotted Lora Jones getting ready to leave school for the day. "Mrs. Jones," he called. "Could you step into my office for a moment?"

The nurse nodded and followed Jim and the two boys to the office. Jones looked at the two boys and asked, "What have you two been up to?"

"Nothing that I know of," Matt grumbled.

"Mrs. Jones I asked you to come with me because I have reason to believe that these two boys are in possession of marijuana. If what I suspect is true, I wanted another adult present when I search them."

"That's illegal," Matt blurted. "You can't search us without a warrant."

Jim grinned. "You have been watching too much television. School is considered a special place. I have many of the same rights that your parents have. When you are here school officials can act in place of your parents. Of course if you would rather wait until Officer Dalett gets here, we can do that too." Jim looked at Matt and barked, "Empty your pockets."

Matt took off his jacket, placed in on Jim's desk and emptied his shirt and pants pockets. Lance did the same. When they had finished, the boys turned toward Jim and raised their arms waist high with their palms up.

"See, I told you, we don't have any marijuana," said Matt.

"Now can we go to practice?"

"Sure, after you empty your coat pockets."

Both boys looked at Jim with cold, white fear. "Come on, Mr. Rahin, give us a break. Okay, I do have a bag of pot, but it isn't mine. I'm only holding it for a friend."

"Me too," Lance confessed.

"Gentlemen, have a seat. You know that this school has a zero tolerance policy regarding the possession on drugs." Jim turned to the nurse. "Mrs. Jones, I'm going to ask you to stay a while until

this matter is settled. Please remain with the boys until I return."
Jim went to the outer office.

"Alison, please phone the sheriff s office and ask them to send Officer Dalett or Bookmore to the school. Tell them that it's important."

By the time the sheriff arrived both parents had been notified and were on their way to the high school. They arrived in time to see their sons in handcuffs.

"Why wasn't I called first?" Brandon Flansburg yelled.

"Mr. Flansburg, I didn't make the school policy about kids with drugs. I'm only following the board's policy."

"Are you some kind of a nut? As the board president you should have called me first. This little stunt is going to cost you your job, Rahin, you can bet on it."

"You don't have the authority to fire me, Mr. Flansburg. If the board wishes to do so they will need to file charges as required by law."

No attempt was made to fire Jim, but things began to go badly for Steve Edwards. His contract was up for renewal.

"I'm fifty-five years old," Edwards announced at the next administrative meeting. He had come to the meeting directly following a closed session with the Board of Education. "I want to get out before I end up like Al Williams. This past year has taken a toll on me and my family. Our former art teacher has written letters to various people in the community hinting that I was one of the community members with whom she had had a liaison. It's a lie, but some still believe that where there is smoke, there's fire. Now this drug business is more than I care to deal with." Edwards paused. "There are those who insist that I am to blame for Fitch and the ill-conceived board policy concerning drugs. Phone calls to my house at all hours of the day have upset my wife. It just isn't worth the hassle."

Jim began to sense a possible opportunity. He would seek the job of superintendent should Steve retire. After the meeting Jim decided to talk to Edwards.

"Excuse me Steve," said Jim. "I'd like a few minutes of your time if you don't mind."

"What can I do for you, Jim?"

"If you retire, I intend to apply for your job. Will I have your support?"

Steve Edwards pushed himself away from his desk and stood. He walked to the window and peered out. After a moment he turned to Jim.

"Jim you are a strong high school principal, maybe too strong. You have done some good things here at North Country, but you lack patience and sometimes you are resistant to compromise. In your many accomplishments you have made some friends, but you have also made enemies. Here at the school, on the board, and in the community, there are those who want you gone. They aren't about to see you as the superintendent. Your enemies have been very vocal."

Edwards waved his arms about. "Don't get me wrong. There are those on the board who admire the work you have done, but the board will never appoint a person who does not have the full support of every member. They will opt for a candidate who is less controversial. I don't believe my support will make any difference. I have already told them that I plan to stay out of the search process. The selection of the next superintendent will be totally up to them."

Jim frowned and sat in a large, stuffed chair. "Thanks for your candor. I am aware of the split among some of the members on the board, but I thought your support might have some sway."

"I believe they have already decided to go outside the district for their next school leader. The board plans to advertise in the *State Administrators News Bulletin*."

"Well I guess that's that." Jim rose, thanked Edwards again, and left. On the way back to his office he thought of various options to his predicament. He was bitter and decided to start looking for a job elsewhere. He believed that there were several schools that would be glad to get an administrator with his background and experience. The schools might not be in the direction that Hope would like, but at this point he just wanted out.

That night Jim unloaded his frustrations on Hope. She listened intently before responding.

"What about me?" she asked. "I can't just get a job someplace else, just like that. If you leave I will have to stay here alone until we can sell the house."

Jim became pensive. "I guess I was so pissed off about the board that I didn't think the situation through. I'll stay on at North Country, but I will continue to search for better jobs for both of us."

FOR THE BALANCE OF THE YEAR Jim's focus centered on hunting and the theater. On weekend he spent time with Paul Glenn and Ed Owen hunting white rabbits or fishing. Gary Owen was back in Idaho and was being considered for a promotion; not even his brother Ed heard much from him.

During the week, when Jim wasn't committed to a school function, he and Hope spent their evenings helping the theater group with their current production. Hope had also developed a fetish for antiques and while Jim was out hunting wild game, she hunted for antiques at house sales, garage sales and auctions. Her new-found hobby was beginning to take a toll on the family budget and household space. The matter reached a critical stage in the spring.

"Hope, from now on you cannot bring something into this house without getting rid of something else first," Jim professed.

Hope reluctantly agreed, but her dilemma was in knowing what to get rid of and what to keep. "At this rate, we will have to get a bigger house," she said. "Either that or I need to go into the antique business."

In June, Jim and Hope looked at a house located south of their present home, twenty miles closer to Utica. It was a four-bedroom, two-story building with three-and-a-half bathrooms, three fireplaces, and a two-car garage. The structure was secluded in a wooded area off the main road and had a long twisting driveway stretching onto a plateau. The property included seven acres of woods. The couple decided to make an offer contingent on the sale of their present house.

Within thirty days both transactions were finalized with closing on both properties taking place on the same day. Hope now had a larger house to accommodate her antiques.

The drive from and to work bothered Jim, especially after a late board meeting. It seemed that he no sooner got home, when he would have to start back to school.

Without informing Hope, Jim began to explore the possibility of purchasing a small cottage on one of the smaller lakes—something closer to school. The property he found was in an estate. Those who had inherited the property were in a hurry to settle the account. Jim was informed by the real estate agent that he could purchase the property for thirty thousand dollars. All he needed was ten percent down. He decided to buy it.

The cottage turned out to be a place where both Jim and Hope ran to for peace of mind, quiet and relaxation.

The northeastern corner of the building faced the Adirondack Mountains. Off the living room was a large deck. On a clear day the top of Blue Mountain could be seen in the distance. The cottage had three bedrooms, two baths and a fireplace.

Jim liked the cottage and could have been happy living there on a more permanent basis, but Hope wouldn't hear of it.

During the spring and the following summer, Jim spent his weekends at the cottage. He built a storage shed in the back of the property and tended to the many fruit trees that dotted the two acre plot.

Chapter 16

THE SEARCH FOR A SUCCESSOR to Steve Edwards was a long, lengthy process. Jim did not apply for the position.

By the start of the following September the board of education had settled on a small, nervous man from the Binghamton as their new educational leader.

Chance Canard had been an unpopular superintendent in his last school district. Three months before the end of his contract, the board informed Canard that they would not continue his services. In July Canard had the good fortune of meeting a North Country board member at a state outing in Albany. Canard did not disclose his pending termination, but was able to impress the board member with a boastful account of his administrative accomplishments. During a long evening of plied libations the intoxicated board member urged Canard to apply for the administrative vacancy posted by North Country Central School. In late August, Canard was hired and given a three year contract.

Chance Canard possessed a Napoleonic complex. He was small in stature, less than five-feet-five inches tall and weighed somewhere near one hundred and twenty pounds. His frail appearance, dark beady eyes and pasty complexion belied a timid personality. He had the propensity of looking through a person rather than at them; seldom did he smile. When it came to the ability of others, Canard was always cynical.

A graduate of Oswego State University, Canard was certified to teach elementary education, but after graduation he was unable to find a job teaching school and spent ten years in industry where he drifted from job to job.

The small man abhorred taller, stronger men and resented the reference of "Shorty." It was a nickname he quickly acquired no matter where he went. To his chagrin the moniker was gleefully applied by men and women alike.

At the age of thirty-two Chance was finally able to land a teaching job in a small backwoods school located in a remote northwestern part of Vermont near the Canadian border. It was there that his self-image changed. He was now larger and stronger than most of the children with whom he spent his days. Chance Canard was no longer "Shorty." He was referred to as Mister by students and staff alike. Despite his size, Chance developed a reputation of being a strict disciplinarian. Within five years, he was appointed to the position of elementary principal. His authoritarian persona pleased the board of education. When the school's superintendent took another appointment in Manchester, New Hampshire, Canard was hired to fill the position.

Three years after assuming the role of superintendent, Chance and the board quarreled over an increase in salary. By the time Canard met the North Country board member his dictatorial style of school management had run its course in Vermont.

From the outset of his appointment Chance Canard insisted that everyone call him, "Mister" when addressing him. He liked to lord his authority over others, including board members.

Like his previous board of education, the North Country Central School District Board soon became fractured by the manner of leadership that Canard offered.

Of the seven-member board. four members argued that the new superintendent had not been given adequate time and support; three members, who had been on the board for many years, could tell that Chance Canard spelled trouble for the district. The new superintendent had a confrontational attitude toward the school, the administration, staff and community.

Each Friday Chance left the district in the early afternoon and did not return until noon on Monday.

If there was a conference or meeting anywhere in the state, Chance Canard told his secretary that he planned to attend. He would often claim that he was traveling to meetings outside the boarders of New York State. All travel, lodging and dining expenses were charged to the district. When there were no meetings to attend, he spent his weekends with a girlfriend who resided outside of Buffalo; she too was an educator of sorts.

Canard earned a new nickname. He became known as the "Ghost." Everyone knew that he was the superintendent, but few people in the community ever saw him.

Jim's first major conflict with Canard came in the early fall when he was called to the superintendent's office for an assignment. It was that encounter that would spark an irritating relationship for them both.

"Mr. Rahin, have a seat," Canard directed as Jim entered the office.

Jim sat and waited as the superintendent fidgeted with some papers on his desk. Without looking at Jim, Canard continued. "Mr. Rahin, as you know the district owns about seventy acres of forest a few miles from the school. I want you to take a group of Gus Cleary's kids up to the site and drop them off. Give them a mower, an axe, and a couple of sickles. Map out a trail for them to cut and mow. I want a nature trail up there so the elementary classes can study the local trees and such."

Gus Cleary was the husband of Lora Cleary, the superintendent's secretary. Gus taught special education. His students ranged in ages from fourteen to twenty-one.

Jim was dumbfounded.

"Well," Jim replied, with hesitation. "Have you talked to Gus about your idea?"

Canard replied in a stinging tirade.

"I'm the superintendent here, not Gus Cleary. I'll decide what, where and when I want things done." Canard stood and began to pace. "I've given you a directive, Mr. Rahin and I expect you to carry it out." In a somewhat calmer voice he added, "I have directed the custodians to put the tools needed for the project into the fifteen-passenger bus. There won't be more than eight or nine students. Am I understood?"

Jim calmed himself before answering. He stood and looked down at the little dictator.

"With all due respect for your position, I'm not going to do what you have asked. First of all what, you are asking me to do is not in my job description. I am needed at the high school, not in a forest twelve miles away. Furthermore, I am not certified to transport students on a school bus. Most importantly, what you are asking them to do is illegal."

Chance Canard stepped back. His face became scarlet, then paper white. This time he spoke without control.

"At the bottom of your job description, Mister, it says: and any other duties as may be assigned by the superintendent or the board of education. I am assigning you to the forest detail." He ended with a crescendo, "Do you understand me you fuckin' jock?"

Jim smiled. So that's what this is all about. His ego demands that I bend to his will.

Jim responded in a monotone. "Mr. Canard, do you understand what I said about your directive being illegal? It is a violation of state law, education law, and the labor laws of New York State. Perhaps I have misunderstood exactly what it is you would like me to do."

Canard threw a pen against the wall. "Jesus Christ, what do you mean you misunderstood? Are you that fuckin' stupid?"

"Perhaps, but I'm sure you wouldn't want me to lose my license by doing something that I either knew or should have known to be illegal."

Chance Canard pounded his desk and shook his finger. "You let me worry about all that legal bullshit. If there is any trouble I'll take care of it."

Jim sported a broad grin. "That's fine. That's all I need to know. If you will have Mrs. Cleary type up a directive spelling out what you want done and signed by you, we shouldn't have any problems."

Canard's anger intensified. Throwing his hands in the air he yelled, "I don't do business that way." Turning to Jim he continued. "But I'll tell you what I will do. I will write a letter to the State Education Department charging you with insubordination. I will take you to a 3020-A hearing and have you thrown out of here on your jock-strap."

"I would like to have you write that letter." Jim replied with a grin. "In a 3020-A, you will be required to list the instances of insubordination. If you write that report I believe you would be the one in jeopardy of being removed from his job."

Canard pointed to the door and screamed, "Get out of my fuckin' office."

As Jim turned to leave, the door opened and Lora Cleary appeared. "I'm sorry, Mr. Canard, I heard the loud voices and thought there was problem."

The superintendent regained his composure and smiled. "No, Mrs. Cleary, Mr. Rahin and I were merely having a difference of opinion. The principal and I are both strong-willed individuals. Sometimes we are so passionate about our point of view that we tend to become exuberant." He turned to Jim. "Have a nice day, Mr. Rahin. We will continue this discussion at another time."

When Jim left the office, Lora Cleary touched his arm. "Jim, I heard that entire conversation. If you ever need a witness let me know—that man is sick."

"Thanks, Lora, but I would never put you or your career in jeopardy. I can handle Mr. Canard; make sure that you keep good records regarding things that he has asked you to do."

Jim knew that Canard had already placed the business manager in harm's way. The superintendent had directed that monies be given to him for meetings, conferences, and the like in cash without signed receipts. The reason he had no receipts is because he never attended the conferences. If it came to an audit the business manager would lose because he'd have nothing to prove that he gave Canard the money."

Chapter 17

THE FROSTY RELATIONSHIP BETWEEN JIM and Chance Canard continued through the fall. Jim was aware that the superintendent was doing everything he could to discredit him. Canard knew that he did not have the kind of documentation needed to prevail in a state hearing and it bothered him.

By Christmas Canard decided to try another approach. Just before the New Year he telephoned Jim with an offering of peace.

"Jim, you and I have been at odds with one another for over two months," he said. "We both want what is best for kids, but we seem to have a different idea on how to accomplish that goal,"

Canard's words were foreign to Jim's ears. The superintendent had never called him by his first name. Yet the tone and sincerity of his voice flowed like heated honey. The words he spoke were devoid of the normal emasculative verbiage.

Canard continued. "Why don't we sit down and see if we can make a new start?"

Jim sensed the pleading in the man's appeal. "I have always wanted to be a team player," Jim replied, "but I won't do anything that I feel is not in the best interests of students, the community, or my career." He paused. "I am willing to meet with you if you would like and see if we can establish some common ground."

"Great!" Canard exclaimed. Why don't you and your wife come to dinner at my place on the twenty-ninth? You can meet my significant other, have a good meal and share with me some of your ideas."

Jim thought about the twenty-ninth and after assuring himself that there was nothing else on the calendar he agreed. "What time would you like us there?"

"Two in the afternoon would be great. That will give us some time to talk before dinner."

"Mr. Canard, I appreciate the call. I'm looking forward to seeing you. Hope and I will be there around two."

Chance Canard had rented a small cottage on Beaver Lake, about a half hour north of the school district. The drive to the lake during the winter months was always a challenge. It was located in a mountainous area where accessibility was restricted to narrow unpaved roads.

Two days before Canard's call, the Rahins had planned a New Year's Eve party. Hope voiced her concern as they drove north to keep the rendezvous Jim had agreed to with Chance Canard.

It was a nasty day; snow had fallen all night and into the morning. It was the kind of snow that stuck to everything. Trees bent under its weight and the wiper blades on Jim's truck continually clogged. The blanket of white made visibility difficult. Route 28 was a mess with little or no delineation between the road surface and the ditches paralleling the highway. The roads along the lake were all but impossible to navigate.

"I wish you had called Mr. Canard and cancelled," Hope said. "This dinner isn't worth having an accident."

"The snow is supposed to stop this evening. If it does, the plows will be able to clear the roads before we head home. I think we'll be okay. I'll just have to take it a little easy. Having four-wheel drive is a big help."

"I hope this trip is worth it," Hope continued to mumble. "I don't trust that man. I think God is trying to tell us to stay home."

"I know how you feel, but I have to give him the benefit of the doubt. If he is sincere it will make my job a hell of a lot easier."

It was two-thirty in the afternoon when Jim's Ford pickup pulled down the undefined driveway leading to the Canard cabin. It had stopped snowing and Jim could see smoke rising from a chalet-like cottage.

There was a woman dressed in a snowmobile suit shoveling snow from the deck of the front porch.

Jim grinned. "Typical Canard," he mumbled. "He won't even clean his own porch. That woman must be his girlfriend."

Jim parked in front of the cottage. The snowsuit clad woman left the porch and met him as he exited the cab.

"Hi," the woman called. "I'm Winifred Nutter, but most people call me Fred."

"I'm Jim Rahin and this is my wife Hope."

Hope nodded hello as Jim continued. "It's nice to meet you, Fred. How come you have to do the shoveling? You should be tending to dinner."

Fred held her mitten finger to her lips. "Shhhh! C.C. is very sensitive. He has been in a relatively good mood all day; I don't want to spoil the evening. Come on let's get in where it's warm."

When the three entered the cabin, Chance Canard rose from a recliner and shuffled over to greet them. He was dressed in jeans, a white T-shirt and slippers; he was most informal. Jim was used to seeing Canard look like he had just stepped out of a fashion magazine.

"Look what I found in the snow," Fred joked.

Canard barely cracked a smile. He withdrew a long-stemmed pipe from his lips and said, "Good of you to come, James. I was worried that you might cancel out."

"I gave it some thought, but decided to give it a try. It really wasn't all that bad," he lied. "Mr. Canard, this is my wife Hope. Hope, this is Mr. Canard."

Hope flashed a smile. "I'm pleased to meet you, Mr. Canard." She extended her hand.

"Please call me Chance," he replied. "It's a distinct honor to meet you, Hope. I can tell already that we are going to be fast friends."

He called me James and he wants Hope to call him Chance, Jim thought. I know we're going to be friends? Something is not right.

"Come in next to the fire," Chance offered, with a sweep of his hand.

Fred gathered up the clothing and Jim and Hope took chairs near a cone shaped, free standing fireplace. The sight and sound of the open fire gave warmth to the cabin atmosphere.

When Fred returned, the snowmobile suit was replaced by a ski sweater, a pair of jeans and wool moccasins. "What would you like to drink?" she asked.

Hope took quick note of the woman. She was not what Hope had expected.

Winifred had short brown hair, eyes to match, and a trim figure. Her smile and amenable personality contrasted with that of the stiff and stoic Canard.

"Do you have a dry red wine?" Hope asked.

"I have merlot."

"That will be fine."

"I'll have a beer," Jim said. "I like Utica Club, if you have it." Fred nodded.

"I have a glass of Merlot, one Utica Club, and a scotch on the rocks. I've been with Chance so long that I don't even ask anymore."

When Chance and Jim started talking school, Hope joined Fred in the kitchen.

The dialogue between Jim and his superintendent was conducted, for the most part, in quiet disagreement.

It didn't take Jim long to ascertain that Canard's ultimate attitude hadn't changed. Jim tried to respond in a polite and respectful manner. Nevertheless, it was abundantly clear that the afternoon would not chart any new avenues of understanding between the two men.

Winifred took Hope on a tour of the chalet. The rooms were small, but cozy. There were two bedrooms and a bath upstairs, and a kitchen, living room, bath and laundry on the first floor. The maple, hardwood flooring had occasional oriental rugs in the bedrooms and living room.

At four o'clock Fred announced that dinner was being served.

A grumpy Chance Canard and an uneasy James Rahin ambled to the long oak table that looked like it had once served in a library.

Jim sat next to his wife. Canard sat opposite Jim. After placing a large bowl of pasta with meat and sauce in the center of the table, Fred took her seat next to Chance.

"Would you like me to say grace?" Hope asked.

"We don't believe in praying," Canard said. "We're agnostics. I can't accept anything that can't be proven, but if praying makes you feel better, by all means pray." Before Hope could say grace Chance grabbed the bowl of pasta and started scooping some onto his plate.

"Hope's family is very Catholic," Jim explained. "One of her uncles is a priest."

"Well, there are just too many things about religious teachings that don't make sense," Canard continued. Suddenly he stopped filling his plate and peered directly into Jim's eyes "You and I have enough to debate without getting into religious philosophy." He frowned and passed the bowl to Jim.

After helping himself to a plate of the pasta, Jim handed the bowl to Fred. She in turn passed it on to Hope. A wooden bowl of salad was passed clock-wise.

"Religion and politics are two subjects that I try to stay away from," said Jim. "Most people are very passionate about both. Debating either is a good way to lose friends and make enemies."

Fred and Hope exchanged small talk about teaching and the weather; Jim and Chance ate in silence.

When it appeared that everyone had had their fill, Fred said, "I have apple pie, chocolate ice cream and carrot cake for desert. Name your poison."

Jim raised his hand. "I'll take a piece of pie."

"One scoop of ice cream for me," Hope followed.

"Would you both like coffee?" Fred asked.

Jim and Hope both nodded.

"Two carrot cakes, apple pie, and chocolate ice cream coming up," said Fred as if she were a waitress.

Hope rose and went to Fred's side. "Let me give you a hand. Where are the cups?"

While the two women fussed in the kitchen, Chance lit his pipe and studied Jim as if trying to figure out how to fit pieces of a puzzle together.

116

Jim grinned. "You appear to be in deep thought. Why so pensive?"

Chance put the pipe on the edge of his plate. "You are an enigma. I can't figure you out. You fight me on almost every issue. I know you have aspirations of becoming a superintendent one day. I could help make that happen for you, but I won't unless you give me your unwavering allegiance."

Just as Jim was about to respond, Hope placed a cup of coffee in front of him. Fred slid a piece of cake next to Chance's pipe and piece of pie next to Jim's coffee.

"No more shop talk until after we have finished eating," Fred directed. She flashed a generous smile and added, "The coffee is going to get cold."

The remainder of the meal proceeded in an air of suspended chill.

Chance finished his cake before the others and sat quietly until he was sure that all were done eating.

It was five-thirty.

Fred finished her second cup of coffee.

"Is everyone done eating?"

"Yes," Hope said. "Thank you for a wonderful dinner."

"How about you, Mr. Rahin?" Chance asked. "Have you had enough?"

What happened to James? Jim thought, but replied, "Everything was excellent, thank you."

"Are you done, Fred?" Chance asked.

"Yes, dear, All I need to do now is clean up."

"Here, let me help you," Chance said politely. With one motion he rose and swept food dishes, silverware, and all onto the floor. At the top of his voice he bellowed, "Now you son of a bitch, am I going to have your complete support or not?"

A startled, wide-eyed Hope quickly pushed her chair away from the table avoiding remnants of dinner from coloring her slacks. Pasta, sauce and coffee blended into a surrealistic collage across the kitchen floor.

Fred sat stunned.

Jim stood, wiped his lips with a napkin and smiled. He addressed Fred. "Thank you, Ms. Nutter, for a wonderful meal.

Perhaps one day Hope and I will be able to reciprocate. However, I believe it's time we said good night." He turned, took Hope by the arm and ushered her toward the front cabin closet.

While Jim retrieved the coats, Canard remained at Jim's side swearing a blue streak.

"You son of a bitch, I'll see that you are fired and never work another day in the state of New York. I will blacken your name throughout the country. Do you hear me? You-you-you fuckin' jock."

Jim maintained his smile and ignored the ranting as he helped Hope on with her coat. After zipping his jacket, he waved goodbye to Fred. She appeared to be glued to the kitchen chair. He opened the door and allowed Hope to make a hasty exit. Jim then turned to Canard. "You take your best shot, Shorty.

Jim knew the derisive nickname would generate additional hostility in the man and it did.

After leaving the cabin Jim and Hope walked through four inches of fresh snow until they reached the truck. While Jim cleaned his windshield, Canard continued to barrage him with a litany of verbal abuse from the porch.

It wasn't until Jim was behind the wheel that the superintendent's ravings were no longer audible. As Jim drove away he rolled down the window, waved and shouted, "Thanks for a wonderful afternoon."

Chance Canard shook his fist and yelled something that was lost in the howl of the wind.

Chapter 18

JIM SPENT THE BALANCE OF THE HOLIDAY SEASON rehashing the Canard dinner story. Most of the guests at the New Year's Eve party were teachers, staff members, and friends. Everyone knew or had heard about Chance Canard; all agreed that he was an ass. Many at the party had their own stories to tell about the superintendent. He was painted as a man who could become irascible at the slightest provocation.

The thought of Canard remaining the superintendent at North Country Central for the next two years clouded Jim's prospects for a congenial work environment. It was annoyingly clear that either Canard or Jim had to go.

When Jim returned to work on January 2, there was a note taped to his desk. It was from the superintendent:

Dear Mr. Rahin:
Please be advised that your position is being eliminated effective July 1. The position you now hold is scheduled to be incorporated under the title of: Assistant Superintendent of Schools. I trust that this notice will provide you with ample time to obtain other employment.
Chance Canard, Superintendent of Schools.

Jim folded the note and placed it in his top drawer. He dialed the number for the district office; Lora Cleary answered.

"Good morning, Lora, did you have a nice New Years?"

"Yes, Jim, Gus and I spent the weekend with our daughter in Albany. How was your party? I already heard about the one you had with Mr. Canard."

"My party was great. As for the Canard dinner—well, that was something else." Changing the subject, Jim asked, "Lora, take a look at Mr. Canard's schedule and let me know when he has some free time. I need to see him."

Lora took a few minutes to reply. "Jim he doesn't have anything on his calendar until noon. He's having lunch with a couple of board members around twelve."

"Good. Set me up for a meeting with him sometime this morning. What I have to tell him may be of interest to his board friends."

Jim entered Canard's office at eleven-fifty. The superintendent was seated behind his desk with his hands folded.

"Good morning Mr. Rahin, did you have a pleasant weekend?"

"Most of it was very enjoyable." Jim sat in a chair opposite his boss.

"I assume, Mr. Rahin, you are here this morning in response to my notice of termination."

"I'm here to inform you that I have no intention of leaving North Country Central until I'm ready or until I am directed to leave following a hearing with the State of New York Education Department," Jim said. "I am a tenured high school principal. Under the tenure law my position cannot be eliminated and replaced by someone else with a different title doing the same job. I think part of your problem is that you don't know the law. You should get some legal advice. If you do, you will find that even the Board of Education cannot terminate a tenured employee without filing a 3020-A and having a state hearing. I just thought I'd let you know." Jim stood and showed a broad grin. "You have a nice day."

Canard took on the visage of a volcano, just before it was ready to erupt. He stood and before Jim could clear the door, there was a roar of indignation.

"You bastard! I don't give a damn what it costs. You are done in this community. I already have the votes I need to get rid of you. I don't give a shit about your tenure. You are history. You can bank on it."

The spew of verbal lava continued to flood the office long after Jim said hello to the two board members waiting in the outer office.

Later that afternoon a notice was posted in the teachers' lounge announcing an emergency meeting of the board of education on Thursday of that week. It was also stated that while the meeting was open to all, the board intended to go into executive session for the purpose of discussing a personnel matter.

When school adjourned for the day Alison Block knocked gently on Jim's door.

"Come in," Jim called.

Alison entered and closed the door. "Mr. Rahin I have some information that I think you should know."

Jim motioned her to a chair. "Have a seat Alison. What's the information?"

"Well, Lora Cleary came to see me about that board meeting that Mr. Canard has called for Thursday. Lora wanted you to know that the meeting is about you. Mr. Canard is going to try and get the board to support him. He plans to replace you with Winifred Nutter. He is going to convince the board that he can get around the tenure law."

"Thanks Lora for telling me. I was aware of Canard's intentions. I'd like the word to get out to the public. If they don't support Canard's actions his attempt to get rid of me will fail. I plan to be at that meeting to see that my side of this issue is heard."

ON THURSDAY EVENING THE SCHOOL'S auditorium filled beyond capacity as people poured into the building to oppose Canard's plan and to give notice to the board that the community was behind the principal.

The board had planned to hold its meeting on the auditorium stage, but soon changed the location. After calling the meeting to order, the board quickly moved to executive session and retired to the superintendent's conference room.

In the auditorium Joe Malone, the instrumental music teacher, invited a member of the audience to play the piano while he directed everyone in song.

Following an hour of music, a member of the board entered the auditorium and requested that Jim Rahin accompany him to the conference room. Jim obliged.

A portly Gary Storms, who had risen to the position of president following the resignation of Brandon Flansburg, welcomed Jim to the executive session.

"Good evening, Mr. Rahin. Thank you for agreeing to meet with us."

Jim bid hello to the board and the superintendent.

Canard did not return the courtesy.

"Mr. Rahin, it has come to the board's attention that there is a serious breach of harmony between you and Mr. Canard," Storm continued. "Mr. Canard states that you have been insubordinate on several occasions by refusing to obey a directive given to you. We would like to hear your version of these events."

"With all due respect, Mr. Canard's claims are disingenuous at best. I challenge Mr. Canard to produce one piece of evidence of my insubordination. It is true that on occasion Mr. Canard has asked me to do certain tasks, but his instructions were vague. I can produce letters written to Mr. Canard asking that he present his directive to me in writing so that I might better understand the scope and intent of his requests. At no time has Mr. Canard given me a written directive."

Storm shuffled papers on his table and looked toward Chance Canard for help. Canard said nothing.

"On numerous occasions, in front of staff Mr. Canard has threatened to remove me from my job. I have told him time and again that as a tenured principal he is required to charge me as provided for under section 3020-A. I have informed him on each occasion that I do not intend to vacate my position without a proper hearing. It would appear that Mr. Canard now plans to circumvent the legal means at his disposal and try to eliminate me by guile. In doing so he places the board at odds with the law."

Vance Morton, a longtime supporter of Jim's, directed his question to Canard. "Mr. Canard, can you produce a letter given to Mr. Rahin spelling out what you expected him to do?"

Canard's persona changed. His neck showed red blotches while his face took on the hue of chalk.

"If I had to write every directive I give to staff I wouldn't get anything else done," Canard huffed.

Morton continued. "But you have said that Mr. Rahin is the only administrator or staff member who has been insubordinate. Surely you know that if you hoped to have him dismissed, you will need proof of his insubordination."

Canard stood and slammed his hand hard against the table. "I want that son of bitch gone. I'm the superintendent here and I want him out."

Chance tried to regain his composure by walking to the coffee pot located at the end of the conference table. After pouring a cup of coffee, he smiled. "Look, I intend to upgrade the administrative structure here at North Country and Mr. Rahin is not included in my plans."

Chance returned to his seat, placed his coffee on the table and began waving his arms as if accentuating his oratory.

"I want to replace the principal with an assistant superintendent. When I am out of the district I want someone here in whom I have confidence."

Carl Jones, another of Jim's supporters spoke.

"Mr. Canard, there are rules governing the termination of tenured employees. You can't wave your hands and say, 'I want Mr. Rahin gone.' The district would be hit with a lawsuit that we could not hope to win."

"I don't give a damn what it costs. I want him out of here. Either he goes, or I go!" Canard sat and took a gulp of his coffee.

Vance Morton scowled at Canard. "There is no doubt in my mind who my choice would be."

Chance jumped to his feet and screamed, "I have two years left on my contract. I can raise a lot of hell around here in two years."

Jones replied with sanity, "I would like to talk to the board without Mr. Canard or Mr. Rahin present."

"By law I am a non-voting member of this board," Chance bellowed. "If you meet without me, I will leave. Our next meeting will be in the presence of my attorney."

Storm tried to calm Canard, but Chance only became more belligerent.

In the heat of the discussion that followed, Jim thanked the board for taking the time to listen to his side of the disagreement. He then returned to the auditorium.

When the crowd saw Canard walk out of the executive meeting, they cheered.

FOLLOWING THE EMERGENCY MEETING of the board, Chance Canard left the district. In his absence Jim was given the title of deputy superintendent. On Friday, two weeks later Chance Canard appeared before a meeting of the board with his attorney.

Schofield Milken had an office in Albany; he specialized in education law and school contracts. His appearance in the Adirondacks was not his first concerning Chance Canard. Earlier in Canard's career, Milken had defended him in a lawsuit involving a female teacher who had filed a claim of sexual harassment. The lawsuit alleged that Canard had sought sexual favors from a probationary teacher. When the woman spurned his advances she was refused tenure. Her evaluations during the previous three years of employment were all excellent, including three evaluations congratulating her on her outstanding abilities in the classroom. The evaluator was Canard. In the final hours before the case was to go to a jury there was a financial settlement out of court.

To Canard, Milken was a genius.

"I am ready to show that the North Country School District's board of education, administration and staff conspired to undermine the authority and veracity of my client," Milken said in his opening remarks. "From the outset of his appointment there has been a concerted effort to undermine the authority and administrative efficiency of my client. As such, his responsibilities as the educational leader in this community has been irreparably damaged. Furthermore, I intend to prove that the high school principal, James Rahin, has demeaned and otherwise damaged the reputation of Mr. Canard by spreading false and malicious rumors regarding Mr. Canard's character."

Milken rambled on for twenty minutes before running out of notes. "...Mr. Canard is asking that he be compensated for the balance owed to him on his contract, and that the sum of one million dollars be awarded in punitive damages. I am hopeful that we will be able to resolve this matter without resorting to the courts for judgment."

Following his opening statement, Milken slumped into a large oak chair next to his client. Chance Canard smiled and whispered into his attorney's ear. Milken nodded in agreement.

Gary Storm listened with interest as Milken weaved his tale and postulated about the district's failure to take appropriate action to protect the integrity of their superintendent.

After silently canvassing the rest of the board, Storm stood. He was aware of the split on the board regarding the events leading to this meeting. Three board members who supported the superintendent sat together waiting for the time when they would be required to vote their convictions.

"The board welcomes the opportunity to review Mr. Canard's assertions concerning his treatment while in our district. It is our desire that this matter be put to rest as quickly and judiciously as possible. The board is anxious to return to its primary responsibilities, that of educating the children of our district. This, sir, is merely an unpleasant distraction."

When Storm finished speaking he sat and wiped his brow.

Milken rose from his seat and glowered at Storm.

"The disregard of rights and trampling of a man's character can hardly be considered a mere distraction, sir."

"No, you are exactly right," Storm replied. "The question before us today is to determine who has been aggrieved. It is the contention of this board that it is the North Country School District and not Mr. Canard that has been injured."

Milken moved from his chair and paced in front of the windows. The blinds in the room were drawn to blot out curiosity seekers. He turned and faced the president. "Perhaps we are wasting our time," he snapped. "Perhaps we should move directly to the courts for satisfaction. It is becoming apparent that you are not interested in an amiable resolution.

"Mr. Milken, the board has witnesses who will testify to the misconduct of Mr. Canard concerning the misappropriation of school funds, the wrongful use of handicapped students, the use of school custodians for personal work, an attempted bribe of a fellow administrator, and for indulging in behavior that is unbecoming to the office he served."

As Storm spoke various school employees filtered into the room. Chance Canard's demeanor changed. He shrank into his seat and attempted to hide from the many eyes focused on him.

Milken observed the change in his client and immediately went to him.

"What's the matter?" Milken whispered.

"Those people are here to tell lies about me," Canard said, in a tone barely audible. "They have recruited the former business manager, my secretary, the high school principal, custodians ,and the director of special education to give testimony against me."

Milken took evasive action.

"Mr. Storm before we continue I would like a few moments to confer with my client."

"If there are no objections, this hearing will recess for fifteen minutes," Storm announced.

Milken and Canard left the conference room and became secluded in the now vacant superintendent's office.

"Chance, I can't help you unless I know what the hell is going on," Milken said. "It appears that there is much more to this matter than you have let on. What is it?"

"I told you, they have brought in everyone who dislikes me. It's going to be their word against mine. Who do you think a hearing board or jury will believe? Just get me out of this one-horse town with the best deal you can manage."

Chapter 19

CHANCE CANARD LEFT the North Country School District with far less pomp then he had exhibited upon his arrival.

On Monday, following the termination of Canard's contract, the board debated whether or not to appoint Jim as the new superintendent. When it was clear that Jim did not have the full support of its members, Charles Du Bois was appointed interim superintendent.

Du Bois, a sixty-five-year-old retired superintendent from Lake Champlain, was familiar with Chance Canard's history. Du Bois had been a superintendent in the Lake Champlain area when Canard was serving as a superintendent in Vermont. Du Bois did not like Canard, but he was determined not to violate the terms and conditions of the agreement entered into between the North Country Board of Education and Milken.

Du Bois' first responsibility as the superintendent of the North Country School District was to ensure that everyone on staff knew and adhered to the terms set forth in the agreement signed between Canard's lawyer and the board of education.

After introducing himself at a faculty meeting Du Bois explained the terms of Canard's termination agreement.

"Mr. Canard was given fifty thousand dollars as a buy-out for the remaining time on his contract," Du Bois said. "Furthermore, as part of the agreement, the board of education has agreed to say nothing negative about Mr. Canard. If anyone should call asking about Mr. Canard, nothing of a negative nature will be said about him. If there are questions about Mr. Canard's termination, such inquiries will be referred to me. In my absence calls will be routed to Mr. Rahin." Du Bois' eyes settled on Jim. "Negative comments about Mr. Canard are not to be expressed to ANYONE outside this educational institution. Is that clear?"

"In other words, the board has agreed to allow that man to continue abusing the educational system," Jim barked. "Canard shouldn't be allowed to be in a position of authority—especially when the position involves kids."

"I'm sure there are those who might agree with you, Mr. Rahin, but this district will abide by the terms of the agreement. Is that understood?"

"I understand," Jim replied. "I don't like it, but I understand."

IN LATE APRIL, JIM RECEIVED a telephone call from South Hudson Valley Central School; it was Elizabeth Andrews.

"To what do I owe this honor?" asked Jim

"James Rahin, I often wondered whatever happened to you. It's nice to know that you became an administrator."

Jim was both pleased and curious. "I thought about calling you on several occasions, but never followed through. If this is not a social call, what can I do for you?"

"Jim, South Hudson Valley has an opening for a superintendent. I'm in the process of sorting through the applicants and double-checking references. I'm calling to get some information about a Chance Canard. He looks very good on paper, but I noticed that he forgot to tell us on his application how long he spent as the super at North Country. Were you the high school principal when Canard was there?"

"Yes. When Mr. Canard left the North Country School District he had an agreement with the board, as part of his severance contract, forbidding anyone employed by the North Country School District to say anything bad about him. You will need to contact Mr. Canard to fill in the blanks. What I can say, is that if you liked Albert Reilly, you're going to love Chance Canard."

There was a long pause in the conversation before Liz replied. "Thanks Jim. I think I have a clear picture of what I needed to know." She paused. "You wouldn't be interested in applying for the job would you? I could see to it that you were given an interview. In any case, it would be nice to see you again. Besides, you owe me lunch."

"Thanks for the thought, Liz, but I don't think I would be happy down state. I like working in the rural area. Perhaps we will run into each other at an administrative workshop. If we do, I'll flip you for lunch."

Liz laughed. "Do you still have my coin?

"You bet. I use it all the time."

"I look forward to our next meeting. If you ever get down this way again, give me a call."

"You got it, lady. "By the way, how's the boxer?"

"He's great. He is planning to leave the ring and get a job selling insurance. We plan to get married. I'll send you an invitation."

"Congratulations. It has been great talking to you again, Liz. Good luck with your search. I hope you have better luck than we did. North Country is still trying to fill the chair Canard vacated."

There was a long pause. "Jim, are you being considered for the position?"

"No, but that's another story. I'll tell you all about it when next we meet."

A WEEK LATER, Charles Du Bois entered Jim's office. He wasn't smiling.

Jim rose from his seat and moved to the opposite side of the desk. "Good morning, Charlie, what can I do for you?"

Du Bois slumped into a chair. "Jim, did you receive a call on Chance Canard?"

Jim sat on the edge of his desk. "Yeah—about a week ago from the director of personnel at the South Hudson Valley School District. Apparently Canard applied for the superintendent's job, but failed to include information about his time at North Country."

Du Bois frowned. "What did you say?"

"I told Ms. Andrews that I was contractually bound not to say anything bad about Mr. Canard. If there was information missing on Canard's application she needed to check with him.

Du Bois groaned.

"What the hell was I supposed to say? I am not about to give that asshole a good recommendation. If that's what is expected, somebody else better take the calls."

"Jim, I got a call from Canard's lawyer," Du Bois moaned. "He is threatening to sue the district for breach of contract."

"Let him sue. I did not say anything bad about him. I only informed the caller that I was obligated not to say anything negative. If Canard construes that as saying something bad than his attorney and the board need to work out an official statement to be issued whenever there is a call about that head case."

Du Bois stood and went to the door and babbled, "I'll be glad when this job is over." When he was halfway in the hall he turned back to Jim. "In the meantime, refer all inquiries about Chance Canard to me."

"What if they know that I was the principal during Canard's stay, and want to talk to me?"

Du Bois moaned, "Jim, just refer all inquiries to me—please."

The following day Du Bois was back; Schofield Milken was with him.

"Jim, Attorney Milken has some questions regarding your conversation with the personnel director at South Hudson Valley. Apparently, Mr. Canard was told that he was being considered for the position, but following your phone interview with South Hudson's personnel director he was dropped from contention."

Jim motioned for Milken to have a seat. "I can't tell you anything more than Charlie has told you," Jim stated. "I merely told the woman that she needed to talk to Chance Canard. Apparently he left out information regarding his stay at North Country. He gave no explanation about his sudden departure. That kind of omission on an application is bound to generate questions."

"Mr. Rahin, Mr. Canard has connections in the South Hudson School District. His friend told him that you gave the personnel director a negative recommendation."

"Have you talked with the personnel director?" Jim countered.

"Not yet. I wanted to hear what you had to say first."

"Well you heard it. If you would like, I can call Ms. Andrews now and put her on a three-way speaker so that we can all hear what is being said."

Milken waved his hand. "No, I will speak with her later." The lawyer rose and headed for the door. Without looking at Jim he added, "Thank you for your time."

When Milken and Du Bois left, Jim called Liz Andrews to let her know about Milken and the so-called connection that Canard had at the school.

"The only people I reported to were board members," she said. "I merely told them that Mr. Canard had left the district under unusual circumstances and that you were unable to give me the information that I needed. Canard's contact must be a board member. I look forward to speaking with Canard's attorney. I am going to ask him some very tough questions concerning Mr. Canard's association with North Country. I'm going to tell him that I also checked with his former school in Vermont. I will be interested in what Mr. Milken has to say. As for the board member friend, I'm going to let the rest of the board know that one of their own violated the confidentiality rules concerning executive sessions." Liz chuckled. "I love it. I'll get back to you and let you know what happens."

Two days later Andrews called to tell Jim that Attorney Schofield Milken never contacted her to discuss Chance Canard's application. Through the administrative pipeline she learned that Canard had taken a job as superintendent in a small school district in Vermont. The district was located somewhere near the Canadian border. Apparently it was a district close to one that he worked at prior to going to North Country.

"See if you can find out the name of the school district. I'd like to keep tabs on that guy."

"You just can't let it go, can you?" Liz chided. "Why don't you forget about Chance Canard; let somebody else deal with him."

"I can't let it go. No matter where Canard is, it's bad news for education."

Chapter 20

WHEN THE PHONE RANG ON MEMORIAL DAY it was nine thirty in the morning; Jim had overslept. It was Alda Sutter.

Mrs. Sutter's daughter, Melba, was a senior attending a technical program at the regional Board of Cooperative Educational Services. Mrs. Sutter sounded frantic. She was agitated to the point of tears.

"Mr. Rahin," Sutter cried. "We have a problem. I believe my daughter Melba is having an affair with one of your bus drivers." She continued to sob louder. "I want him fired. He's a married man with children. He is telling Melba that he is going to leave his wife and marry her. You and I know that that will never happen."

Jim yawned and ran his hand across his eyes. Remaining cool he answered, "Who is the driver?"

"It's the after-school driver on bus thirty-five. It's the bus that picks up the student from the district cooperative center. The driver's name is Henry Dunn."

"Are you sure about this?" he asked. Sutter now had Jim's full attention "While your daughter is of age, the district forbids staff from dating students. Of course Mr. Dunn will argue that what he does on his own time is none of the school's concern."

"But it is happening on the school bus!" she exclaimed. Mr. Dunn keeps Melba on the bus until all the other students have been dropped off. He takes her to the sand pit on Timber Road." Alda took a deep breath between her gulps of air and sobs. "That's where they have sex."

"Thank you for your call, Mrs. Sutter. I will look into the matter immediately."

After finishing his conversation with Mrs. Sutter, Jim went outside where Hope was working in her flower bed. "I'm sorry, Hope, but something has come up. I have to go to the office."

Hope was on her knees pulling weeds. She set some weeds into a bucket and looked up. "What's the matter? Something happen?"

"I just had a call from a concerned parent. She believes that her daughter is having an affair with one of my bus drivers."

Hope frowned. "Is the witch back?" she joked.

"Unfortunately, momma says that it's one of our married drivers."

Hope got to her feet, brushed some dirt from her hand and then wiped them on her apron. She shaded the morning sun from her eyes.

"Would you like me to go with you?"

"Nah, there is nothing you can do. Finish your flowers. I'll only be gone for a couple of hours. When I get back we'll take a drive to the Lake House for dinner."

Hope smiled. "Okay. I tried to wake you earlier. I felt playful. I guess the games I had in mind will have to wait."

Jim arrived at the school a few minutes before noon and went directly to his office. His first telephone call went to Charles Du Bois. After speaking with Mrs. Du Bois, Charlie took the phone.

"Yes, Jim, what seems to be the matter?"

Following a brief conversation where Jim did most of the talking, Du Bois groaned, "Oh no. Well, can't this wait until Monday? I have a house full of guests."

"If what Mrs. Sutter is saying is true we are obligated to take immediate action.

"Well, what do you suggest?"

"I think you should speak with Dunn and place him on a paid leave of absence until the district has had time to evaluate the situation."

"I'm only the interim super. My responsibility to the district is from nine to five and it doesn't include weekends or holidays. Call the board president. Let him make the decision."

Jim's next call was to Gary Storm. When Jim told Storm about the problem and Du Bois' remarks, Storm yelled, "This kind of shit is what we pay you administrators to take care of. If Du Bois doesn't want to handle the problem then you handle it."

When Storm slammed the phone Jim began searching through a card index until he came to the name of Marcy Lasher.

Marcy was the director of transportation. She assigned drivers to routes, set up athletic bus runs, and in general watched over the transportation needs of the North Country School District. When it came to her job, Marcy was like a mother hen keeping her chicks safe. She was in her twilight years, but still tougher than shoe leather. Lasher had served the district as a bus driver for over twenty years before she was given administrative responsibilities. Because her job encompassed both elementary and high school students, Marcy normally answered directly to the superintendent. This matter, however, would be different. For this problem, Marcy would act under the direction of the high school principal.

Jim brought the director up to date on the alleged lecherous activities of Henry Dunn and asked that she check his time card to determine the time that he brought the bus back to the garage following his district cooperative center run in the afternoon.

"Check his times from the start of the year and note if there is a time difference between when he first started the route and now," Jim asked.

"I know that there has been about a forty-five-minute difference in recent weeks. I spoke to Henry about it. He claimed that there is road construction on his route and that he has had to take a longer route in order to get the kids home."

"Have you talked with the town supervisor about the road work?"

"No, but I will."

"Also check with the district cooperative office to see if there has been a delay in their dismissal time."

Marcy straightened her square frame. "I'd like to have a talk with Dunn before school resumes," she said. "If I find out that there isn't any construction and he still insists that there is, I'm going to fire him on the spot for falsifying his records."

"I have another idea," Jim countered. "If we confront him, he will deny everything. Both he and Melba will change their behavior and make it harder for us to learn the truth."

"What do you suggest?"

"On Tuesday when school resumes, you and I will wait for Dunn's bus near the sand pit. I will drive my wife's car so he will not suspect anything. When the bus passes we'll wait a few minutes and drive to the sand pit. We'll catch them in the act."

"I hope this information is all wrong," Marcy said. "This is surreal. I know Henry's wife. She's a nice lady. This will devastate her. They have three kids in school. I hate to think of what this scandal will do to them."

At four-fifteen Tuesday afternoon bus number 35 drove along Smelt Creek until it came to Everett's sand pit. The bus veered right, pulled into the pit and came to a stop at the far end behind a mound of earth. Henry Dunn opened the folding door and stepped out. After surveying the surroundings he reentered the bus and walked quickly to the back. As he navigated past the seats he unbuckled his belt and allowed his pants to fall to his ankles. Melba Sutter awaited his return, her slacks and panties were already folded and placed neatly on the back seat.

Jim and Marcy were parked a short distance from the pit. After seeing the bus pull in and park they approached.

Marcy forced the accordion door open with a hard push and entered; Jim was right behind her.

Henry Dunn left the bliss of his lover's nest so suddenly that he slipped and fell prone onto the bus floor.

Melba grabbed her clothing and was in the process of dressing when Marcy and Jim arrived in the back of the bus. Without comment Henry stood and reached for his pants. He wasn't fast enough. Marcy scooped up his shorts and pants and was waving them in his face.

"You lousy pedophile," Marcy screamed. "Get off my bus. You're fired." Marcy grabbed the front of Henry's shirt and pulled him to the front of the bus.

Jim moved into a seat in order to allow Marcy and her captive to pass. Marcy threw Henry out through the open bus door.

Henry landed hard against the mound of earth. After righting himself he squinted at his attacker and whined, "Geez, Mrs. Lasher, can I have my clothes?"

Henry stood bare from the waist down, his manhood limp. His white, boney knees shook as he reached for his pants. The pleading look in his wet eyes softened Marcy's resolve, and she threw the clothing into his face.

"I don't ever want to see your face around the bus garage again," Marcy screamed. "If you come anywhere near the school, I'll have you arrested."

Henry dressed and started walking toward town.

Melba tried to force her way past Jim.

"Let me go!" she yelled. "I love him. You have no right to hold me here against my will."

"You are going home," Jim barked. "You rode the bus to school this morning and you'll ride it home. What you do after that is between you and your family."

Melba fell sobbing into a seat.

Jim exited the bus and walked back to the car.

Marcy started the engine and drove off. As they passed the emasculated Henry Dunn, he waved at the teary-eyed Melba.

Alda Sutter met the bus as it pulled next to her driveway. She too was crying. The work worn woman looked old beyond her years. Although not yet forty, Alda's ratty clothes and unkempt appearance made her look closer to sixty.

"I hate you. I hate you all," Melba yelled as she exited the bus and she glared at her mother. Without further discussion, Alda turned, wrung her hands and followed her daughter into the house.

Marcy drove back to the bus garage.

"Well, what do we do now?" she asked Jim once she arrived.

Jim patted Marcy on the shoulder. "Write it up. I want you to write down everything you saw and heard this afternoon. I will do the same. I will also inform the superintendent and the board about the matter, but I want something official for the record."

THREE DAYS LATER Alison Block rapped on Jim's door. "I'm sorry to interrupt you, Mr. Rahin, but Mrs. Lasher and Mrs. Dunn are here to see you."

"Give me five minutes, Alison, and then show them in."

Exactly five minutes later Alison knocked again and ushered the two women into the room. Marcy sat immediately, but Jamie Dunn remained standing.

Jamie Dunn was a sad, tired woman in her mid-thirties. Jim could tell by her swollen eyes and dark circles that she had been crying. Her reddish hair, hazel-green eyes, and freckled complexion gave notice of her Irish-Scottish heritage. She was as thin as a typing ribbon, but held her short stature erect trying to be proud. Through all of her sorrow, Jim saw a spunky—yet attractive woman.

"Please have a seat Mrs. Dunn," Jim offered as he motioned to a chair next to Marcy. After Mrs. Dunn was seated he continued. "What can I do for you ladies?"

Marcy was the first to speak.

"Mr. Rahin, Mrs. Dunn is here to plead for her husband. They have three children and no income other than what Henry earned as a bus driver. If I put him on another run, could he stay on?"

"Even if Henry's reemployment was okay with me I don't think it would be so with the board," Jim replied.

Jamie Dunn's composure collapsed. "I'm not asking this for myself, but my children," she moaned. "What can I do about the children?"

"What is Henry doing now?"

"Nothing, he leaves in the morning and I don't see him again until late at night. He tells me that he's looking for work, but I think he's with her."

"By her I assume that you are referring to Melba Sutter."

"Yes, since you suspended her she and Henry spend their days together. I don't care about Melba Sutter. If she wants him, she can have him. I just need to be able to keep my house and feed my children."

"Are all of your children in school?" Jim asked.

"Yes," Jamie answered, the youngest just entered first grade."

"Mrs. Dunn would you be interested in a job here at school?"

Jamie sat upright and brushed the tears from her eyes. "What kind of job?"

"We are looking to hire a woman to run the laundry area. You would be responsible for washing and drying towels, clothing items and team uniforms. You could start after the kids are in school and end in time to be home when the kids get off the bus. The job only pays minimum wage, but there are health benefits that go with it—what do you think?"

Jamie's face broke into a faint smile. It wasn't the kind of a smile that could brighten a room—but it was a start, Jim thought.

"If Mrs. Dunn is not interested in that job, I'm looking for a bus driver," Marcy added. "I could have her trained and be ready to go in a couple of days."

Jim rose and went to where Jamie was seated. "We don't need an answer right now Mrs. Dunn. Think about the job options and let me know in a couple of days." Please understand that any job for your husband in the school setting is out of the question. I hope you can resolve your marital difficulties. Children need two parents."

Chapter 21

INDIAN LAKE IN JUNE WAS ALIVE with the anticipation of new life. Greenery was emerging from the killing frost of fall and the lonely despair of a bone cold winter. Melting patches of crystallized snow hiding under boughs of forest pine were giving way to heads of forest flowers struggling to catch a glimpse of sun. Melba felt her belly and removed her colorless feet from the water.

"Hank," she called. "Do you really love me?"

Henry Dunn removed the hat that protected his eyes from the light and rolled to one side. "You know I do," he cooed. "You are my life. I don't give a damn what it cost me. I'll find another job."

"Will you leave Jamie and marry me?"

"Well, yeah, eventually. I just need a little more time.

Melba turned away and looked at the sky-blue waters of the lake. "How much more time?"

"Well—I don't know—six months—maybe a year. Why? "What's the rush?"

"We don't have a year, Henry. I'm going to have a baby."

Henry sprang to his feet and moved away from the blanket.

"You can't be..." He braced himself against the trunk of a large maple tree. "Are you sure? I was so careful. You said..." he stopped talking and turned away. "Mel, you can't be. It would be the worst thing that could possibly happen right now. I—we can't afford a kid. Not now. I can't take care of one family. How could I possibly afford another?"

Melba rose and brushed her skirt free of a few chips of bark. "You should have thought about that before you…" Her voice trailed off.

Henry grabbed Melba by the arm and spun her around. They stood face to face.

"Before I did what?" he snapped. When she didn't answer, he reiterated, "Before I did what?"

Melba yanked her arm free of his grip and picked up the blanket. As she walked up the wooded path to the dirt road, she turned and said, "You know what. How the hell do you think I got this thing in my stomach? You think the fuckin' stork came to me in the night?"

By the time she reached the road Henry was at her side. "You told me you were safe. You told me it was okay. You said you had just finished your period."

"So? I was wrong. Fuckin' ain't an exact science ya know. When a guy screws a girl it's like shooting crap. Ya roll the dice. Sometimes you win and sometimes you lose. We lost. So what are you going to do now?"

"I gotta think. Maybe we can find someone who will help you abort. I know this doctor near Utica that performs abortions. It might cost a couple of hundred, but it would be worth it."

Melba's face looked as if she had a bad case of sun burn. "You son of a bitch. You ain't takin' me to no fuckin' doctor. I'm havin' this kid with or without you. All my life people have been take'n things away from me. Nobody is take'n my baby."

JAMIE DUNN LOOKED FRESH and rejuvenated when she returned to the school a few days later, following her offer of employment. Alison Block met her at the office counter.

"Good morning, Jamie, what brings you here this morning?"

"I need to see Mr. Rahin."

"I think he has someone in there with him right now," Alison replied. "As soon as he's free I'll let him know that you are here."

Jamie took a seat and waited.

Twenty minutes later Jim appeared and went to Alison's desk.

"Alison, please get this letter out to Mrs. Sutter. Her daughter is expecting. Mama wants the school to provide home instruction.

Melba is over seventeen. If she wants to graduate she will need to attend school." Jim set the letter on Alison's desk and turned. "Mrs. Dunn, what a pleasant surprise. What can I do for you?"

Jamie stood to face him. "I have decided to take your job offer."

"Bus driver or laundry attendant?"

"I think the job in the laundry would better meet my needs. Driving bus would get me home after my children. I don't want them home alone."

"I thought you might choose that job. Has Henry been home?"

Jamie's eyes became clouded. "Yes. He and Melba had a disagreement. She informed him that she is pregnant. Henry wants her to have an abortion. She refused. She insists on keeping the baby."

"I know about Melba's situation," Jim replied. "Melba's mother informed me that Melba is going to have Henry's baby. What does Henry plan to do?"

"He has no choice. He will have to support that child. The only thing positive is that he vows to never see Melba again. Mr. Rahin, I know my husband still loves me. I'm hurt and ashamed of what he has done to our family, but I prefer to stay with him for the sake of the children. I feel bad for my oldest. Kids at school make remarks. You know how kids are."

Jim moved to her side. Jamie was shaking with grief.

"If there is anything I can do to help," he offered, "please let me know."

Jamie brushed moisture from her cheek. "He needs a job. Isn't there something he can do? I know what he did was stupid, but his sons and I are the ones who are suffering."

"Mrs. Dunn, I can't place Henry in the school setting. I can't allow him to be near young girls. However, I will ask around to see if there is anyone in the community looking for help. Perhaps the cheese plant or furniture factory could use another man. Don't worry; I'm sure something will turn up."

Jamie threw her arms around Jim and hugged him. When she pulled away she was blushing. "Henry—I mean I will be eternally grateful. Ahh—if there is anything I can do for you, anything— please let me know."

Jim looked into her eyes and saw desire fueled by gratitude. "Mrs. Dunn, I'm not doing this for Henry. My interest is for the welfare of your children."

Jamie looked away. "When would you like me to start?" she replied in a loud whisper.

"How about starting tomorrow morning?"

Jamie nodded her assent.

"Good. Be here by eight and report to the custodian's office. I'll have Ed show you around and explain your duties."

GRADUATION TOOK PLACE ON JUNE 27, without the presence of Melba Sutter.

As a young girl, Melba had served as a babysitter for Max Meica's children while Mrs. Meica was in the hospital fighting cancer. At the age of thirty-six Cybil Meica lost her battle with the disease.

After her split with Henry, Melba started working at the Meica farm on weekends as a house cleaner and cook. A week after Cybil's death Melba left home and moved into the Meica farmhouse. She did the cleaning, cooking, and from time to time helped with the farm chores.

Maxwell Jr. took a liking to Melba. He was aware of the rumors surrounding the tryst she had with Henry Dunn, but said nothing to his father. Junior harbored thoughts of taking over where Henry had left off . He flirted with Melba waiting for the opportunity to present itself; it never did.

Maxwell Meica was a massive man. He was thirty-seven years old, had the shoulders of a lumberjack and the agility of a football player. Unless riled, Max was an amiable good-natured man. He believed in hard work and honesty. At six feet-four inches tall and two hundred and fifty pounds, Max was not the type of man most people would want to anger.

Max was not what most women would consider handsome, but Melba found his rough features attractive. He was good to her and by Melba's standards he was rich. Within a month she had totally replaced Cybil in the home. In addition to her household duties and helping on the farm, Melba was sharing Max's bed. She fully intended to lead Maxwell Meica to a justice of the peace for a quiet wedding ceremony as soon as possible.

Maxwell Jr. did not take kindly to the idea of Melba replacing his mother and decided to tell his father everything he knew about her.

In July while the Meica's were haying, Junior turned to his father and said, "Dad, I need to talk to you about Melba."

Big Max stuck the pitchfork into the ground, wiped his brow with a large red bandana and yelled to his son, Brandon, to stop the tractor.

"Okay, son, what is it you want to tell me?"

Junior leaned on his fork. "Dad I know that you are very fond of Melba, but I think that there are some things about her that you should know."

Max's eyes narrowed. "I think I know everything I need to know about Melba, son. She is a hardworking caring person who makes me happy. I don't care about any rumors that might be floating around out there."

Junior walked a few steps away from his father. He feared that what he was about to say next would generate a hostile reaction. Junior knew that when his dad could be irrational when angered.

"Dad, are you aware that Melba is pregnant? She may be carrying Henry Dunn's child."

Instead of erupting in volcano fashion, Max grinned and called to Brandon. "Get moving Brandon, we're eating daylight."

Once the tractor was moving Max hefted a forkful of hay onto the trailer and turned to Junior.

"Son, I know about Dunn and I don't care. It's a rare person who has never made a mistake. Remember when you got arrested for shoplifting? Your mother and I didn't brand you a thief. You made a mistake. And as for Melba's baby—well as far as I'm concerned I'm the father. You're going to have to accept that—at least until your old enough to get out on your own."

Junior frowned. "Well, pop, if that's how it is, it's okay with me. I just don't want her taking advantage of you."

Chapter 22

SINCE BECOMING PRINCIPAL, JIM had championed the proposition that all students regardless of where they received their education in elementary school should be held to the same standard. He believed that every student must be subjected to the same information and required to take a standardized exam. The exam was to be designed to measure subject knowledge regardless of past labels, teacher orientation, or family social standing.

Jim was convinced that some teachers were over-rating student achievement based on socio-economic factors and parental pressure. Because of his push for educational excellence, he became a primary supporter of the "Effective Schools" movement.

Effective School proponents believed that "What gets measured gets done." Testing programs and the effectiveness of schools based on common standards became the new educational buzz. The New York State Department of Education in Albany offered a workshop to push for the inclusion of a mandatory Effective Schools program in every school district in the state.

Because of North Country Central's commitment to the concepts of Effective Schools, members of the North Country School District staff were invited to the conference as presenters.

"I'm not going to attend," Charles Du Bois exclaimed. "My weekends are mine. I'm not getting paid to do school business on weekends."

Jim turned away from his boss in disgust. "I believe state ed wanted the whole administrative team there. How is it going to look if the educational leader of the district is absent?"

"Say that I am ill or something. I've paid my dues. I'm only here as an interim. Let the board get off their dead asses and hire a superintendent that can take charge. I'm sorry I even agreed to take this job."

"Okay, but I think you're wrong." Jim opened the door and was about to leave when Du Bois called.

"Jim, I know you are disappointed, but this board pisses me off. I don't understand why they don't appoint you as superintendent and let the district get on with its business. They should have done that when Canard left."

"Canard's supporters on the board will never approve me. That's why."

"But you have enough support to get the appointment."

Jim grinned. "Would you take a job where from day one you didn't have a hundred percent support of the board?"

"Then why do you stay here? There are other jobs out there. I'd be happy to give you a recommendation."

"Thanks, I'll keep that in mind. Who knows? I might find something at the Albany conference.

FOLLOWING THREE DAYS OF DEBATE in Albany, Jim came to the conclusion that there was more to the Effective School concept than just testing. No matter how he and his colleagues stressed testing and measuring effectiveness, the root of the problem for school districts boiled down to a lack of funding.

Each mandate required an increase in financial support. When it came time for politicians to back the movement with dollars they all cried poor mouth. They said that the millions of dollars projected for the project would not be forthcoming. Taxpayers couldn't afford the burden.

At dinner Jim was discussing the plight of his educational proposals with Liz Andrews.

He and Liz met at a seminar on school finance.

"I think the key to the financial dilemma facing schools today is a matter of priority," Andrews said. "There is lots of waste in the management of schools statewide."

"That's true, but most districts are so parochial about keeping their own districts the way they have been for the last hundred years they are reluctant to change. Regardless of the financial savings the district might garner, they are reluctant to merge with a neighboring district." Jim counted on his fingers to accentuate the point he was trying to make. "Small schools could share superintendents, business managers and a whole lot of other services that would save millions of dollars a year. I'll bet that…" Jim was suddenly interrupted.

"Well, well, well," a voice said. "If it isn't the Boy Scout."

Jim spun away from his meatloaf. He knew that voice; it was Chance Canard.

"Nice to see you, James," Canard said, with a broad grim. "Are you going to introduce me to your lady friend?"

Jim was stunned. "What are you doing here Canard? I thought we got rid of all the vipers in the state when you went to Vermont."

"Now James, don't be curt. I hold no animosity toward you. In fact you did me a favor. At Cold Hollow Academy I now have a job in a district that appreciates me. My word is law."

"What are you doing here—slumming?"

"Actually I needed some R and R, and these state functions are always interesting. Canard looked at Jim's plate. "The food is always excellent. Wouldn't you agree?"

"Yes, when my stomach isn't soured by bad company."

"My, my, we are testy aren't we?"

Liz Andrews stood and extended her hand. "Mr. Canard I'm so glad to finally meet you. I have heard so much about you. I'm Elizabeth Andrews, The personnel director for the South Hudson Valley Central School District. I believe you know the former vice president of my board."

A dark expression replaced the grin on Canard's face.

"You were wrong, James. All of the vipers have not been driven from the state."

"Consider me a king snake," Liz said, with a generous grin.

"What the hell is a king snake?" Chance growled.

146

"A king snake is harmless to humans, but kills rattlers and other harmful reptiles," Liz said with a wink.

Just as Liz finished her explanation a voice behind her said, "Oh, there you are, Chance, darling."

Jim knew that voice too.

Before Jim could react Rebecca Fitch took her place next to Canard.

Looking directly into Jim's eyes, Becky said, "Hello, James, long time no see."

Jim turned back to Chance. "I was right, Canard, you are slumming. Does Fred know that you are doing a witch now?"

The smile on Chance Canard's face returned. "I forgot to tell you James. I recently hired one of your former art teachers. Her technique is extraordinary. As for Fred', she and I parted company shortly after I left North Country."

It was Jim's turn to smile. "I'm happy for Ms. Nutter and I wish the two of you the worst. Besides slithering and shedding your skins, you both have a lot in common. You are both evil people who shouldn't be allowed around kids. However, I do have to admit that Ms. Fitch is an excellent art teacher. She will be a very active member of your community. She likes to take a special interest in her male students and fellow staff members. At North Country High she once had a private party for the football team. Yes, she was a very popular teacher. There were many who hated to see her leave."

Rebecca Fitch took Chance Canard's arm. "How's your love life Jimmy-boy? Has that lovely woman sought fulfillment elsewhere yet?" Becky turned her attention to Liz. "You better find yourself another stud, honey. This bull is impotent."

"Maybe when he's around a dry cow that can't give milk, but I haven't notice a lack of virility in Mr. Rahin's appeal and charm."

"Well, Jim Rahin will never be half the man that Chance is," Fitch belched. "Chance Canard knows how to make a woman feel like a woman." Becky turned to Canard. "Let's find a table where the air's better."

When Canard and Fitch were out of voice range, Liz said, "What the hell was that all about? I knew about Canard, but who's the vampire bitch that he's with?"

For the next twenty minutes Jim told Liz the story about the witch from the North Country Central School District.

"What I don't understand is how she was able to hook up with Canard," Jim queried. "The last time I heard about her, she was teaching in a private school and tutoring some young boy after hours."

Liz Andrews broke into a booming laugh. "Rahin, you really have a penchant for getting into trouble. I'm really sorry you didn't come to work at South Hudson. There would never have been a dull moment."

When they finished dinner, Jim and Liz said their goodbyes.

"Liz, it was good to see you again. I look forward to the next conference."

"Take care of yourself, James, and try to stay out of trouble. If you decide to change jobs let me know where you end up."

After checking out of his room Jim made his way to the school's fifteen-passenger bus. Other members of his Effective Schools team were standing outside the bus. Upon his approach he could tell the staff was agitated.

"Hi guys," Jim called. "What's going on?"

"Jim, someone has vandalized the bus," said Marcy Lasher.

Marcy had driven the bus to Albany.

Jim approached the bus and observed a lit candle embedded in wax on the hood of the vehicle. Scrawled into the paint next to the candle was the number 666.

"Did anyone see who did this?" Jim asked.

"I don't think so," Marcy replied. "I got here a few minutes ago and found the candle just as you see it. I called the police and filed a report." Turning to the other members of the group Jim added, "Folks, we are going to be held up a while—at least until Mrs. Lasher is ready."

"It looks like a worshiper of Satan tried to establish a shrine," Mary Anne Tracer joked.

"That's just what I was thinking," Jim snapped. "Marcy, keep everyone here. I'll be back shortly."

At the hotel Jim approached the desk and asked, "Could you give me the room number for Ms. Fitch.?"

The desk clerk ran through a list of names. "I'm sorry, Mr. Rahin, but I don't have anyone here listed under that name."

Jim started to leave then returned to the desk. "Excuse me again, but do you have a Chance Canard listed?"

"Yes," the clerk answered. "I believe he is in room 211."

"Thanks."

Jim took the elevator to the second fl oor and quickly made his way to room 211. After knocking on the door, he waited.

"Who is it?" a woman's voice asked.

"Housekeeping," Jim replied.

When the door opened, Rebecca Fitch appeared in a robe. She didn't seem surprised to see Jim.

"Hello James," she spewed with a grin. "Have you given up your job as a school administrator?

"You know why I'm here," Jim snapped stepping through the threshold.

"Let me guess," Becky cooed. "You're here to ask for my forgiveness."

"You vandalized a school bus," Jim bellowed. "Your signature is all over the mess you left. I'm going to have you arrested."

"When was I supposed to have desecrated your precious bus? I have been with Chance ever since I left you and that Barbie-doll you were having lunch with."

Conrad Canard stepped out of the bathroom with a towel draped around his scrawny body. "I will testify to that," he said. "Do you have any proof that Becky damaged your vehicle? Are there any witnesses?"

Jim knew that he had been bested in his attempt to bluff Fitch into admitting her guilt. "You and Ms. Fitch are the only people at his conference who have an ax to grind with the North Country School District."

Canard placed his arm around Becky's waist. "Proof, Mr. Rahin, proof. One must have proof. Isn't that what the board said when I wanted you fired."

Jim turned the knob on the door. He looked back at Canard and then to Becky. "I'm disappointed in you Becky. I thought you had given up playing with children. I thought at some point you would want to make love to a real man." He smiled and looked at Canard. "See ya, Shorty."

When Jim was back in the hall he heard Canard yell, "Fuck you, you fuckin' jock. You will never be the man I am."

Back at the bus Jim met with two officers of the New York State Police and informed them of his suspicions. After writing down the information and taking pictures of the candle and writing, the officers left.

Jim called to Marcy, "Let's go home. There isn't anything more we can do here."

Chapter 23

THE NORTH COUNTRY BOARD OF EDUCATION selected Oliver Hatch as its next superintendent. Ollie, as he preferred to be called, had worked as an elementary principal in the district where Jack Walker served as the superintendent. Hatch came highly recommended by Walker; there were still Walker supporters on the board.

Oliver Hatch was a short, wiry man of Scottish decent. He loved to play golf almost as much as he enjoyed a good party. Gregarious in nature, he was quickly accepted by the staff and community. Jim too liked the man and soon the two administrators became friends as well as colleagues.

One of Hatch's first recommendations to the board was to hire an assistant principal. Jim had served in that capacity as well as the principal since John Walker left North Country. Ollie Hatch was in the honeymoon of his appointment. The board accepted his recommendation and actively started the search for an assistant principal.

From the outset it was clear to Jim that Ollie wanted to pick the person who would serve as Jim's assistant.

Jim felt that he should have the final say regarding the assistant.

A break in relations between Jim and Oliver Hatch came when Hatch recommended a man with whom he had worked with in a former school district.

Jim supported a man who had spent twenty years in the Marines and was, at the time of his application, teaching science in a private school.

"Jim, I will place both names before the board for their consideration, but I will be recommending Neil Mullins if the board asks who I prefer."

"Mullins seems like a nice guy Ollie, but my gut instinct tells me that Dean Bruce would make a better disciplinarian."

An irritated superintendent stood and paced. "Why? What are his educational qualifications? Bruce has only been out of the Marines for two years. Neil Mullins has a proven track record as an elementary principal for at least that long. He was also a successful sixth-grade teacher for over twenty years. He knows how to handle kids."

"Ollie, if Mullin's is so good and well liked as you say, why hasn't he been appointed to an administrative position in his own district before now?"

Hatch slammed his hand onto the top of his desk. "Damn it, Jim, now I know why you had trouble with Canard and members of the board. I'm your boss for, Christ's sake and I want Mullins."

Jim turned away from Hatch and headed for the door. "Do what you have to do Ollie, but if I'm asked, I will recommend that the board hire Bruce."

Jim was angry. He decided to leave the school and grab a late lunch at the Parma Coffee Shack. When he entered the diner he spotted June Fallen at a booth talking with Frieda Aden.

When June spotted Jim she waved and motioned him to join her.

As Jim walked toward June, Frieda casually blocked his path.

"Hey, Mr. R, I heard ya bumped into the witch in Albany." Frieda lowered her voice. "I understand she's boffin' the Ghost."

Jim held his finger to his lips. "Shhh. I'll tell you all about it later."

Frieda nodded. "Gotcha!" She brought pencil and pad together and asked, "Whatcha gonna have Mr. R ?"

"A bowl of today's soup and a ham sandwich."

"You got it," Frieda sang. "One soup with ham coming up."

Jim slid into the booth opposite June. She placed her cup of coffee down and said, "What's up, Jim, you look a little peaked. Having a bad day?"

"I'm having a little disagreement with Oliver Hatch. We're trying to hire an assistant principal. Ollie wants a guy that he knows from some school in the western part of the state and I want an ex-Marine who is presently teaching in a private school."

June thought for a moment and then asked, "Who is going to be the assistant's immediate supervisor?"

"I am."

"Then the decision should be simple. If you are going to be evaluating the assistant and he is going to answer to you, then all things being equal you should be the one to do the selecting."

"Well, that's how I see it, but Ollie doesn't agree and he is my boss."

"Will the board ask you which candidate you want?"

"I don't know, but I'm sure they'll ask him."

Frieda interrupted the dialogue. She winked at Jim and placed his order on the table. "There ya go Mr. R, let me know when ya wanna have that talk."

When Frieda returned to the counter June said, "Jim I have a meeting with one of the board members later today. I will see to it that you are asked about your preference."

At the Tuesday night meeting of the Board of Education, Jim sat listening as the president moved through the order of business. When it came to the matter of hiring an assistant principal, he passed out copies of each candidate's credentials.

After reviewing the material the president asked if there were any questions regarding the candidates; there was no reply.

Vance Morton asked that the board go into executive session for the purpose of discussing a personnel matter.

In the executive meeting the resumes of both candidates were discussed.

After forty-five minutes of banter Storm rose from his chair. "Mr. Hatch both candidates appear to be well qualified. You spent time with both men; do you have a preference?"

Hatch shuffled some papers and said, "I prefer Mr. Mullin. I believe he has the most experience."

153

There was a noticeable silence in the room.

After a few moments Marty Diller stood. Marty had been a longtime supporter of Jim. He cleared his throat and asked, "Mr. Rahin, you have been serving as the vice principal as well as the principal for a number of years. What do you think?"

Hatch shot Jim a quick glance and shook his head in the negative.

"Mr. Hatch is correct when he says that Mr. Mullin has the most educational experience," Jim acknowledged. "However, what this job calls for is a person who knows how to handle problems of an unusual nature. Mr. Mullin handled a class of sixth graders, and from all that I have read, he did a great job. Mr. Bruce, on the other hand, was a Marine for twenty years. He was in charge of young men and discipline. If we were looking for an elementary principal or even middle school principle, Mr. Mullin would be my choice as well. But we are dealing with older students, especially boys, who need a guiding hand. It should be someone who they can look up to and respect. My choice is Mr. Bruce."

Oliver Hatch colored with anger, but said nothing.

Vance Morton saw the expression on Hatch's face and immediately asked that the board come out of the executive meeting for the purpose of voting.

When the regular meeting resumed, the president of the board whispered something to Hatch and then addressed the other members. "The clerk will now ask for your vote on the selection of an administrative assistant.

When the clerk asked each member to vote, Jim watched as each member voted in accordance with how they felt about Jim, and not on the qualifications of the candidates. The vote went exactly the way he had predicted. Dean Bruce was appointed to the position by a vote of four to three.

When the board adjourned, Jim stayed until all the members were gone. Only Hatch remained behind.

As Hatch cleared the conference table Jim sat in a chair next to the desk. "I'm sorry about the disagreement, Ollie. I hope there are no hard feelings."

Hatch set a handful of pencils in a container and said, "You're damn right there's hard feelings. I hope this guy works out, because if he fouls up I'm going to blame you."

"Fair enough," Jim replied. "That's the way it should be."

THE NEXT MORNING AS JIM entered the school, he was greeted by Mr. and Mrs. Salvatore Farintino and their daughter Melinda.

The Farintinos owned a small gift shop in the village; their daughter was a senior.

"Good morning," Jim said. "You folks are up early. What brings you to school?"

"It's about Melinda," Salvatore said. "She is having a problem with Ms. Dykson. Ms. Dykson calls her names and belittles her in front of the other students."

"Come into my office," Jim said. "We can continue this there."

In Jim's office he asked the Farintinos to have a seat. Yolanda Farintino and Melinda sat, but Salvatore remained standing.

"Continue, Sal. You were saying that Melinda is having a problem with her gym teacher."

"Ms. Dykson does not show my daughter respect. She uses words that are hurtful."

"Melinda, why don't you tell me what's going on," Jim asked.

Melinda hesitated, than spoke quietly. "Ms. Dykson swears at me and refers to me as a wop. I met with my guidance counselor about the problem, but nothing has changed."

"How long has this been going on?"

Melinda frowned. "It started toward the end of last year. I had hoped that this year would be different, but it has gotten worse."

"She called my daughter a guinea slut," Yolanda Farintino growled. "A teacher shouldn't say things like that."

"You are right," Jim replied. "I will speak with Ms. Dykson. He turned to Melinda. "If this ever happens again, I want you to come directly to my office."

Sal Farintino was a small quiet man, but today he was different. Today Jim could see rage etched in the man's face.

Sal raised his fist and shook it. "If the school does not do something, I will. I will not allow this woman to treat my daughter in this shameful way. I don't want this woman anywhere near my daughter."

Jim nodded his understanding of what was being said. "I will speak with Melinda's guidance counselor and have your daughter removed from Ms. Dykson's class."

At that moment the bell rang for the first period. Jim opened his private entrance door to the hall. "Mr. and Mrs. Farintino, please leave by this door. Fewer students will see you. Your presence will generate gossip concerning your daughter and the reason for your visit.

Jim took Melinda by the arm. "Melinda, I want you to accompany me to the guidance office."

A few minutes later Jim and Melinda entered the guidance office.

"Good morning, Mr. Rahin," Penny Worth, the guidance secretary called. "I was just getting ready to call the Farintino home. Melinda was reported absent from homeroom."

"She was with me," Jim replied. "I'm here to see Ms. Flanagan."

Penny rose and walked to an office a short distance from her desk.

Jim heard the secretary say, "Ms. Flanagan, Mr. Rahin is here to see you. He has Melinda Farintino with him."

When Ms. Worth returned she smiled and said, "Ms. Flanagan can see you now."

Melinda followed Jim to the counselor's office. When they entered Flanagan rose from her desk to greet them. "Good morning," she said with a generous smile. "To what do I owe this honor?"

Erin Flanagan grew up in the north-country. She attended one of the smaller districts that now comprised North Country Central and graduated at the top of her class. She was a tall, handsome woman who had returned to the North Country after spending several years living in Albany. Erin had one child; the product of a short, hurtful marriage.

Jim always felt that Erin should have gone where she would have an opportunity to meet other people her age. The chances of meeting someone who deserved her were few and far between in her present environment. Nevertheless, Erin was an excellent counselor and Jim would have hated to lose her.

"Ms. Flanagan, I understand that you are aware of the problem that Melinda is having with Ms. Dykson.

Flanagan looked at Melinda and placed her hand on the girl's shoulder. "I spoke with Ms. Dykson on at least three occasions. She was in my office twice, and once I spoke with her over a cup of coffee in the teacher's lounge. I thought the matter was settled."

Erin turned to Melinda. "Is she still calling you names?"

Melinda nodded.

"I'm sorry, Mr. Ranin, but I thought the matter was settled."

"When you spoke with Ms. Dykson, what did she say?"

"She admitted calling Melinda names. She claimed that Melinda does not give her all in gym class and when there are coeducational classes Melinda spends too much time talking with the boys. She encourages the boys, rather than discouraging them."

"I don't," Melinda blurted. "The guys just like me. I don't encourage them."

Jim held his hand up to halt the conversation.

"I don't care what Ms. Dykson's excuses are, the name calling has to stop. Ms. Flanagan I want you to remove Melinda from Ms. Dykson's class and place her into a study hall."

"What about the physical education requirement for graduation?" Erin asked.

"I will explain the situation to the Farintino family doctor. I'm sure he will give Melinda a note to excuse her from physical education for the balance of the year."

Erin Flanagan gave a sigh of relief. "Well, that should take care of the contact in a classroom, but what if Ms. Dykson bothers Melinda in the halls?"

"I'll take care of that," Jim snapped. He turned to Melinda. "Melinda, please wait in the outer office until Ms. Flanagan can make the changes to your schedule." When Jim and Erin were alone, he continued the discussion. "I have met with Dykson before regarding her attitude and language around students. She

157

hates attractive and popular girls. That's what this is all about." Jim was speaking at the top of his voice.

Erin went to his side, held a finger to her lips and whispered, "Shhh, this room isn't exactly sound proof. Anyone sitting out there can hear what you are saying."

Jim lowered his voice. "Yeah I know, but I get so frustrated with that bitch. She was given tenure by John Walker. If I had my way, she would have been out of here long ago. I guess I will just have to start building a case for a 3020-A hearing."

"Jim, calm down before you meet with Dykson. She would like nothing better than to have you say or do something in anger that she could use against you."

Jim looked into Erin's gray-blue eyes and heard the sound of reason. Good looks, common sense, and a logical outlook on life, Jim thought. I don't know who the guy in her life was, but he sure missed the boat. "Okay counselor, I'll go back to my office, breathe into a brown paper bag and let my blood pressure drop before I call that fat-ass to my office. Thanks, I owe you a drink."

"Any time, boss!"

An hour later Jim asked Alison to notify Ms. Dykson that he wanted to see her.

It wasn't until the end of the school day that Fanny Dykson came to Jim's office. She was accompanied by Jerry Farmer.

She brought the president of the teacher's union with her, Jim thought. She must have gotten the note from Erin.

"I don't have much time," Fanny said. "Is this about the Farintino girl?"

"Yes, Ms. Dykson, it is. I want you to refrain from having any contact with Melinda Farintino."

"Are you taking the word of a student over that of a teacher?" Jerry Farmer asked.

"Ms. Dykson has already admitted her complicity in this matter, but there are also other staff members and students who could be called to testify, should this matter require a hearing. I will be filing a letter for Ms. Dykson to read and sign. She may make any rebuttal statements that she wishes, but the letter must be signed and returned to me within ten days. Her signature is merely proof that she has received and read its contents."

"Is this going into my folder?" Fanny asked

"Yes."

Fanny scoffed. "We'll see about that." Fanny Dykson and Jerry Farmer stormed out.

When Fanny Dykson failed to comply with Jim's directive, he sent her another letter informing her that if she refused to return the original letter signed, he would place her on a five day suspension pending a hearing.

The following morning Dykson appeared with the signed letter and threw it on Jim's desk. "Here's your letter," she snapped. "It will never stay in my folder." With a grin, she quickly left the office.

Jim reviewed the letter. Fanny had written a rebuttal charging Jim with harassment. Jim grinned and walked to the district office.

"Mrs. Cleary, please place this letter of reprimand into Ms. Dykson's file."

Cleary appeared to be nervous. "Mr. Rahin, Ms. Dykson and Mr. Farmer were in earlier. Mr. Hatch asked me to bring the letter to him when it arrived."

"I see," Jim replied. "Never mind I'll take it in myself."

Oliver Hatch sat at his desk writing. When Jim entered he looked up. "Yes, Jim, what's up?"

Mrs. Cleary said that you wanted to see this letter of reprimand that I wrote on Fanny Dykson." Jim handed the letter to his boss.

Hatch read the letter then placed it on his desk. "Jim, Jerry Farmer and Ms. Dykson were in to see me about this. Don't you think that you're blowing this incident out of proportion?"

"I have had problems with this woman ever since I came to this district. She shouldn't be around kids. If I had been here when she first arrived she would never have gotten tenure."

"So now you're trying to build a case to take her to a hearing."

"Yes. I plan to document every act of misconduct that Dykson does. You know as well as I that that is the only way for the district to be successful at a hearing."

Oliver Hatch left his desk and went to Jim.

"In my judgment you are being vindictive because you don't like this teacher." Hatch turned and looked out of the window. "Jim do you have any idea how much it would cost this district to take

Ms. Dykson to a 3020-A hearing? For what that action would cost, the district could hire three teachers. Besides, according to Farmer the association will produce witnesses including Chance Canard, Rebecca Fitch and many others who will swear under oath that you have had it in for Ms. Dykson from day one."

Hatch shook his head. "I'm sorry, Jim, but I can't allow that to happen on my watch. I'm trying to build rapport with the teacher's union and the community. A thing like this would undermine what I'm trying to do." Oliver took the letter on his desk, tore it in half, and threw it into his waste basket.

"I thought what we were doing was all about the kids. I thought that kids came first." Jim said. "I guess I was wrong."

"That's pie in the sky, Jim. In the real world if you want to survive, you have to play the public relations game."

"Fine, but when the Farintinos come here again, I'm going to bring them—and their attorney—to your office. See how far you get with that public relations bullshit then.

Jim started to leave, but then turned back to face Oliver when his boss called.

"Jim, I'll speak to Farmer. I'll have him caution Dykson about staying away from the girl, but you need to contain your irrational dislike for that woman."

Jim closed the door with authority.

"I'm sorry, Jim," Lora Cleary said. "I know you are right in what you are trying to do, but it's like trying to fight city hall. There's too much politics here and not enough of what's right for kids."

Jim nodded and left.

Chapter 24

DEAN BRUCE WAS A TALL, FIT MAN WITH short brown hair circling his ears. The rest of his hair had disappeared years earlier when he was still a young man. For most of his military career, Dean shaved his head. Friends referred to him as Mr. Clean.

Bruce's first day as the assistant principal passed with very few problems. He replaced Jim in the hall during the lunch period, made visits to the in-school suspension room and insured that all students knew who he was and why he seemed to be visible everywhere in the building.

At the end of the day Dean sat with Jim to review policy and talk about the day and expectations for the future.

"I just have a few questions," Bruce said. "Mrs. Lauren has expressed her desire to retire. Do you have anyone in mind to replace her?"

"Penny Worth, one of the secretaries in the guidance office has expressed an interest in coming to this office. She's very efficient. I think you'll like her.

"Most of the staff members are very supportive," Dean said. The only one that was unapproachable was the gym teacher."

Jim grinned. "She doesn't like you because you were my choice for the job. She and the super have become good friends. He wanted someone else as the assistant."

"That's not good," Dean Bruce offered. "Am I going to have to walk on egg shells when I'm around Hatch?"

'Naw, just do your job and you'll be fine. You have sound judgment. If you run into a situation that could be a public relations problem, let me take the lead."

At the same time that Dean Bruce was hired, the board approved two other positions. Both teachers were hired as part of an agreement Hatch had made with the board.

Pamela Foxworthy was appointed as the middle school vocal teacher and Ian Polovich was appointed to the position vacated by the retirement of one of the guidance counselors. In both cases the appointees were personal friends of Oliver Hatch.

Foxworthy was the sister of a board member's wife. The board member and his wife went to dinner and played cards with the Hatchs every Friday night.

Polovich was recommended to Hatch by a close personal friend. Hatch had promised his friend that Polovich would be appointed.

"Dean, keep a close eye on our two new staff members," said Jim. "Foxworthy lacks experience and may need help keeping those ninth graders in line. As for Polovich, I don't have a read on him yet. I know that he comes to us from the western part of the state. He seems to know what is expected of a guidance counselor, but there is something about him that makes me uneasy.

"I know that he is having a hard time finding a place to live. His wife doesn't seem too happy about living in the North Country. They're staying in a motel right now."

Jim thought for a moment. "If the Polovichs don't find a place by the end of the week, tell him to see me. I might be interested in renting my chalet."

To Hope Rahin's delight, the Polovichs rented the chalet on a month-to-month basis with the understanding that the rent arrangement would end once they found another apartment.

Jim's evening commitments would not be as intense now that he had an assistant. The only late night would be when there was a board meeting.

On Saturday afternoon Hope was in the process of purging the cabin of their personal items when there was a knock on the door. Hope left the bedroom and yelled, "Come in."

When the door opened, a small, blond woman in a blue hooded jacket stepped into the kitchen."

Hope went to meet her. "Can I help you?"

"I'm sorry to bother you—I'm Alice Polovich. I know that Ian and I are not scheduled to move in until tomorrow, but I wanted a chance to talk with you. I was hoping that you would be here."

"I'm Hope Rahin, Alice, what can I do for you."

"I heard from some of the other teachers that you weren't happy here and that you took a job in another school district. I thought you might be able to help me find a job closer to a city."

"I understand how you feel Alice. The Lake District is a wonderful place to be in the summer, but the winters are long, cold, and boring. I found a job about thirty miles south of here. In the winter when I can't get home, I drive to Utica and stay with my parents."

"Ian and I have a friend in Utica. He used to be a minister in Geneva. I'm sure that he would be helpful in finding me a place to stay if I couldn't get back to the chalet. I hate the thought of teaching here at the North Country elementary."

"I can't promise anything, but I will let my principal know about you. Do you have a resume that I could give him?"

"I'll see that you have one tomorrow," Alice replied.

To Oliver Hatch's disappointment, Alice Polovich took a job in another district. The commute for Alice was forty-five miles, one way. The district was near Schenectady.

"What will she do in the winter?" Hope asked, when Jim told her the news.

"Ian is not pleased about her decision, but he was unable to change her mind. He said that she has a connection for lodging through the church. This situation is going to put an awful strain on that marriage."

"As much as I dislike living this far from a city, I would never do anything to put our marriage at risk."

"Well, I have some feelers out for a superintendent's opening near Lake Champlain," Jim announced. "If the job comes through, we will be moving in the summer. You will be less than an hour from Albany."

IN APRIL ERIN FLANAGAN CAME TO THE office to see Jim. Her face was flushed and the smile she normally wore was absent.

Erin asked Alison if Jim was in. Getting an affirmative nod, she entered Jim's office before Alison could tell her that Yolanda Farintino was with him.

"I'm sorry for interrupting Mr. Rahin, but there is a big problem in the guidance office." Flanagan softened her approach when she saw Mrs. Farintino. "Oh I'm so sorry Mrs. Farintino, I didn't know that there was anyone in here."

Erin turned to leave when Jim called to her, "Don't leave Ms. Flanagan, what we are talking about concerns you."

Erin's look went from anger to concern. "You must be talking about Melinda."

"Yes. Ms. Dykson is going out of her way to seek out Melinda during lunch, before school starts and before the buses leave in the afternoon. I want you to get a small hand recorder for Melinda. I want her to turn the recorder on whenever Dykson comes near her. We are going to keep a record of Dykson's abuse. The Farintinos have hired an attorney. They are going after Ms. Dykson and the school. You and I may be asked to testify."

"Does Mr.Hatch know about this?" Erin asked.

"Not yet. I'm not going to tell him until Dykson is on tape. Hatch promised that he would get Dykson to stay away from Melinda. Well, apparently he hasn't. I warned him about what the Farintinos intended to do if it continued. He tore up the letter of sanction that I placed in her folder, now let him figure out what to do."

"Don't you think that you should at least warn him?" Flanagan asked. "If this goes to court and I have to testify against the school what will happen to my job?"

"Nothing—you have tenure. Besides, you can't be expected to lie under oath. I guarantee that you and I won't be the only ones to testify. There are teachers, secretaries, lunch employees and custodians who will testify that they heard Dykson say improper things to Melanie."

"Okay, I just hope you know what you are doing."

When Mrs. Farintino left, and Jim and Erin were alone, he said, "Erin what were you so worked up about when you first came into my office?"

"I needed to see you about Polovich. Jim, he's terrible as a counselor. He has ignored student applications for college and spends his time locked in his office with either students or staff. I know that student personal problems are important, but he cannot ignore those college forms. They must be in to the colleges in a timely manner."

"Have you talked with him about your concerns?"

"Yes I have. He told me that he is here to counsel and not to push papers. He had the audacity to tell me that if I was so concerned about the college forms, to do them myself. They're his students, why should I have to do his work."

"Someone told me a little while back to relax before I blew a gasket. I thought that was good advice."

Erin Flanagan took a deep breath and sat into one of Jim's overstuffed chairs. "I hear ya. Just talk to that ass, would you please, before I do something drastic."

"Okay, Erin, I'll have Dean Bruce meet with him. If that doesn't change his ways I'll give him a written directive."

"Okay, but you better hurry. Every day that Polovich delays, his students fall further down on the college acceptance list."

"Your wish is my command," Jim joked with a wave and a bow.

"Yeah well if that's true, I say—off with his head." Erin did a bow of her own and left.

Chapter 25

Dean Bruce monitored Ian Polovich's activities for three days and found that Erin was right. Polovich was spending far too much time behind closed doors. Most of the lengthy periods were spent with one young girl. Dean knew that teenagers have lots of issues during hormonal changes, but the amount of time Ian was spending with the same girls was excessive. He was ignoring the needs of the rest of his students.

The other interesting observation was the frequency and amount of time that Jamie Dunn spent in Polovich's office.

So that's the long and the short of it," Bruce told Jim, as he finished his report. "I haven't spoken with Polovich. I thought I'd let you know the findings first." How would you like me to handle this?"

"Write up an evaluation and give it to him. I'll be interested in his response."

Bruce Dean wrote the evaluation and placed it in Polovich's mail box. It took less than two hours for Polovich to respond.

Upon entering the office Ian Polovich approached Penny Worth's desk.

"Miss. Worth, is Mr. Bruce in?"

"Yes, would you like—"

Without waiting for Penny to finish, Ian charged into Dean's office.

"Who the hell do you think you are?" Ian yelled. "How dare you tell me that I'm spending too much time with a student? Who has the guidance certification here, you or me?"

"Calm down," Dean replied. "I was asked to observe you and write a report regarding that observation. I'd like to discuss the evaluation with you, but only after you have regained a little composure."

When Jim heard the loud voices, he left his office and entered Bruce's room.

"What's the problem?" Jim asked.

Ian Polovich extended the document, clutched in his fist, toward Jim. "This is the problem," he bellowed.

Jim took the report and quickly scanned the contents. "This looks like an evaluation. All new staff are observed and evaluated during the course of the year."

"If I'm going to be judged on how I perform my job then I want someone who is qualified." Ian looked in Dean's direction. "Frankly, I don't think that he is."

"I think you better calm down, Mr. Polovich." Jim took a seat and motioned for Ian to do the same. "Do you expect the district to hire people who are certified in each discipline taught to evaluate staff?"

"I expect to be able to do my job as I see fit," Polovich replied. "Mr. Bruce has no right to tell me who I should counsel, and how long it should take."

Jim rose and paced. "Ian, how many students do you have?"

"I have all of the ninth and twelfth graders. Flanagan has grades ten and eleven."

"Then you are responsible for over three hundred students. At this time of the year you should be seeing each ninth grader at least once for scheduling and each senior for help with college applications or job interview training. How many ninth graders have you scheduled for tenth grade?"

"I'm working on it," Polovich mumbled,

Jim shook his head. "And how many seniors have you helped with college applications?"

"A few, but Flanagan is going to help me—"

Jim interrupted, "Ms. Flanagan has three hundred and fifty students of her own. You need to budget your time accordingly so that every one of your students has an opportunity to meet with you."

"What about a student who needs to see me on a regular basis? The girl that Mr. Bruce refers to in this report has some serious problems.

"If we have a student who needs that much help she should be referred to the school psychologist. You are not trained for the kind of help she obviously needs. And why are you spending time with our laundry lady when you could be spending time with students."

Ian Polovich tensed. "I'm not at liberty to discuss my conversations with Mrs. Dunn. Our discussions are confidential."

Jim's face took on the hue of the red tie he was wearing. "You were not hired to counsel with staff. If staff members wish to counsel with you on matters, other than those affecting students they teach, they can do so after regular school hours."

"I will speak to my union rep about this." Polovich said. "Is there anything else?"

"Not right now," Jim replied. "Mr. Bruce will continue to observe you. An evaluation of your performance will be given to you shortly thereafter. Please sign it and return it to me within ten days after you receive it. You need to understand that whether or not you are recommended for continued employment depends on your evaluations and progress."

Ian Polovich took the report and left.

Jim returned to the chair he had occupied upon first entering the office. "Well, Dean, what do you think?"

Dean Bruce had written some notes onto a legal pad while Jim and Ian were talking. He refreshed his memory of what was said between his boss and Polovich before answering. "He's stressed out. I spoke with Jamie about her meetings with Ian. I was wondering if her meetings with Polovich had anything to do with her children. They didn't."

Bruce shook his head. "Mrs. Dunn said that she had been counseling him. Apparently Ian's wife is spending more and more time away from home. She always has a reason, but when Ian says that he will go to her for the weekend, she says no, breaks her previous plans, and come home. At home, she shows no interest in him. Ian thinks that his wife is having an affair. He went to Mrs. Dunn because she is going through the same problem with Henry."

"Henry is cheating again?" Jim snapped. "What an asshole. Jamie deserves better. I helped him to get a job at the lumber mill for the sake of Jamie and the kids." Jim slapped his hand on Dean's desk. "I should have fixed it so that son of a bitch would have been forced to leave the area."

"I told Mrs. Dunn that it would be better if she met with Polovich after school. She said that would be hard because of the kids.

Jim pointed at the door as if Ian Polovich were standing there. "You keep on his ass," Jim growled. "If he continues to ignore his responsibilities as a guidance counselor, let me know."

Two weeks later Jim was forced to hire a retired guidance counselor part time for the high school in order to play catch-up with scheduling. Erin Flanagan turned over some of her tenth graders to the extra counselor for scheduling while she assisted Polovich with senior graduation needs.

Jim wrote an evaluation of Polovich chastising him for his lack of priorities. Jim sent a copy of the evaluation to Oliver Hatch along with a recommendation that Polovich's employment be terminated.

Pamela Foxworthy was one of the nicest teachers Jim had on staff. Her tall ,stately presence and good nature enhanced an angelic face. Jim liked her and genuinely hoped that she would be successful as a teacher. Pamela played the piano well and enjoyed working with students. Her drawback was that she lacked any kind of discipline in her classroom.

When informed by Dean Bruce that Pamela had lost control, Jim decided to take a personal interest in helping Foxworthy succeed.

At a post observation conference Jim outlined steps that he felt would help his music teacher regain order in the class.

"Pamela, there are a few things I want you to change in your classroom," said Jim. "First of all, I think you need to close the blinds on the windows so that the kids in the back row are not distracted by what is going on outside. Secondly I want you to move some of the students to the front row and separate the troublemakers so that they are not acting out to gain the attention of the others. Those students who continue to disrupt the class should be sent to Mr. Bruce's office. Last, but not least, I want you to change the position of the piano. The back of the piano should be facing the students. You should position yourself so that you can see what is going on in the room at all times."

A nervous Pamela Foxworthy fidgeted with her wedding band as Jim outlined his expectations.

"What will happen if I can't gain control?" Pamela asked.

"If you do what I have suggested, discipline should improve. If you need help, ask Mr. Malone to help you. He's tougher than nails and the kids will listen to him."

"But what if all this fails?"

Jim could tell that her self-confidence was gone. He took a deep breath. "Pam, without discipline little or no teaching and learning will go on. If kids aren't learning in one teacher's class and are not a problem with other teachers, then it is up to me to remedy the problem."

"How do you do that?"

"I get rid of the teacher." Jim stood and moved to where Pamela Foxworthy was sitting. "Pam, I believe that you have great potential as a teacher. I believe that you can be a valuable asset to the educational community here at North Country High. If you do everything that I have suggested and there are still problems, I won't blame you. We will put our heads together and try another approach. However, if you fail to do what I have suggested it will be reflected in your evaluation and as much as I like you as a person, I will not recommend you for continued employment as a teacher at the high school."

During the first week of June, Joe Malone and Dean Bruce came to Jim's office.

"Jim we have a real problem with Mrs. Foxworthy's classes. The kids are running wild," Bruce reported. "The only time that there is order in the room is when Joe goes into the room."

"I can't take time away from my instrumental lessons and band rehearsals to babysit her classes," Malone added.

"She hasn't done one thing that you asked her to do in your post-observation review," Dean interrupted. "The only time I see a student from her room is when Joe sends one to me."

Jim's smile at greeting the two men faded as he digested what they had to say.

"Well, I guess Mrs. Foxworthy will be another teacher that I will recommend for termination. I am recommending to the board that Ian Polovich be released. Hatch is not going to be happy. Both Polovich and Foxworthy owe their jobs to him."

Jim threw his hands in the air as a gesture of his frustration. Foxworthy's dismissal would be especially difficult. Her husband and Ollie play cards together every Friday night."

"Do you think we ought to give her another year?" Dean asked.

Malone shook his head. "I'm telling you guys that Pamela Foxworthy lacks the where-with-all to be an effective teacher. She's too nice. She wants everyone to like her. She wants to be a friend first and a teacher second. You both know that that attitude is a blueprint for failure. I like Pam, but if she is here next year I will not take time away from my students to sit in her classes. She will have to sink or swim on her own."

"I have thrown her all kinds of safety devices so she wouldn't drown this year," Dean Bruce added. "I really don't believe that another year will be any different."

"Thanks for the input," Jim uttered. "This letter to Hatch will be one of the most difficult that I will ever have to write.

Chapter 26

Peter Foxworthy paced back and forth in Oliver Hatch's office. Pamela, his wife, had returned home early from school after receiving a notice from Jim stating that she was not being recommended for continued employment. In her absence ,Pam's classes were being covered by Dean Bruce for the balance of the day.

Oliver Hatch had received a copy of the letter along with a letter of his own explaining why Jim was recommending Pam's termination of employment. Oliver had gone to Jim's office to discuss the letter with him.

It was a warm June afternoon, causing Oliver to shed his suit jacket. The sleeves on his white shirt were rolled to the elbows and the top button undone. He jerked on his blue striped tie in frustration as he continued his conversation.

"Look, Jim, you have admitted that you and the staff like Mrs. Foxworthy. You admit that she has potential. Why in the hell can't you give her another year? Hell I'll even send her to a workshop this summer on how to better manage the classroom. For Christ's sake, she and her husband are personal friends of mine. If she was one of your friends would you be recommending dismissal after only one year?"

Jim leaned back in his chair. "I never hire anyone that I can't fire. All my friends know when I walk into this school I become the principal first and a friend second." He rose and walked around the desk to where Hatch was pacing. "With me kids come first— and they should come first with you too."

Hatch stopped pacing and faced Jim. "If I didn't believe that kids come first, I wouldn't be here." He slumped into a chair. He looked beat. "All I'm saying is that she deserves another chance. I haven't even started to discuss the Polovich letter."

Jim had also written a notice of termination to Iva Polovich.

"Look, Jim, I have Pete in my office right now. He's really pissed. He contends that no one lent a hand to help his wife all year. He says that it's a personal thing between Pam and Joe Malone. Malone, because he is your friend, has influenced your decision."

"That is all bullshit! Joe Malone has bent over backwards to help Mrs. Foxworthy in any way that he could, but he has his own kids to worry about." Jim returned to his desk and pulled a file from a drawer. "This is Pamela Foxworthy's folder. Take a look. There are at least four evaluations in her folder each signed by her. Each evaluation represents no fewer than four observations. Each observation was followed up with a one-on-one meeting with the teacher. I like Pete, but he is allowing his anger to cloud his knowledge of the truth."

"Most of those observations were done by Dean Bruce. Is that correct?"

"Yes, but either Dean or I met with Mrs. Foxworthy after each observation."

"I told you when we hired Bruce that I didn't like him. I still don't. I know your evaluations of him have been positive, but I think the district can do better."

Jim's eyes narrowed. "Are you suggesting that you are planning to eliminate Bruce?"

"I'm considering it."

Jim again went to Oliver's side. "On what grounds?"

Hatch smiled. "Jim you know very well that I don't need cause to dismiss a first-year employee. You give Pamela another year to prove herself and I'll do the same for Dean."

"That's blackmail." Jim snapped.

Oliver returned to his chair. "Call it what you want, but if Mrs. Foxworthy goes, so does Bruce."

173

After an hour of discussion, Oliver Hatch returned to his office. When he opened his door Peter Foxworthy was waiting.

"Jesus Christ," Foxworthy said. "What took you so long?"

"Jim Rahin is a hard-nose. I had to convince him that allowing Pam to stay on was in his best interest."

Pete colored with anger. "Did you convince him? If I were in your shoes I wouldn't have bandied words with him. I would have told him. After all, you're the superintendent not him."

"Jim has friends on the board. With certain matters I have to walk softly."

"God damn it, Ollie, does my wife have a job or not?"

Oliver motioned for Pete to keep his voice down. "Yes, Pete, Pam's job is safe at least for another year, but she needs to improve. I don't know what Pam has told you about her teaching, but her file is replete with suggestions for improvement, notes of help given and warnings that continued classroom failure would result in a recommendation for dismissal."

"I appreciate your help. I'll talk to my wife. Is there anything that I can do to help her?"

"No. I'm going to send Pam to a couple of workshops this summer—at the school expense. Perhaps talking with other teachers who have experienced difficulty in the classroom will help."

Peter Foxworthy nodded and shook Oliver's hand. "Thanks again Ollie. That's a load off my mind." As Peter turned to leave he stopped and turned to Oliver. "Ollie, Rahin isn't going to set Pam up for failure next year, is he?"

Oliver smiled. "Jim Rahin may be a hard-headed son of a bitch with faults, but deliberately setting up one of his teacher's to fail is not one of them. When it comes to kids and his job he is very professional. If anything he will go beyond what is expected to ensure that Pam demonstrates the best of her teaching abilities to her students. If he does not recommend her to return next year, it won't be because she was sabotaged."

TWO DAYS AFTER HIS DEBATE WITH Oliver Hatch over the future of Pamela Foxworthy, Jim was approached by Ian Polovich.

"Mr. Rahin, I would like to meet with you regarding the notification you sent me about my continued employment."

Jim looked up from the paper he was reading. "You will need to speak with my secretary. Ms. Block keeps all my appointments. She will fit you in."

"I just spoke with Alison. She said that you are free any afternoon this week."

Jim set the paper down and looked at his calendar. After scrolling his finger down the page he said, "How about Thursday after lunch?"

"Eighth period is my free period," Ian replied.

Without answer Jim nodded and wrote Ian's name on the calendar.

"I'll see you then," Polovich said.

On Thursday Ian Polovich appeared in the office at 2:20 in the afternoon. He was accompanied by Jerry Farmer.

"I thought you were going to see me after lunch," Jim said as Polovich and Farmer entered the office.

"I thought I said eighth period," Polovich replied. "It's my planning period and I wanted Mr. Farmer to be with me."

Jim searched for Ian's folder containing notes on observations, evaluations, and interviews. "Have a seat."

"I'm here to support Mr. Polovich's contention that he should be given another year before a final determination is made about his counseling abilities," Farmer interjected.

Jim waved the folder and said, "Jerry you know as well as I the school doesn't have to give a reason to a first-year teacher. The decision to terminate Mr. Polovich is based on judgments made through the evaluation process, a process, I might add, that was established through negotiations between the teachers' association and the board."

"It is the contention of the association that Mr. Polovich was not given suggestions for improvement," Farmer continued. "The administration should have helped him to improve."

Jim set Polovich's file onto the desk. "Mr. Polovich was given numerous suggestions. His file is filled with letters directing that his approach to counseling be changed. Mr. Palovich chose to ignore my advice as well as that of Dean Bruce and Ms. Flanagan."

"Flanagan had no business telling Ian what to do. She's not an administrator," Jerry Farmer replied.

"Maybe so, but she's a damn good counselor. I thought Mr. Polovich would take help from her inasmuch as he had asked her for help in the past."

Ian Polovich, who had sat quietly through the discussion between Jim and Farmer, stood and said, "We are wasting time here Jerry. I think I would be better off talking directly to the superintendent."

"Mr. Hatch and the board can do what they want, but my recommendation will not change.

At the end of the school day Lora Cleary called and asked Jim to stop into the superintendent's office.

Jim had a pretty good idea what Hatch wanted. At four that afternoon Jim entered Hatch's office. Oliver was on the phone.

He looked at Jim and motioned for him to have a seat.

Sunlight was sneaking past the corners of the vertical blinds on Hatch's windows. Jim sat where the light could not find his face and he waited.

Oliver hung up the phone and drew a long breath. "That was my buddy in Geneva," he said. "Jeff is the superintendent there. We were discussing Ian Polovich. He told me Ian is a basket case. His wife notified him that she wants a divorce. After twenty years of marriage, she wants to call it quits. Jeff said that Alice told a friend in Geneva that she is in love with a pastor in Albany. The pastor plans to leave his wife so that he and Alice can get married. The whole thing is a freakin' mess."

Oliver rose and began pacing the floor. He did that when he had something unpleasant to say.

"Jim, I'm going to recommend that Ian Polovich be given another year of employment. He turned to face Jim with his hand raised chest high. "I know how you feel, but I just can't kick a guy in the balls when he is down. A year from now he will have put his life back together. If he still isn't cutting it I'll get rid of him."

Jim sat quietly observing two goldfish feeding in a tank next to Oliver's desk. "Fish don't do anything, but they still get fed."

"Did you hear what I said?" Hatch asked.

Jim stood. "Yeah, I heard. You're the boss, but I want you to know that when I get complaints about Polovich from parents or staff, I'm going to refer all calls to you."

Chapter 27

IN THE FALL, FOXWORTHY'S TEACHING abilities and Polovich's guidance methods didn't change. As promised, Jim directed every irate parent and disgruntled staff member to the superintendent. By Christmas, Oliver Hatch was ready to capitulate.

"I miscalculated the extent of the problem," Oliver admitted to Jim. "I need to do something, but I don't know what."

"Pamela Foxworthy is not as big a problem," said Jim. "She actually is a little better. Her major problem is that she wants to mother these kids. That works with some, but there are those who need a swift kick in the ass. If she would refer them to Bruce I think her classes would be manageable. She just won't send the recalcitrant offenders to the office." Jim took a cup of coffee from the desk. He watched the heat rise from a white porcelain mug. "This is good coffee," he mumbled.

"Yeah, Lora makes good joe. But what the hell am I going to do with Polovich and Pam? You say that Pam is getting better, but the calls keep coming. As for Polovich, I promised my buddy that I would give him another chance. Jesus—I can't go through the whole year with screaming parents, kids, and staff on my ass. Even board members are starting to call because people are calling them."

Jim took a sip of his brew. "It's too bad we don't have an elementary opening," he said. I believe Pamela would do fine with younger kids."

Oliver's cheeks lit up as if someone had placed a light bulb in his mouth. "Elementary!" he shouted. "That's the answer." He picked up the phone and dialed.

Jim looked on with a puzzled look. "What?" he snapped.

Oliver looked at him. "I just remembered that—" he paused. "Hello, Sister Agnes? This is Oliver Hatch. Yes, remember me? We met last week at the meeting in Ogdensburg. Yes, I'm fine, and how are you? Good." Hatch looked at Jim and smiled. "Sister, are you still looking for an elementary music teacher?" There was a long pause, but the grin on Oliver Hatch's face widened. "Well listen, Sister, I have a teacher that is teaching high school vocal music right now, but she is looking for a position where she would be working with younger students."

There was another long pause, during which Oliver flashed a thumbs up to Jim. "Yes, Sister, she is Catholic and lives less than an hour from Lake George." There was another pause. "Don't worry about that, Sister, she is used to driving in the winter. She has a four-wheel drive vehicle."

He's going to pawn her off on that Catholic school in Lake George, Jim thought.

Oliver Hatch was writing directions onto a legal pad. "Yes, Sister, I'll have her there tomorrow. I'm sure your students are going to love her."

When Oliver hung up the phone, Jim threw his hands in the air. "Well?"

"Sister Mary-Nolen has been looking for a music teacher to work with the kids in the church's elementary school. She is excited about the possibility of Pam teaching for them."

"Will Pam accept a position there?"

"She'll take the position. I'll promise she can have the first elementary opening we have at North Country." Oliver's face suddenly went to a shade of grey. "Now if I can only figure out what to do with Polovich."

IAN POLOVICH DROVE HIS 1967 Jeep south on route 28. When he reached Okara Lake he pulled into a parking area next to a small cabin; Jamie Dunn was at his side bundled against the cold like an Eskimo with several layers of clothing at the height of winter.

"I feel guilty," Jamie mumbled. "I shouldn't be here," she said as she popped her head through the over-sized neck of the Woolrich hunting jacket. "I should be home with my children

"And wait for your faithful husband to return with lipstick on his shirt and tell lies about how he had to work overtime again?"

"Oh, Ian, you don't understand. No matter what Henry is doing, two wrongs don't make a right."

"My marriage is over," Ian replied. "I don't care." He reached for Jamie's hand. "We found each other in this winter hell-hole and no matter what, I don't want to lose you."

"But you told me that your job is in jeopardy. I can't just up and leave my house and job and run off to who knows where." Jamie straightened herself. "I need stability in my life, Ian."

"I'll find another job. I promise."

"When? It could be a long time before you are able to find another job as a counselor. We still will need a roof over our heads and food."

Ian turned off the car engine. "I'll work at Mc Donald's if I have to."

"How will you be able to feed three children and two adults on what you will be making flipping hamburgers?"

Ian Polovich looked away and placed both hands on the wheel. He was afraid of the response he was about to get. "We could leave the kids with Henry until I find another good-paying job."

The cab of the Jeep grew colder even though Jamie's face was flushed to the intensity of hot coals. "You are a selfish, self-centered bastard, Ian Polovich." She moved her body so that her back was hard against the passenger door. "Whatever happened to all that stuff you told me about taking care of me and loving my children as if they were your own? Jamie's voice became elevated. "Were those all lies just to get me into your bed?" She turned and looked out of the passenger side window. "You are no better than my husband."

Ian began to plead with her. "I do love you Jamie, you must believe me. I didn't lie to you. I do want to take care of you and the kids. It's just that right now my life is going downhill fast. I don't know what to do. I don't want to lose you, too."

Jamie opened the Jeep door and stepped into the snowy night. "Let's go inside," she said, her anger on hold. "I'm freezing out here."

Inside the cabin there was a fire in the fireplace. Ian had driven to Okara Lake after school to ensure that the cabin would be warm when he and Jamie arrived.

Upon entering the living room Jamie went directly to the fireplace. She added a fresh log and stood mute rubbing her hands together.

Ian removed his coat and went to her. Softly he murmured, "Let me help you off with your things."

Without looking at him Jamie shed the man-size coat she was wearing. When Ian attempted to help her off with a second jacket, she pulled away.

"No," she said in a sharp tone. "I'm still cold."

He put his arms around her and kissed her on the neck. "I'm sorry about what I said. We'll work something out. I don't think Hatch will dismiss me until June. Maybe by then I'll have another job." He placed his hands on her shoulders and turned her toward him. "Forgive me?" he asked.

Jamie began to cry. "I won't leave my children," she sobbed. "If you want me, you have to take my children too."

"Okay, okay," Ian whispered. "Shhhhh, don't cry. I love you and your children. We'll figure out something. I won't leave here until you can go with me, but you have to tell Henry that you want a divorce. When he leaves the house, I will move in and start providing for you and the children."

Jamie Dunn removed her second coat and dropped it onto an Adirondack rocker near the fireplace. "I'm still cold," she pouted

Ian took her hand and guided her toward the master bedroom. "I can take care of that, too," he whispered. He kissed her tears and held her tight.

WHEN THE SCHOOL RECESSED FOR winter break, Oliver Hatch called Ian Polovich and asked him to come to the office.

"Ian, Jim Rahin and I would like to talk with you," Oliver said.

"Gee, does it have to be today?" Ian asked. "I was planning to drive to Albany."

"Well, when will you be back? We really need to talk. I spoke with Jeff. He said that he may have a job for you. They are looking for a counselor at the community college."

"I'll put off my trip to Albany. Alice and I were going to meet to hammer out the terms of the divorce, but it can wait," Ian replied.

"I'll be at the school the first thing in the morning," Oliver said.

"I'll be there at eight or so," Ian replied.

At eight-forty-five the following morning, Lora Cleary announced that Mr. Polovich was waiting.

"Get him a cup of coffee, Lora, and tell him that I'm waiting for Mr. Rahin; he should be here momentarily."

Jim arrived on time and both he and Ian entered Oliver Hatch's office.

"Good morning, Ollie," Jim greeted.

Ian grunted, "Morning." He was still clutching the cup of coffee that Lora Cleary had given him.

"Have a seat," Hatch directed.

Jim was already seated and looking through Ian's file.

"Mr. Polovich, last June I went against Mr. Rahin's recommendation regarding your continued service and allowed you to continue your role as a guidance counselor at the high school. It was my hope that, with help, you would develop into a first rate counselor." Oliver rose and began to pace. "My trust in your abilities has not been supported by your achievements. Since September I have been continually besieged by phone calls concerning your lack of due diligence toward the students you serve. Can you give me one reason why the North Country Central School District should extend your employment through to the end of the school year?"

Ian Polovich was silent.

"You have to admit, Ian, that Dean Bruce and I have done everything we could to assist you," Jim said. "Even Erin has helped by taking some of your load. I just don't think you were cut out to be a school guidance counselor. Perhaps you should open a counseling office of your own. Apparently you enjoy working one-on-one with individuals."

Polovich placed the cup he was holding onto the top of Hatch's desk. "I need this job," he pleaded. "Fire me at the end of the year if you must, but please allow me to finish out the year."

Oliver went to Ian's side. "Ian, if it's money you are worried about, Jeff Rawlings is sure that he can get you a job as a counselor at the college."

"It isn't the money," Ian quickly answered. "I have found someone who I love and I don't want to leave the area; at least not until June."

"Jamie Dunn is a married woman," Jim blurted.

Polovich turned to Jim and yelled, "Everyone knows that her husband spends more time away from home then he does with his family. Jamie Dunn is married only in the legal sense. As soon as I'm free of Alice I intend to marry her."

"We are getting away from the purpose of this meeting, gentlemen," Oliver said, interrupting the bantering between Jim and his counselor.

"I'm sorry," Jim mumbled.

Ian sat, but said nothing.

Following another half-hour of discussion and review of Ian's file, Oliver said, "I'm sorry, Mr. Polovich, but I have no choice but to terminate your employment effective immediately. You can clean out your desk today."

Ian Polovich looked like a beaten puppy. He nodded and left.

Jim remained with Hatch. "I feel sorry for the guy, but the welfare of the kids has to come first."

"Yeah, well you only have a few days to replace him so you better hop to it."

"I already have a call into all of the teacher colleges and Utica asking for the names of individuals who completed their counselor certification during the last semester. I'm more concerned about Jamie Dunn. Her life has been one nightmare after another.

Polovich is right; her marriage is one in the legal sense only. But Ian Polovich is not the answer to her prayer."

A perceptive Oliver Hatch studied Jim for a moment, then in a sterile rebuke said, "Neither are you."

Jim jumped to his feet. "My only interest in Mrs. Dunn is that of a friend. I don't want to see her hurt or the kids mentally harmed."

"Jim, stick to being a principal. Let Father Newman take care of her soul and let Social Services deal with her family problems."

Jim glared at Oliver, then without comment, he left the office.

Chapter 28

IAN POLOVICH MOVED INTO HIS FRIEND'S cabin on Okara Lake and continued his relationship with Jamie Dunn. He placed his name on the substitute list of every school district within a fifty-mile radius of the cabin. The need for teachers was critical. Ian was able to work somewhere every day. He even substituted in the North Country elementary, but Jim directed the girl who was responsible for calling subs not to call Ian for the high school unless it was absolutely necessary. Jim didn't want Polovich in the same building where Jamie Dunn was employed.

In February Jamie asked Alison Block to arrange a meeting so that she could speak to Jim.

Alison looked at her calendar. "He is in classrooms evaluating staff every day this week. The only time he might agree to meet with you is before school starts or after four when staff and students have left the building."

Jamie thought for a moment. "I think the morning would be better. I will come in as soon as the children are on the bus. If it's all right with Mr. Rahin I can be here by seven-thirty."

"I'll ask," Alison replied. "I'm sure seven-thirty will be all right. Mr. Rahin is here before seven every morning. It gives him time to organize his day and dictate memos."

The following morning Jamie arrived at the school early. Alison was not in the office.

Jim heard the office door open and left his desk to greet Alison with some letters. He stopped short when he saw Jamie. "Oh, Jamie," he said, "I thought it was Alison."

"I believed that I was scheduled to meet with you at seven-thirty," Jamie said, with a smile.

Jim looked at his watch. "Gosh, it's almost seven-thirty now. I guess I got carried away with my evaluation reports." He motioned to Jamie, "Come on in."

Jamie removed her coat and sat in the chair opposite Jim's desk.

"What can I do for you Mrs. Dunn?"

Jamie Dunn didn't look directly at Jim when she answered. "Mr. Rahin, I guess you know that Henry and I are estranged." She changed her focus and looked directly at him. "Henry is involved with a woman in Watertown. He says he loves her, but I don't think

Henry knows what love really is. He hasn't been home for over a month."

"Does Henry know about Ian Polovich?"

Jamie's eyes found the floor. "I don't know. I think he suspects." Her answer was uttered in a hushed whisper. "Everyone seems to know. I'm not proud of that." Her gaze went back to Jim. "But I don't see Ian in my home—or show emotion in front of the kids."

"Do you love him?"

Jamie took a moment before answering. She rose and wrung her hands repetitively as she paced toward the door. Without looking back at Jim she replied, "I'm thirty-six years old." Turning to face Jim she continued unapologetically. "I'll be thirty-seven in another month. I know it's wrong, but life with Henry has not been easy. I tried to keep the marriage together regardless of his drinking and womanizing." As if pleading for understanding, she added, "You know that."

Jim moved to her side. "You didn't answer my question."

Jamie turned away. "Mr. Rahin, I love my children and I wouldn't do anything to harm them. They are my whole life."

"Do you love Ian Polovich?" Jim reiterated.

Jamie turned and looked him in the eyes. "No!"

Jim returned to his desk. "Then why?"

"I'm a woman with a woman's needs," she said, moving toward Jim's desk. "At first I suppose I became involved with Ian because he was going through the same thing with his wife. We seemed to have a lot in common. He was a comforting ear and said things I wanted to hear. Our sexual involvement just seemed to happen. I suppose it was an extension of our mutual needs. He kissed me and…" Her explanation trailed off. "It just happened. Do you know what it is like wanting to be loved, and not having anyone to share that with?"

Jim shook his head. "But Ian Polovich…"

"He was there," Jamie interrupted. "What was I supposed to do, go to a bar and pick up a man? Ian Polovich isn't the greatest catch in the world, but he's clean, educated, and willing to listen. He treats me with kindness."

"If you needed to talk to someone you could have come to me."

Jamie dropped into the chair and quietly replied, "I thought about that. I know you have a chalet close by and that you would have been willing to listen, but you are happily married with a lovely wife." She looked directly at him. "Would you have gone to bed with me?"

Jim shook his head in the negative. "If I did that I would be no better than Henry or Alice Polovich." There was a rap on the door.

"Yes," Jim called.

It was Alison. "I'm sorry to interrupt, Mr. Rahin, but Ms. Andrews is on line one. She said to tell you that it's important."

"Tell Ms. Andrews that I will call her back in five minutes."

When Alison closed the door, Jamie rose and put on her coat. "You're busy so I won't take any more of your time. She moved to the door opened it a crack turning back to Jim. "Mr. Rahin, if you would like to help me, please let Ian sub at the high school."

As the door closed Jim dialed the number for the South Hudson Valley Central School District and waited.

"South Hudson Valley Central School," a voice answered.

"The personnel director's office, please."

The next voice was that of Jean Wallace. "Ms. Wallace speaking, may I help you?"

"Jean this is James Rahin. I'm returning Ms. Andrews' call."

"One moment, Mr. Rahin, and I'll connect you."

A second later Liz Andrews' voice touched his ears. "Good morning, James, how's your day starting out?"

"I've had better."

"Well, I'm about to brighten it a little. Do you get the *New York Times*?"

"No."

"Well, if you have access to a copy turn to page sixteen. I think you will find the article headlined, 'VERMONT SCHOOL ADMINISTRATOR AND TEACHER EMBEZZLE THIRTY THOUSAND DOLLARS,' very interesting."

"Is it someone I know?" Jim asked.

"Uh-huh"

"Who?"

"Let's just say that it must have been a Halloween prank. The embezzlement was perpetrated at the Cold Hollow Academy by a ghost and a witch."

"You're shitting me?" Jim howled, "Canard and Fitch?"

"That's right! Get the paper. You'll find the story very amusing."

"Okay Liz, thanks for the call. I'll get back to you." Jim hung up the phone and hit the intercom. "Alison would you see if you can find me a copy of today's *New York Times*. Check with the library."

That evening Jim relayed the story to Hope.

"According to the *Times*, Fitch was ordering items for her class. Canard approved the orders and took the money out of petty cash even though the business manager objected. The items were never ordered; the money was pocketed. She and Canard shared the ill-gotten funds. The external auditors notified the board president when no receipts could be produced. Canard and Becky were subsequently arrested. Both have been relieved of their positions pending the outcome of the trial."

"It couldn't happen to two nicer people," Hope said. "I wonder whatever happened to Winifred. She was nice. I don't know how she ever got mixed up with a nut like Canard."

"I don't know. It's hard to figure you women out sometimes. Take Jamie Dunn for instance. Why she would tie herself to a guy like Ian Polovich is beyond me. She was hurt in her first relationship with a man who is a bum, and now she is involved with another man who will break her heart—I just don't understand it."

"Yeah, you can never tell what kind of a guy a woman will go for. Look at us."

Jim grinned, "Point well taken."

Hope picked up some dishes from the table and went to the sink. "Seriously, Jim, what do you think will happen to Canard and Fitch?"

Jim drained the coffee from his cup and said, "I don't know. According to the article, Canard is placing all the blame on Fitch." He laughed. "The bastard said that Fitch had him under her spell. It'll be interesting to see if the Judge will buy that bull."

TWO MONTHS AFTER READING THE ARTICLE about Canard's troubles, Jim was served with a summons. He had been summoned as a witness for Chance Canard. Schofield Milken subpoenaed Jim to testify about Rebecca Fitch's character.

Milken hoped to paint Fitch as an evil person capable of seducing a man to do her bidding.

Jim felt trapped into a no-win situation. He knew that the truth about Rebecca and her stay at North Country would not be helpful to her case. The dilemma was that Jim did not want to assist Chance Canard in anyway.

The trial was scheduled for August. Jim hoped that between the time that the summons was served, and the date of the trial, something would happen that would make his testimony unnecessary.

It was October before the case of Chance Canard went to court.

Schofield Milken was successful in having the trial moved to Burlington. A judge sided with Milken in determining that the jury pool in the small town in and around the greater community of Cold Hollow Academy might be polluted.

Jim enjoyed driving through New York and Vermont in the fall of the year. The hills were always alive with color as leaves sailed from treetops in a rush to blanket mother earth. It was morning and the bright sun beating through the windshield warmed the inside of the car. It forced Jim to lower the windows. Even though the sun was bright, morning air carried a cooling sting.

Jim crossed into Vermont near Ticonderoga and proceeded north to Burlington. He wondered who else would be called upon to bear witness concerning Canard's good character or Rebecca Fitch's claims of witchery.

Chance Canard and Fitch each had their own attorney and had been scheduled for separate trials.

The prosecuting attorney had also asked that Jim be present during Rebecca's trial. Jim assumed that he would be asked about the circumstances under which Ms. Fitch left the North Country Central School District. Jim had already decided that he would only reiterate the statement given in the letter signed by Rebecca when she was asked to resign. He was determined not to assist the case of Canard by telling the true version. Jim's greatest concern was for the testimony of other witnesses. If asked under oath about Rebecca's claims of witchery he would have to answer truthfully.

Rebecca Fitch's trial was set to convene in a few weeks. Jim wondered if he would be asked to testify in that trial too.

CHANCE CANARD SAT WITH A confident smugness as Jim entered the courtroom and slid into a pew toward the back. Schofield Milken tapped Canard on the shoulder and whispered something. Chance looked in Jim's direction and waved. Jim avoided any acknowledgement of Canard's greeting.

Both Milken and Canard were dressed in dark blue suits with a red ties. Matching handkerchiefs protruded from the upper pocket.

The prosecuting attorney was a tall young man with blond bushy hair. He looked less impressive than Milken. The boy attorney wore a well-worn brown suit with an outdated tie and shabby brown shoes that were in need of polish. The young attorney also looked in Jim's direction. After satisfying his curiosity he continued reviewing the papers in front of him.

During the trial, Milken called to the stand former board members who supported Canard while he was at North Country and other individuals who testified to Chance's good character.

When Jim was called, he passed Canard and took his seat in the witness box without looking in the direction of the defense.

After Jim swore an oath to tell the truth, Milken approached with a smile.

"Good morning, Mr. Rahin," Milken gushed as if he were pouring fresh maple syrup onto a batch of hot pancakes before sinking his teeth in. "I want to thank you for taking the time out of your busy schedule to be here today, Mr.Rahin."

He's planning on applying the butter after the syrup, Jim thought.

"I didn't have much of a choice," Jim replied.

"Well, we appreciate your presence." Milken's response was a little less enthusiastic.

"Mr. Rahin, were you the principal of North Country Central School's high school while Ms. Rebecca Fitch was employed as an art teacher?"

"Yes."

"Did her teaching responsibilities meet with your satisfaction?"

"Yes."

Milken took a step back and glared with a mild amount of surprise. "You mean you had no problems with Ms. Fitch as a teacher?"

"That's correct."

Schofield's smile became a scowl. "Are you saying that the board member and others who have testified here today lied under oath?"

"No."

Milken threw his hands in the air for dramatics. "Well, Mr. Rahin, either they are lying, or you are. May I remind you that you took an oath to tell the truth."

"Perhaps counsel needs to rephrase the question," Jim suggested. "None of the previous witnesses could attest to Ms. Fitch's teaching abilities. They all spoke of her character. As a teacher Ms. Fitch was above average in ability and above average in knowledge regarding her subject. You asked me if her teaching met with my satisfaction. The answer to that question is yes."

Milken looked embarrassed as he returned to the defense table and wrote something on a yellow legal pad. When he returned to Jim he said, "Very well, Mr. Rahin, did you have a problem with Ms. Fitch's character?"

"Yes."

"How so?"

"Ms. Fitch chose to date some of our students. The district administration felt that if she chose to date students she should get a job elsewhere. When given that option Ms. Fitch decided to resign."

"Come now Mr. Rahin isn't it true that Ms. Fitch was having sexual relations with underage boys. Isn't that why she was fired?"

"I have no evidence that Ms. Fitch had sex with underage students. As for Ms. Fitch leaving the employment of the North

191

Country School District, the letter of resignation in her official file states that she was leaving to take a job in New York City."

"Mr. Rahin, I don't believe that you are being one hundred percent honest with this court."

"Counsel can get a court order and check Ms. Fitch's file if you like. If you can prove that she had sex with a student, under the age of consent, I'll take action to have her New York State Teacher's Certificate revoked."

Milken was sweating. He wiped his brow with the red handkerchief that he pulled from the upper pocket of his jacket and went back to his table. After a moment he returned to where Jim was seated.

"Mr. Rahin, were you aware that Ms. Fitch considered herself to be a witch?"

"There were rumors that a few illiterates in the community were saying that. She was a witch—yes. Those same individuals probably also believe in ghosts." Jim looked at Canard. Personally I never saw anything that I could attribute to super natural causes."

"Isn't it true that Ms. Fitch placed a burning candle on the school vehicle while you were at a conference with the mark of Satan scrawled on the hood?"

Jim grinned. "Did somebody see her do that? Gee, we tried to find a witness to that act, but the only person that was seen in that vicinity was your client. He was parked near the bus. He was with Ms. Fitch at the time. When I asked him if he had seen someone near the bus, he said no."

Milken slammed his pad onto the defendant's desk and looked at the judge. "Your honor, I have no more questions for this witness."

Before Jim could be dismissed, Belden Powers, the young prosecuting attorney said, "Your honor, I have some questions for this witness."

Milken tried to object, but was overruled.

The young attorney ambled over to the witness box and smiled. "Mr. Rahin, I'm Belden Powers. I'm with the district attorney's office. How ya doing?" Powers had a strong New England accent.

Jim looked up at the man. Geez, this guy's gotta be six-six if he's an inch. "I've been better," he replied.

Belden nodded as if understanding the meaning of Jim's reply. Powers looked at Chance Canard.

"Mr. Rahin, were you the principal at North Country High when the defendant Chance Canard was the superintendent?"

"Yes."

"You were asked by Mr. Canard's attorney to gauge the character of one Rebecca Fitch while she was a teacher in you school. I would like you ta do the same regarding the character of the defendant.

Jim's face lit up and he smiled. "I'm sorry, but Mr. Canard has a formal agreement with my board of education that says no one who works for the North Country Central School District shall say anything negative about Mr. Canard."

The courtroom broke into uncontrollable laughter.

The judge rapped the gavel several times to establish order.

Powers looked at the Judge and said, "I think under the circumstances the court will hold the district hold harmless because you are under oath to tell the truth."

Jim drew a deep breath. "Well, counselor, if Rebecca Fitch is a witch, Chance Canard is a warlock. He did more evil things in his short tenure at North Country than anyone other person before or since the school's reorganization. He left and sued the board because he wanted to do something that he knew or should have known was illegal. He told the board that if they didn't allow him to do what he wanted, he would leave—and he did. The board consequently bought out the remainder of Mr. Canard's contract. He subsequently moved on to Vermont to continue weaving his control over others."

Schofield Milken rose and sputtered, "I object! The witness' remarks are prejudicial and libelous."

"Overruled," the Judge bellowed.

Belden Powers thanked the Judge and started toward his table. Halfway between Jim and the table, Powers turned. "One last thing, Mr. Rahin. In your judgment is Mr. Canard the type of person who could be swayed by a young woman who claimed to be a witch?"

"In my judgment the Chance Canard I knew would have spit in her eye. If anything he prides himself on being a leader. He is not one to be led. His staunch position with the North Country board is a good example of that."

When Jim left the witness box he again smiled at Chance Canard.

Canard sat with a scowl and extended his index finger for all to see.

A WEEK LATER JIM RECEIVED A CALL from Liz Andrews.

"Are you going out to celebrate?" she asked in an exuberant voice.

"Easy, Liz, you're on a telephone not standing a block away. What am I supposed to be celebrating?"

"You need to get civilized. Read the *New York Times*. It's about Canard. He was found guilty. Sentencing is scheduled in two weeks. He will probably do time and lose all of his teaching credentials."

"Are you shitting me? That's great. It was a long time coming, but in the end justice prevailed. Was there any news regarding Rebecca Fitch?"

"The article merely stated that her trial was set for November."

"Thanks, Liz, if you hear anything more let me know."

"Dig into your piggy bank and draw out some money. Order the *Times*. Calling you long distance is expensive." She laughed.

"If I had your money Andrews, I'd burn mine."

After a short banter, Jim hung up the phone and thought, I think I'll get *the New York Times* and post the article in the teachers' room."

Chapter 29

WHEN JIM RETURNED TO HIS OFFICE from a district cooperative administrative meeting he was informed that Yolanda Farintino had sworn out a complaint against Fanny Dykson and the school. Th e complaint charged Dykson with harassment and the school with failing to maintain a safe and orderly environment.

On Jim's desk there was a note asking him to contact Oliver Hatch as soon as possible. Jim smiled and dialed the number for Hatch's direct line.

Oliver Hatch answered with a sullen, "Yeah?"

"Oliver, this is Jim. I just got back from the meeting. What's up?"

"Jesus, Jim, the Farintinos are planning to take Dykson and the school to court. The family will listen to you. Will you try to convince them to drop the charges?"

"The last time I talked to you about the Farintino-Dykson matter you said that you would take care of it. I told you that the family was threatening to contact a lawyer if Fanny continued to harass Melinda. Dykson is a hard head. Maybe a judge can talk some sense into her."

"Jerry Farmer is asking for our help"

"Where was Jerry when all this was going down? He knew that Fanny was out of line. No teacher should be doing what she was doing to a student. I don't care how a teacher feels about a kid. There's simply is no justification for her actions."

195

Oliver Hatch stood and began to pace. "I agree with everything you've said, Jim, but coulda, woulda, shoulda isn't helping. We need to do something—now."

"Ollie, I understand how you feel, but if I were in your shoes I would tell Fanny Dykson to contact the Farintinos and apologize. The Farintinos are good, honest people who just want to live and let live. I believe an earnest, 'I'm sorry,' would go a long way in settling the matter and getting the charges dropped. I intervened once and promised the Farintinos that Dykson would change. I'm not going to do that again unless Fanny is willing to meet with the Farintino family and apologize. If she is willing to do that, then I will be glad to mediate."

"I'm meeting with Fanny and Jerry Farmer after school is out. I'll let you know what she decides. If she refuses to meet with the family, she'll just have to make her case to the Judge."

Jim changed the course of the conversation. "Oh, by the way, Ian Polovich has accepted a job outside of New York City. He starts the second of January. My friend at South Hudson Valley needed a guidance counselor to finish out the year. The gal that was the counselor for seventh and eighth grade took a leave of absence. If he works out, Polovich might get a probationary appointment for the following year. The personnel director doesn't think the woman will return. The counselor wants to be a stay at home mom. It's up to Polovich to prove his worth. If he doesn't change his ways, he will be out on his ass."

"Does Polovich know that you got him the job?"

"No, and I don't want him to know."

"Ian thinks you hate him. Why don't you let me tell him?"

"No!" After hanging up the phone, Jim mumbled, "I didn't do it for him."

IAN POLOVICH WAITED IN THE SCHOOL parking lot. It was two-thirty in the afternoon. Jamie Dunn usually finished work around two-fifteen. She was running late. The Jeep was still running to keep the windows from fogging up. School would be recessing for Thanksgiving at the end of the week and Ian intended to make a last minute attempt to convince Jamie to leave the north country and travel to New York City. He needed to find an apartment. Ian hoped that he would find a small apartment within commuting distance of the South Hudson Valley Middle School. He was hoping that Jamie would be moving with him.

At ten minutes to three Jamie opened the door to the Jeep.

"Please hurry, Ian." I don't want the kids to get home before me." She rubbed her hands together in an attempt to warm them. "Burrrr," she said, as she tried to turn the heat up. "Is that all the heat this truck can give?"

"It's an old truck. I guess I need to replace the heating element. The thermostat is probably stuck shut."

Jamie sat on her hands. "The first thing you should do when you start getting a steady check is to buy yourself a reliable vehicle."

Ian smiled. "I'll let you pick it out. We can car shop at the same time that we are looking for an apartment. We'll have over a week to shop if we leave tomorrow."

A shadow crossed Jamie Dunn's shiny cheeks. She adjusted the red kerchief covering her head.

"Ian, I have told you many times that I'm very fond of you. I enjoy being with you and the way you make me feel when we make love, but I don't love you. I won't leave everything here and run away to New York City like a lovesick school girl. I have responsibilities; children, a home, and a job."

Ian pulled the truck to the side of the road. "But I love you. Don't you understand? This job in New York will allow me to take care of you and the children. In time I know that you will grow to love me—I want to marry you."

"Ian please don't stop, I don't have time to discuss this now. I must get home before the school bus."

The Jeep returned to the snow-blown road. Ian watched silently as telephone poles passed in rhythm like giant candles sticking on a large, white cake.

"My life is empty without you," he groaned.

"Neither one of us is prepared to make a commitment. We are both still married to someone else. Why must we hurry into a situation that might make life worse for both of us—and the children? Besides, you don't even know if the job will become permanent. What happens if after six months you are unemployed again?"

"Without Rahin dogging my every step, I'll do just fine."

The Jeep pulled in front of the Dunn house. Jamie could see the bus about a half mile down the road. She opened the Jeep door and slid out. "Ian, let's talk about this later."

Ian Polovich yelled in frustration, "God damn it woman, I don't have time. I have to leave for New York. I need to find a place to stay."

Jamie's face soured. "I will not be cursed at. If you can lose control so easily now what will you do if there was the pressure of me, a family, and no money?"

Ian softened his tone. "I'm sorry. It won't happen again. Please, Jamie, come with me."

The school bus pulled in back of the Jeep. As the Dunn children filed out, Jamie closed the door of the Jeep, shook her head no and walked into the house.

Ian watched Jamie enter the house. She prefers that shabby little house to me, he thought. The sound of the bus horn startled Ian and he finally drove off.

IAN POLOVICH DROVE TO ALBANY where he stopped at a Howard Johnson Motor Lodge. After checking into a room he placed a phone call to Jamie Dunn. A man answered the phone.

"Hello." Ian did not answer. The man reiterated, "Hello!" Suddenly the phone went dead.

"She's got someone else," Ian mumbled.

He left his room and went to the bar. A bartender approached. She was an attractive, petite woman with gleaming hair the color of onyx. Ian noticed that her hair complemented the ring she wore. The woman was sipping a glass of Cream De Mint. God, he thought her eyes are the color of her drink.

"What'll it be handsome?" the woman asked.

"Vodka. Straight up."

The barmaid moved away, placed her drink on the back bar and poured two shots of vodka into a glass. "Ice?" she asked.

"No, I like it just the way you have it."

When the woman placed the drink in front of Ian she retrieved her Cream De Mint, and returned to where Ian was seated. "Where ya from?" she asked.

"Here and there."

"You're a man of few words." The woman started to walk away.

"Wait, I'm sorry if I was rude. I didn't mean to be. My life is a little messed up right now. It seems that every time I get involved with a woman I get hurt."

"Ahhh, your girl dumped you huh?"

"My wife ran off with another guy and the girl that I then fell in love with doesn't love me. She refused to go to New York with me. I think there's another guy."

The bartender grabbed the bottle of vodka and topped off Ian's drink.

"This one's on the house," she whispered. "What's in New York?"

"A job."

"What kind of work do you do?"

"I'm a guidance counselor. I'm going to South Hudson Valley Central to be the counselor for seventh and eighth graders."

The barmaid started laughing. "Wouldn't ya just know it? I can't seem to get away from you guys."

Ian placed his drink on the bar. "What do you mean?"

The even white teeth of the girl were accentuated by the green of her tongue and gums as she howled. "This is too funny she chuckled. You know how you're luck is with women? Well, that's what my luck is with anyone connected to a school."

"Were you in love with a teacher?"

"Love? I haven't been in love with anyone since my older brother took me to his bed. No, love had nothing to do with it. Hate maybe, but not love," she shook her head. "No! In my first teaching job the community drove me out. My second job, my principal lied to me and threatened to have me arrested if I didn't resign. My last job was terminated when I was arrested and charged with theft. The judge gave me five years of probation and suspended my license to teach. All because of an educator. I will never teach again or even enter a school building."

"Holy shit, it sounds like you had a principal like mine. I had this guy that wanted my ass out and did whatever he could to nail me." Ian motioned for another drink. "Yeah, what your principal did sounds like something Rahin would do."

The bar maid's face blanched. "Did you say Rahin?"

Ian took a swig of his vodka. "Yeah, James Rahin, ever heard of him?"

"Did you work at North Country High School in upstate New York?"

Ian looked at the barmaid with a new curiosity. "How did you know?"

"Rahin is the son of a bitch that lied to me and got me to resign. The guy that got me arrested used to be the superintendent at North Country. Rahin got him fired too. I ended up going to work for that guy in Vermont. His name was Canard. The bastard had me sign papers for things and then he sold them and pocketed the money. He's doing time and I—" she paused. "Well, that's why I'm working here." The barmaid poured Ian another shot and asked, "What's your name?"

"Ian, Ian Polovich."

"What room are you in, Ian?"

"I'm around the back of the motel in room 116."

"You're an interesting guy, Ian. When my shift ends at two, I'll drop by—if you're still up." She winked at him. "If you're not I'm sure I can get you up." She started laughing. "We can talk some more. It sounds like we have a lot in common."

Ian downed the remaining vodka and started to leave. At the door he turned to the bar and called, "Hey, I don't even know your name."

The barmaid paused from cleaning some glasses, smiled and said, "Rebecca, Rebecca Fitch. My friends call me Becky."

Chapter 30

HENRY DUNN SAT AT THE KITCHEN table drinking coffee. His wife stood next to the stove.

"You have no right to come and go in this house as you wish," Jamie snapped. "You stay away for months at a time and then you just show up and want to play husband and father. It's over, Henry. I don't think of you any more as my husband." She turned to him. "You have been with other women and I have slept with another man. The marriage is over."

"I know all about that fuckin' Russian," Henry hissed. "Jesus, if you needed someone to fuck, why didn't you go out and find a real man.?"

"Ian Polovick may not be what you call, 'a real man,' but he treated me with respect and cares about the children. You only think of your needs. You don't care about anyone else. You don't care about me or your children. You only think with your zipper." Leaning forward Jamie spit in Henry's face. "You're a pig!"

Henry Dunn leaped from his chair and punched his wife in the face. Jamie fell against the stove and slumped to the floor.

The children started crying, "Please, Daddy, don't hit Mommy, please."

Dunn pulled the belt from his pants and folded it in two. "You little bastards. Don't tell me what to do." He raised the belt above his head and tried to strike his oldest son. The belt wouldn't follow through.

Jamie had grabbed the belt and was screaming. "Children run outside. Go next door."

With fear painted on their faces the boys did as their mother instructed.

The following morning Ed Carter, the head custodian, came to Jim's office. He was not his jovial self.

"Jim, have you seen Jamie Dunn this morning?"

"No. Why?"

"You should. She looks like hell." Carter moved closer to Jim's desk. "She looks like Polovich beat the hell out of her."

Jim left his chair and faced the custodian. "Did Jamie tell you that?"

Ed shook his head. "No, she won't say anything. She says that she doesn't want to talk about it."

Without further comment, Jim pushed past Carter and headed for the laundry room. When he entered the hot, smelly room there were towels stacked on the counter and clothing going round and round in the huge dryer. Jamie was folding uniforms at the far end of the room.

"Jamie," Jim called.

Jamie didn't respond.

Jim went to her and spun her around so that they were face to face. Jim was shocked. Jamie's eyes were red slits surrounded by blue circles. There were large bruises on her cheeks and forehead and her face was sanguine. "In the name of Jesus, did Polovich do this?"

Jamie pulled away. "Please, Mr. Rahin," she mumbled through swollen lips. "I don't want to talk about it."

Anger rose in Jim and he shouted, "That son of a bitch. I'll have him discharged and arrested."

Jamie started crying. "Please, it wasn't Ian."

"Don't try to protect him. I know he was waiting for you yesterday when he should have been on his way to New York."

Jamie sobbed, "It wasn't him."

"I don't believe you." Jim walked into the hall. "If Ian didn't do this, than who did? If you won't tell me someone else will."

Back in his office Jim called Alison. "Alison, please get the oldest Dunn boy for me, ahhh—what's his name?"

"Claude," Alison replied.

"Jim slapped his forehead. "Yeah, that's it, Claude."

Claude Dunn favored his mother in his character and appearance. He was small for his age and timid. When he spoke it was like listening to a young girl. Although he was in the ninth grade, Claude's voice had not yet matured.

When Alison ushered Claude into Jim's office it was apparent that the boy didn't want to be there. His head was held low and his eyes fixed on the floor. Although he looked like Jamie, the boy had not developed her proud posture. His clothing was old and worn, but clean.

"Claude," said Jim, "Were you at home when Mr. Polovich was with your mother?"

Claude did not answer.

Jim bent at the waist and said, "Claude, you don't have to be afraid. No one is going to hurt you or your mother again, but I need to know if you saw Mr. Polovich hit your mother."

Claude stiffened and peered into Jim's eyes. "Mr. Polovich would never hurt mom."

"Well if it wasn't Mr. Polovich who was it?"

Claude started to cry. "It was my father," he sobbed. "He beat mom because she wouldn't let him hit us."

Anger again welled in Jim's breast. "Your father came home last night?"

The boy nodded.

Jim stood straight. "Is he still there?"

Again Claude nodded while he continued to stare at the floor and sobbed.

Jim tried to remain calm.

"Alison, would you please see that Claude has a pass back to his classroom."

"Kathleen, this is Jim Rahin at North Country High School. Is Sam Bookmore there?"

"One moment, Mr. Rahin."

A few moments later Sam Bookmore responded. "Yeah, Jim, what can I do for you?"

"Sam, can you run up to the school? I have a case of battery I think you should take a look at."

Sheriff Bookmore took a deep breath. "Jim you know the judge doesn't like prosecuting kids who fight. It's usually a case equal guilt. His calendar is overloaded as it is. He just doesn't have the time to play bad-guy with kids."

"Sam this has to do with battery on a staff member. It's a domestic case."

"Shit, Jim you know how that is. When it's all said and done spouses are reluctant to prosecute."

Jim started to get hot under the collar. "Sam, you owe me one."

There was a long pause. "I don't owe you anything, Rahin. If anything, you owe me."

A more conciliatory Jim replied, "Please, Sam, I need your help."

"Aw shit. Okay Jim, but if this turns out to be a waste of my time, you and me are kaput."

When Sam Bookmore saw Jamie he was shocked. "Who did this to you?" he growled. "He needs to be locked up."

"No, please," Jamie managed as if she were sucking on a lemon.

Jim could tell that she was in pain. "You should have stayed home today."

Jamie sat on an oak chair located near the washing machine and began to weep. "I couldn't stay home—I just couldn't."

"Will you swear out a complaint?" Sam asked.

Jamie shook her head.

"Mrs. Dunn, Mr. Rahin has told me that your husband came home last night and beat you when you wouldn't let him hit the children. Is that correct?"

Jamie looked with astonishment at Jim. "Please leave me alone. Please! You'll only make things worse." She was sobbing.

"We will protect you. I'm going to get a court order barring Henry from coming near you or the kids," Bookmore said. "Tonight you and your children will sleep in your own beds without the fear of being harmed."

Bookmore motioned to Jim. The two men left the laundry and quick-stepped their way to Jim's office.

"Are you going to arrest Dunn?" Jim asked.

"I don't think I can do that without Jamie filing an official complaint. I am going to get the judge to give her an order of protection. That will at least get him out of the house. If he refuses to go—then I will arrest him."

By two o'clock that afternoon Jim and the sheriff knocked on the door of the Dunn home. An intoxicated Henry Dunn opened the door. He was holding a can of beer. He glared at Jim and slurred, "What the fuck do you want, Rahin?"

Jim didn't answer. He clinched his fist, hoping Henry Dunn would attempt to punch him.

"I have a court order here, Dunn, it states that you are to leave this house immediately and not return," the sheriff announced.

Henry's small frame straightened from its hunched position and he spit. "This is my house, Mr. You ain't got no right to order me out. If that bitch doesn't like it let her get out. Let her go with that whoremaster boyfriend of hers."

Sam Bookmore waved the order of protection. "If you refuse to leave you will be arrested."

Henry Dunn attempted to slam the door, but Sam's foot kept it open. He reached in and took Dunn by the shoulder. Mister, you're going to jail."

After forcing Henry back into the room he asked Jim to get Henry's coat. Jim was glad to comply."

Jim was waiting when Jamie arrived home. She walked past Jim as if he weren't there and went to the kitchen. Jim followed.

Jamie was silent as she placed a piece of wood into a pot-bellied stove. When she had finished she took off her coat, hung it in a closet and faced Jim.

"Mr. Rahin, You have been very good to me. I know you mean well, but you have no business involving yourself in my family's business. You had no right to drag Claude into the argument between me and his father."

Jim felt a twinge of embarrassment. "I have every right if I feel that there is child abuse taking place in a home."

Jamie filed a pan with some water and placed it onto a cast-iron wood-burning cooking stove. "I'm going to resign from my job and move to New York," she announced. "I need to get away from here and allow my boys a chance at a new life. Ian Polovich isn't what most women dream of, but he loves me and will provide a stable home for my children."

"I understand how you feel Jamie, but don't pull the kids out now. Let them finish out the year. In June things might look different. Henry is not allowed to come near you or the kids. If he does, Bookmore will lock him up. Furthermore, you and Ian Polovich might think differently about your feelings for one another. Maybe he will meet someone else. Maybe you will meet someone else. Hell, you don't even know if Ian will have a job after June."

Jamie went to the door and opened it. "I will think about it," she said. "Now will you please leave before the school bus gets here? I don't want you here when the kids arrive."

Jim returned to his office and called the sheriff. When Bookmore answered, Jim said, "Sam, would you make a point of checking on Mrs. Dunn from time to time? I know she's being foolish by not prosecuting her husband, but she needs protection. It's that proud Irish head of hers that's the problem."

"You're right. I spent an hour with her after I took Henry to jail. She's afraid that if she has Henry arrested the kids will hate her. I told her that if Henry shows up she is to leave the house and call the office. I gave her the name of J.A Heintz over in Boonville. He's a damn good attorney. She's going to file for a divorce. I'll make a point of dropping in on her whenever I'm in the area just to make sure that everything is all right. Ya know Jim she's a fine woman. She shouldn't have to put up with that ass."

While Sam was talking, Jim thumbed through the phone book until he found the phone number of Joe Heintz. He quickly wrote the number onto a small pad. "She is a good woman Sam. A woman like Jamie might make a confirmed bachelor think twice about spending his twilight years alone."

There was a long pause before Sam Bookmore answered. "Don't start playing cupid, Rahin, you're too fat to fly."

The following morning Jim dialed the number for the attorney.

"Joseph Heintz, attorney at law," a silky woman's voice announced.

"Yes, this is James Rahin. I'm the principal at North Country High. I'd like to speak with Mr. Heintz."

"One moment, Mr. Rahin, I'll see if he's available."

Jim waited. After a minute or so a man chimed in. "Joe Heintz."

Jim struggled for the words he wanted to say. "Uhh, Mr. Heintz, I'm calling about an employee of mine—Mrs. Jamie Dunn. Sheriff Bookmore told me that he spoken with you about handling divorce proceedings for Mrs. Dunn."

"I did speak with Mr. Bookmore, but the substance of our conversation is privileged information. I cannot discuss what he and I talked about."

Jim became frustrated. "Look, I'm only interested in helping Mrs. Dunn. I don't give a damn what you and Sam talked about. Jamie Dunn doesn't have a great deal of money. If she cannot pay for your services, I am willing to help."

Joe Heintz chuckled. "Don't get upset Mr. Rahin. I hear you and I want you to know that I will represent Mrs. Dunn for a modest fee. Between your offer and that of Officer Bookmore, I'm sure Mrs. Dunn will not be financially challenged by my services."

Jim was stunned. "Are you telling me that Sam Brookmore offered to pay Mrs. Dunn's expenses?"

"Mr. Rahin, You'll have to ask Officer Bookmore if you want an answer to that question."

A pensive James Rahin mumbled, "Thank you for your time." Jim shook his head in disbelief and smiled. Why that sly old dog, he thought. Don't try to play cupid—huh. He grabbed the phone and called the jail. "Sam Bookmore," he snapped.

Sam answered in his normal professional manner. "Deputy Bookmore."

"Sam, I want you to be the first to know," Jim bellowed.

"Know what?"

"Jamie Dunn is leaving the area. She's going off to marry Ian Polovich."

There was a long break in the conversation. After several moments Bookmore spoke again. "James Rahin if this is some kind of joke I'll…"

"If you hurry you might be able to get your deposit back from the lawyer."

"You son of a bitch, Rahin, how did you know I paid for Mrs. Dunn's retainer?"

Jim was laughing. "Because I was going to do the same thing, until I heard you had already talked with Heintz."

"Were you just joking about her running off with Polovich?"

Jim became more serious. "Yeah, I was just kidding, but if you don't get off your high horse and let that woman know that you are interested, someone else may sweep her away."

There was a resounding 'click' on the line.

"Hello, Sam!"

The line was dead.

Chapter 31

HENRY DUNN COLLECTED THE ITEMS THAT had been taken from him when he was placed in lock-up. He shook the large manila envelope to make sure he wasn't leaving anything behind.

"You got it all," Officer Rubin barked. "Make sure you stop at the front desk before leaving. Sergeant Bookmore wants to see you."

Dunn mumbled something incoherent and walked to the front of the jail. Sam Bookmore was seated at a large desk just to the right of the booking station.

"Officer Rubin said you wanted to see me."

Bookmore looked up from his paperwork and spoke in a deep guttural voice. "That restraining order is still in effect, Dunn. You are to stay away from your wife and kids until the hearing. If the judge grants you visitation time we'll make arrangements to have Jamie leave the house while you are there. If you ignore the order of protection you'll be arrested and locked up again."

Sam rose to his full height. "If I hear that you have laid a finger on your wife or the kids you are going to have a bad accident. Then I'm going to arrest your ass and throw away the key. Do I make myself clear?" Henry Dunn stood mute.

Sam took two steps toward Dunn and yelled at the top of his voice, "Do I make myself clear?"

Henry stepped back away from the officer. "Where am I supposed to live? I lost my job because I spent thirty days in this hell-hole and now I don't even have a place to live. It ain't right. Where am I supposed to go?"

Sam pointed a finger in Henry's face. "You should have thought about that before you beat up your wife. Now get out of here before I kick you out."

"I'm going, but you ain't heard the last of me. I'm gonna get a lawyer."

MELBA WALKED TOWARD the barn holding her daughter, Cybil. Melba had been living with Maxwell Meica for more than a year. There had been an ice storm that evening and the ground was still slick from a thin coating of the frozen rain. Choosing her steps carefully, Melba maneuvered her way to the barn door. She slid the bolt from its housing and stepped inside. A young calf rose from a bed of straw and moved to greet her. Cybil giggled with glee at the sight of the animal.

"Does mommy's little girl want to play with the cow?" Melba cooed. She placed Cybil onto the barn floor and held her steady. The calf sniffed the baby then turned to Melba.

"Yeah, I know," Melba said. "You want to be fed. Melba took the top off of a large barrel and poured a scoop of grain into a shallow pail. The calf lost interest in the humans as its tongue attacked the pan of corn.

"Would you have something for an old friend to eat?" a shadowy figure wrapped in a horse blanket said in a hushed whisper.

Melba jumped with fear. She grabbed Cybil and backed her way toward the door.

The shadow moved into the light. "Don't be afraid, honey, I would never hurt you. Is that our daughter?"

"Henry!" What are you doing here?"

Henry Dunn moved with feet of lead toward his one-time lover. "I don't know who else to turn to," he said. "I slept here last night. Will you help me?"

Melba studied her intruder then quickly closed the door. "Henry, you look like hell. What has happened to you? I thought you were working and living in Watertown."

"I was until I was arrested. I just got out of jail. Jamie had me arrested. She has a court order barring me from coming to the house. I don't know what to do."

"You can't stay here. Max is in the house. If he finds you here there's no telling what he might do."

"Hasn't he married you yet?"

"No, but we've talked about it. There just never seems to be enough time."

"Does he know that I'm the father of the little girl?"

"Cybil—her name is Cybil."

Henry threw the horse blanket away. "Does Max know that I'm Cybil's father?"

Melba's answer came with hesitation and concern. "I—I don't know. I think he thinks that Cybil is his. She carries his last name."

Henry smiled and rubbed his hand across the fender of the new tractor that was parked in a nearby stall. "You've done pretty well for yourself, girl. You've moved up in the world. Meica must be worth a few bucks."

Melba hugged Cybil closer to her. "What do you want, Henry?"

"I need money."

"I don't have any money."

Dunn leered at Melba with a contorted, ghoulish grin. "No, but Meica does. You can get it from him."

"Max isn't going to give you money."

"I think he will." Henry placed his hand on Cybil's arm. "It would be rather embarrassing if word got out that the baby wasn't his."

Melba drew back and slapped him as hard as she could. "Don't you ever lay your hands on my baby again!"

The blow stung causing Henry to step away from his assailant. Anger welded inside his body and he scanned the barn for a stick. He grasped a discarded, broken ax handle and held it above his head. "You bitch, apparently Meica hasn't taught you respect. I guess I will have to."

Melba turned her back away from the impending blow in order to protect Cybil. Just as Henry was ready to strike, the barn door opened. Henry turned toward the light. It was Max Meica.

211

"What the hell is going on in here? Melba what is Dunn doing here?"

Melba rushed to Max's side. "He wants money. He said that if I didn't give him some money he would tell everyone that Cybil is not your daughter."

Max charged Dunn and grabbed him around the neck. "You little weasel. Try to blackmail me and my wife, are you? I'll wring your scrawny little neck."

Max gave a hard shove, causing Henry to fall awkwardly into a fresh pile of manure.

"She's not your wife. Melba got pregnant when we were seeing each other. That baby is my daughter."

Max was boiling and approached Henry menacingly. Melba blocked his path. "Please Max, don't hurt him, I don't want you to get arrested."

Max Meica stopped. "Get out," he growled at Dunn. If I ever catch you on my property again, I'll kill you."

Henry gathered himself together and slinked past Max into the morning air. "She's my flesh and blood Meica, not yours."

"You're wrong," Melba screamed. "I had a miscarriage before I came to live with Max. Ask my mother. Cybil is a Meica."

Henry Dunn backed away from the barn. "I'll have you arrested for assault and battery, Meica. We'll see how you like being kept in a cage." Henry Dunn ran for the road, looking back to make sure that Max was not following.

Max took Melba's hand and smiled. "I was angry enough to kill that man," he acknowledged. Not because he said that Cybil was his, but because he was fixin' to hurt you."

"Henry Dunn isn't worth your spit," said Melba. "I didn't want to risk losing you because of him."

Max wrapped his muscular arms around Melba and the baby. "Tomorrow we are going out and find a preacher. One thing Dunn said that is true, we aren't married. We're going to take care of that tomorrow." Max stepped away from Melba. "Speaking about truth, Honey, you are a terrible liar. Nevertheless, one thing is true; Cybil is my daughter.

IN JUNE FOLLOWING GRADUATION, Jim started applying to other schools. He was determined to find a job as a superintendent. He was especially optimistic about a position in a school district east of Utica. It was a school district that was predominantly comprised of Italian families. He felt that he could be happier working there.

On his desk he found a note: Call Ms. Andrews. He placed his portfolio down and dialed the number for Liz Andrews's office; it seemed to take forever for Ms. Wallace to answer.

When Jim heard her voice, he said, "Jean, this is Jim Rahin. I'm returning Ms. Andrews's call."

Liz was her upbeat self, "Hello James. How are things going in your neck of the woods?"

Jim smiled. "You're exceptionally chipper this morning. Did your boxer friend keep you in the clinches last night?"

Andrews chuckled. "My love life is none of your business Rahin. I don't know if the news I have for you is good news, but it certainly will spike your interest."

Jim attempted to rein-in his curiosity, but failed. "Okay, what is this news that will illuminate my senses?"

"Guess who sent me an invitation to his wedding?"

"Who?"

"Ian Polovich! He and Ms. Rebecca Fitch are going to tie the knot."

Jim winced and fell silent.

"Jim, are you still there?"

"Barely, girl, just barely. How the hell did those two find each other?"

"I don't know, but I guess they have been living together since January. I thought you might get a kick out of that news."

"Polovich must be a tiger in bed. I can't imagine Fitch being satisfied with just one man. Why didn't you tell me about them sooner?"

"I didn't know. He never brought her around. They have an apartment in the city."

"I wonder if Jamie Dunn knows about this," Jim mumbled."

"What was that?" Liz said. "I didn't hear you."

Jim jotted a note on his desk blotter to remind him to see Jamie. "Oh, nothing, Liz, I was just talking to myself."

Liz decided to change the course of the conversation. "Jim, I don't think the school is going to extend Mr. Polovich's employment. The board hasn't acted on the superintendent's recommendation yet, but I'm sure they will at the next board meeting. As you predicted, Polovich spent too much time counseling a few students and never followed through with the paperwork. When someone tried to talk to him about his shortcomings he got very defensive and said that he wasn't hired to be a paper pusher."

"That's too bad. He and Fitch—Mrs. Polovich—will probably move south. Becky always said that she preferred living in the South."

"How about you, Jim, are you planning to move?"

"Not yet, but I do have a promising prospect."

Jim sensed a change in Liz's voice, as if she had an inclination that he would soon leave the North Country School District. "I hope you are planning to take a job closer to the city."

Jim laughed. "Liz, you know that Hope would be miffed if I even thought about moving down-state. She would never be happy living that far away from her family."

"Well, are you going to tell me about this exquisite opportunity or not?"

Jim lowered his voice as if fearful that others were listening. "I interviewed at Frankfort. I love the community and it's only a few miles from Utica."

Liz tried to be positive. "Well, Jim, if I can be of any help, let me know. But I think it's awful that you have to sacrifice your vocational future because of marriage. I could help find you a good job as a superintendent down here making a hell of a lot more money than you are going to get up there."

"It isn't only because of my marriage," Jim said. "I like living in the country where I can hunt and fish. Besides, downstate may pay more, but it also costs a lot more to live there."

"Okay, Jim, have it your way. In any case, good luck. Let me know if you decide to take the job."

When Jim finished the call he drove to the Dunn residence. He hadn't spoken to Jamie since she chewed him out for getting involved in her life. Whenever Jim chanced to see her an aloof and antiseptic greeting was all that transpired between them. Now he felt that he needed to tell her about Polovich. When he arrived at the Dunn home, there was a sheriff's car parked in the driveway. Oh shit, he thought, something must have happened. The Dunn children were laughing and throwing a baseball in the yard. They waved as Jim stepped out of the car; he waved back and went to the front door.

Sam Bookmore answered Jim's knock. "Good morning, Jim. You must have heard the news."

Jim was puzzled. How the hell did Bookmore hear about Polovich?

"Yeah," Jim replied. "I just got the news about twenty minutes ago."

"Well come on in," Sam bellowed. He turned and yelled, "Jamie, Jim Rahin is here."

Jamie left the kitchen and went to greet him. She was dressed in her best attire. Her hair was longer than he remembered, but her eyes shined. She was happy. Jamie's Irish laughter echoed through the room as she hastened to Jim's side and threw her arms around him. "Oh, Jim, I owe so much of my happiness to you. Thank you for getting involved in my life."

Jim stood confused. The last time he was at the house Jamie had berated him. Now she was thanking him. Was the change in attitude due to Ian Polovich getting married? The situation was very confusing.

"I didn't know how you would take the news," Jim replied. "I'm glad to see you are happy."

"Why shouldn't she be happy?" Sam shouted. "Now we can get married."

"You and Sam are getting married?"

"Yes, now that the divorce is final, Sam and I are going to get married and we'd like you to be the best man."

"Your divorce finally came through?"

Jamie took on a puzzled expression. "Yes, I thought you knew."

"Isn't that why you're here?" Sam asked.

Jim showed his embarrassment. Sheepishly he said, "No, I didn't know about the divorce." He looked at Sam. "I didn't even know about you two."

Jamie's elation mellowed. "Then why did you come, Jim?"

It was the second time Jamie had ever called him by his first name; he had always been, "Mr. Rahin."

"I received word today that Ian Polovich is getting married."

Jamie's smile returned. "I'm happy for him. If you see him, tell him that I wish him a long and happy life."

Sam Bookmore put his arms around Jamie. "I too wish him well, Jim. Do you know the girl?"

"Yeah, so do you."

"Is she from around here?"

Jim grinned. "She used to be from around here."

"What's her name?"

"Rebecca—Rebecca Fitch."

Sam Bookmore broke into uncontrollable laughter. "Not Becky Fitch the witch?" How in the hell did she find him?"

Jim too was laughing. "That, my friend, is the mystery. I don't know and I don't care."

"I heard about this Rebecca," said Jamie. "I don't care about her past. If she loves him and he her, I don't care what went on before they met. I wish them both the best of luck. Ian is a lonely man. He needs someone to love, and someone who will care about him."

Jim looked into Jamie's eyes. They were wet with emotion. "I know what you are saying, Jamie and you're right. The past shouldn't matter as long as they love each other. I wish them both well."

Chapter 32

BACK AT HIS OFFICE JIM FOUND A NOTE taped to his phone: CALL MR. HATCH. Jim dialed the number for the district office—Cleary answered.

"Lora, this is Jim Rahin. Is Mr. Hatch in?"

There was a long pause. "Yes, Mr. Rahin. The Farintinos and their attorney are with him. He would like you to join them."

"I'll be right down."

Jim went to a file cabinet and withdrew a folder.

The drumbeat of Jim's steps echoed through the hall as he hastened toward Oliver Hatch's office. When he arrived he was surprise to find Fanny Dykson seated across from Lora Cleary's desk. The overfed gym teacher grimaced as Jim passed her on his way to the superintendent's inner office. A myriad of thoughts shot through his mind—all pertained to the past year and the information that had been collected by Melinda.

Whenever the senior was approached by Dykson a small recording device, located on Melinda's person, was activated. The guile used to entrap Fanny in her game of harassment would not sit well with Oliver or the board if they knew that Jim was involved in the plot.

"Ah, Mr. Rahin," Oliver greeted as Jim entered the private office. "We have been waiting for you. You know Mr. and Mrs. Farintino, of course ,and this is Mr. Grayson. Mr. Grayson has been retained by the Farintinos. He has a law office in Albany."

"How do you do, Folks, I'm sorry if I'm late." Jim shook hands with the visitors. He looked at Mrs. Farintino. "I wasn't aware of the meeting."

Oliver looked flushed as he motioned for Jim to sit. An extra chair had been brought into the office for that purpose.

Hatch held up a small cassette. "Jim, Melinda has been taping conversations of Ms. Dykson. Were you aware that Ms. Dykson has been harassing Melinda over the past two years?"

"Three years," Jim corrected.

Oliver Hatch was nervous. Wet stains showed in the arm pits of his white shirt.

"What efforts were made to resolve this breach of school policy?" It was obvious that Oliver Hatch was attempting to divest himself of any knowledge pertaining to the matter at hand.

Jim waved the folder that he had brought with him. "Mr. Hatch, I have brought a complete dossier on the matter dating back to Melinda's sophomore year. It will show that many attempts were made to dissuade Ms. Dykson from her unethical behavior. Intervention was attempted by numerous staff members, including me. When all measures to alter Ms. Dykson's behavior failed I wrote a letter of reprimand. It was signed by Ms. Dykson and placed in her permanent file." Jim placed the folder onto the top of Hatch's desk. He looked into Oliver's frightened eyes. "I'm sure if you check her folder you'll find it."

Oliver Hatch pushed Jim's folder out of the reach of Grayson. "Well the hurtful words have been said. We can't un-ring a bell. What we can do is take action to ensure that the bell doesn't ring again."

Hatch rose from his desk and began to pace.

Grayson interrupted Oliver's thoughts. "Mr. Hatch, we are aware of the eff orts made to curtail the insults heaped upon my client and her family. Many attempts have been made to mute her sounds of bigotry. Yet, the bell you speak of continues to ring its vile message. You assure us that you will see to it that the bell does not ring again. How?"

Oliver turned away from the windows. "What will it take to appease your clients?"

"I want that woman fired," Yolanda Farintino screamed.

218

"What kind of an example does this teacher set for the children?" Salvatore Farintino asked. "She should not be allowed to influence the thoughts of others because of her disdain for my family. My daughter has done nothing to this woman, yet she dogs her days with venomous and hateful remarks."

"If the Farintinos are not satisfied with the action taken by the school we will proceed to a legal course of action," Grayson boomed. "Ms. Dykson's harassment of Ms. Farintino is unconscionable. The Farintinos will name Ms. Dykson and the school in the suit. It is abundantly clear that many other adults, students, and staff persistently brought this abomination to the attention of the administration on numerous occasions. I will be asking the court for an order to gain copies of all such documents. This school has been errant in its responsibilities by allowing the degrading of a child to continue with impunity."

Oliver straightened his posture and paced the room with the cassette in his hand.

"I cannot refute the fact that Melinda has been subjected to a horrendous miscarriage of justice," he said. "Ms. Dykson's behavior is wrong. The evidence on this tape is irrefutable. Her unethical behavior has violated her professional ethics and the duty owed to every student who attends North Country Central School." Oliver returned to his desk and sat.

"Melinda, Mr. and Mrs. Farintino, I don't blame you for the course of action you have chosen." Beads of sweat were visible on Oliver's brow. "I offer you my deepest apology for any lack of urgency I may have failed to assign to Melinda's plight. I was obviously remiss in my duty. I should have ensured that North Country High had an ongoing program that protected a safe and orderly environment for all students."

Robert Grayson cleared his throat and spoke in a hushed tone. "That's all well and good, Mr. Hatch, but we still want to know what action will be taken against Ms. Dykson."

Oliver shook his head. It was tedious for him to speak. "I can't give you an answer to that question at this moment. I will need time to confer with my board of education and apprise them of this matter in its entirety."

Hatch again left his seat and began to pace. "Ms. Dykson is a tenured member of this staff. As such, under the tenure law, she is entitled to a hearing and representation to answer all charges." The superintendent looked at Grayson. "You understand what I am saying don't you counselor?"

Robert Grayson nodded and then whispered something into Mrs. Farintino's ear.

Both Mr. and Mrs. Farintino huddled in conference while Oliver Hatch waited.

Grayson stood and asked, "How much time will it take for you and the board to make a decision?"

Oliver looked at Jim. "I'm not sure. What do you think, Mr. Rahin?"

Jim had anticipated the reaction of the Farintinos. He had already formulated a timetable in his head while Hatch and Grayson were talking.

"Well, by law you must allow at least forty-eight hours for the board to set a day for the meeting and notify the public. Even when the board intends to call for an executive meeting a notice must be posted. Once a course of action is formulated, Ms. Dykson is entitled to notification and allowed ten working days to reply." Jim shook his head. "It's an arduous process. If the board elects to file a 3020 on her, I'm sure that the teachers' association will support her with legal counsel and the board will be required to pay her full salary while she is suspended. The road to a state hearing is long and costly. The tenure law, with all of its deformities, was enacted to guard teachers against the arbitrary actions of certain boards of education. Unfortunately, at times it has become a protective shield for the incompetent."

"It sounds like it will be a long time before we have an answer," said Salvatore Farintino.

"I'm afraid so," Oliver replied.

Sal looked at his wife and then turned to his attorney. "What shall we do?" he asked.

Grayson stood and started filling his briefcase with documents that he had brought with him. "Mr. Hatch, you do what you must regarding Ms. Dykson. You know the feelings of my clients. In the meantime, I am going to start the suit proceedings." The attorney gave a sheepish grin. "Like the world of education, the wheels of justice move at a snail's pace. If the district is able to exact retribution that is satisfactory to the Farintinos, I will cancel any court date that may be assigned." Grayson showed a broad grin. "Gentlemen, as they say, the ball is in your court."

WHEN THE ROOM WAS EMPTY, with the exception of Jim, Oliver asked, "Did you know about the tape?"

Jim looked directly at his boss. "Yes, I knew."

Oliver looked like a frightened deer in the headlights of an oncoming car. "Jesus, man, you are complicit in helping those people to sue the district." He slammed his hand hard against the desk. The noise unhinged Lora Cleary and she rushed into the room. She held her finger to her lips. "Ms. Dykson is still out there," she whispered."

Jim waved Lora off; she retired to the outer office.

Jim lowered his voice. "Ollie, I warned you. I even put it in writing so there would be a record should there be another incident." Jim rose and went to the front of the desk. "You tore up that reprimand with a promise that you and Jerry Farmer would keep Dykson in line. You failed—as I knew you would. I kept my copy. Bruce and Flanaghan will attest to the time and purpose of its origin. I'm sorry, Oliver, but I felt that I needed to cover my ass."

"And in doing so, you left mine swinging in the wind."

Jim returned to his seat. "Well, time is burning. The one good thing is that school is out. You have two months to settle the matter. Come September, if the case is ongoing, the district will have to pay Fanny her salary and hire a long-term sub to fill her position. It will become costly."

"I'm going to start right now. I'm going to meet with Dykson, alone, if she'll agree to it."

Jim rose and went to the hall door. "I'm going out this way. I'll be in my office. Let me know how you make out."

Fanny Dykson entered Oliver Hatch's office wearing an indignant sneer. She swaggered to the chair opposite Oliver's desk and dropped. Her heft forced the chair against the office wall.

"Well, what did the wops and their lawyer want? My blood?" Fanny asked.

Oliver stared at his guest in disgust. "You know Ms. Dykson it's that kind of attitude and language that has this district on the verge of an expensive lawsuit and ridicule."

Fanny sat upright. Her face was a blank sheet of paper. "What do you mean?" she stammered. Oliver Hatch had never addressed her in that tone of voice before. He had never chastised her for anything. When it came to complaints, from or about the Farintinos, he had always referred to them as "those whiners."

Endeavoring to hold his anger in check, Oliver, with his face on fire, enunciated in slow deliberate verbiage, "I mean that the Farintinos are filing court papers in a lawsuit naming you and the district as conspirators in actions to deprive Melinda Farintino of her civil rights. You are being sued for continued harassment, and the school district is being sued for knowingly allowing the behavior to continue—with impunity."

Fanny's response came low and hesitantly. "What proof do they have? I was always careful not to have others around."

Oliver left his desk and went to where Dykson was seated. He was on the verge of a full-blown eruption. He began slowly, but finished in a thunderous explosion. "Your contempt for others often clouds your assessment of their intelligence." Oliver clinched his fist as if wanting to lash out at the woman seated before him. Then the explosion happened. "The girl was wearing a wire. She has every insult you ever uttered to her–on tape."

A nervous grin graced Fanny's lips. "That's entrapment isn't it? I mean tapes aren't admissible in court. Are they?"

"I'm not a damn lawyer. How the hell should I know?" Hatch started pacing the floor. Turning to the teacher he said, "One thing I do know, is that there are a hell of a lot of people who are willing to testify in support of the Farintinos tape or no tape."

Fanny's grin was replaced with concern. "But they don't have anything in writing. I mean whatever Rahin wrote is gone. Right?"

Oliver went to her side. "Yes, Fanny, I did destroy the letter of reprimand, but Rahin retained a copy along with other letters of concern by staff and community members, including Flanagan and Bruce." Hatch returned to his desk. "Hell, there are probably board members who will have to give witness about the calls that they received."

"Will this go to a judge?"

"Haven't you been listening? I told you that the family has hired an attorney. He is filing for a court date to present the Farintinos' suit."

A visibly shaken gym teacher wrung her hands and slumped into the huge leather chair. Her voice was weak when she asked, "What can I do?"

Oliver looked away. He did not want to look her in the eyes when he responded. "You do have a few options, none of them are good."

Dykson sat upright in the chair and exclaimed, "What do you mean?"

Oliver continued to stare out of the office window that was located behind his chair. Off in the distance he could see the local farmer planting. Corn, he thought. There had always been fall corn in that field for as long as he could remember.

Finally he turned to face his recalcitrant colleague.

"Ms. Dykson, we reap what we sow. You just couldn't leave that young girl alone. All of her support lines in the school met with you about your obsession. Even Jerry and I warned you about the potential perils of your actions, but…"

"That's water long past," Fanny interrupted. "I asked you about the options. What does this all mean?"

Oliver rose and went to Fanny's side. He rested his hands on the two chair arms and railed, "What it means, my dear, Ms. Dykson, is that this district stands to pay out thousands of dollars for failing to provide a safe and orderly environment I stand to lose my job and you, my biased, hypocritical woman, stand to lose your job, your certificate to teach school and your life's saving."

Anger replaced concern as Dykson sprang to her feet and pessimistically snapped, "Just for calling that sexpot a name? I don't believe it!"

"Believe what you want," Hatch growled. "That young lady, regardless of your opinion, is entitled to an education devoid of ethnic slurs and threats from a teacher whose responsibility it is to act in place of the parent while she is in our care.

Oliver once again began to pace the office floor. Snapping his body in Fanny's direction, he pointed an index finger and barked, "You, lady, failed in that responsibility. If fact, you went out of your way to create a hostile environment both in and out of the school setting. Your actions were intolerable in anybody's book."

Dykson turned away from the superintendent. "I need to talk to Farmer. Maybe the association will find me a lawyer."

A cooler Oliver said, "You better hurry, Fanny, time is running out. If this goes to trial and you are found guilty, I will be required to terminate your employment immediately."

A beaten Fanny Dykson answered in an uncharacteristic gentle voice, "Ollie, what do you suggest?"

In frustration, Oliver threw his arms in the air. "I just don't know, Fanny. The Farintinos want you gone. I don't think that they will be satisfied with anything less at this point. There was a time when I thought an honest, 'I'm sorry', would have been sufficient." He went to the window and became lost in thought. When he turned back to Fanny he added, "They now have the expense of an attorney."

"They like Jim Rahin. Do you think that they would listen to him?" Fanny asked.

"I spoke with Rahin. He refuses to intercede. He said you have been a pain in the ass ever since he arrived. He says you are a brilliant teacher, but a stupid individual. You had the opportunity to apologize, but you refused. He said that now you are on your own."

Dykson took a seat and for the next thirty minutes, explored the what if's with Hatch.

"…so," Oliver concluded. "If I were you, I would think about leaving New York State. You said you had thought about going to North Carolina. That's not a bad idea."

"But I need a job."

"Fanny, they need teachers in North Carolina. The state is growing faster than they can find teachers to man their schools. If you stay here until you can find a job it may be too late. If you are brought to trial, you may not have a license to teach anywhere."

A shaken physical education teacher went to the door and turned the brass door knob. Hesitating a moment, she looked back to Oliver Hatch. "After I have spoken with Jerry Farmer, and hear what he has to say, I'll let you know my decision."

Chapter 33

JERRY FARMER WAITED IMPATIENTLY in Jim Rahins office. The tranquil morning belied the hostility that was brewing over Fanny Dykson's pending litigation. Farmer was there to speak to Jim about interceding with the Farintinos on Fanny's behalf. Farmer's contention was that regardless of how Jim felt about her as a person, he would be derelict in his responsibility to the district if he didn't ask the Farintinos to drop their legal action. Jerry knew that if the Farintios dropped their action against the school, there was a good chance the judge would throw out the family's claims against Fanny.

"How much longer will Mr. Rahin be tied up?" Farmer asked Jim's secretary.

Alison frowned. "Gee, Mr. Farmer, I really can't say. He and Mr. Hatch have been in conference for over an hour. Let me interrupt and see if he will give me an indication of time."

Farmer looked at his watch. "Tell him that I only need a minute of his time."

Alison nodded and walked the hall leading to Jim's office. She knocked gently and then opened the door.

"I'm sorry to disturb you, Mr. Rahin," she demurely intoned. "Mr. Farmer has been waiting. He says that he only needs a minute of your time and was wondering how much longer he should wait?"

Jim looked at Oliver Hatch. "Jerry has been vehement about his support of Dykson. He thinks that I should intervene for the sake of the district."

Oliver Hatch nodded and squinted into the sunlight that was bathing Jim's office through the window behind Jim's desk.

"He's right. Regardless of how you feel about Dykson, you owe it to this district to do what you can to alleviate any potential harm to its well-being."

Jim turned to Alison. "Inform Mr. Farmer that I will be with him shortly."

When Alison closed the door, Jim rose and went to Oliver's side. "I first owe a duty to the students of this district," he snapped. "Look, Ollie, I don't want to cause the district any financial harm, but if that woman had been dealt with early on we wouldn't be going through all this intrigue now."

"Are you saying that it's my fault?"

"Partly yours, Farmer's and others in this district who knew about what was going on and could have done something about it but didn't."

Oliver pushed his chair away from Jim and stood. "Let's get Farmer in here and see if we can come to some kind of consensus."

Jim returned to his desk and pushed the intercom for Alison. "Ms. Block, please ask Mr. Farmer to come in."

"Good morning gentlemen," Jerry said as he entered the room. "Thanks for taking the time to see me." He was dressed casually.

"Good morning, Jerry, I assume that your visit today is in regards to Ms. Dykson."

"Yes," Farmer said with a nod. "I know how you feel, but as despicable as Fanny's actions were this is more about what is in the best interest of the North Country School District."

"I agree with you on that," said Hatch. "A lawsuit will bring irreparable harm to the reputation of this community."

"You two guys should have thought about that when you were so complacent about what Ms. Dykson was doing to that young girl."

"As a union rep I'm supposed to support my fellow teachers," a defensive Farmer barked. "That's what I did."

227

"Even when you knew that the teacher was wrong?" Jim quizzed.

"Even when I don't necessarily agree with the actions," Jerry replied.

"I do that too, when there is a conflict between a teacher and a student, but when it's all said and done I put the teacher on notice that I thought the student was right and if there is another problem of similar circumstance I will support the student. You had a responsibility to let Ms. Dykson know that you disapproved with her behavior and that further misconduct on her part would not be supported by you or the union. The first responsibility of all of us should be to the kids. What are we teaching when we support conduct that is wrong?"

"That's easy to say," Jerry grumbled. "I have to work with these people every day."

"That's just my point," Jim rebuked. "We shouldn't have to work with people—teachers or anyone working with children—if they corrupt the ethics and values of what we as educators are trying to instill in those left in our care. I…"

"All right, we get the picture, Jim, but what can we do now," Hatch grumbled.

"I will ask the Farintinos to back off on their lawsuit if Fanny Dykson resigns and the district agrees to pay all legal fees incurred."

"The board isn't going to buy that," Oliver groaned.

"And I doubt that Fanny is going to resign," Farmer added.

"Well gentlemen then I guess we will have to let the chips fall where they may."

Oliver Hatch went to the door, looking back at Jim he said, "No matter how this goes down, Jim, I think you will have lost any support you might have had on that board. They know Ms. Dykson was wrong in her actions, but two wrongs won't make it right."

There was a crashing silence in the room when Oliver left.

After a brief moment of reflection, Farmer also went to the door. "Jim, I agree with Ollie. You have supporters on that board. If this incident goes to trial without an effort on your part to quell the hostility, your support will vanish."

"They can do what they want. I will do what I must," Jim replied.

THE NORTH CAROLINA SKY WAS ABLAZE WITH a ball of topaz surrounded by a blue sapphire. Dykson and her companion, Connie Anders, enjoyed the fresh country air and tall pines as they drove from Fayetteville, South Carolina, where they had spent the night. The women were on their way to Charlotte, North Carolina to look for a job. Fanny had taken to heart the advice Oliver Hatch had given her a week earlier concerning her options and teaching future. Fanny was determined not to apologize to the Farintinos unless absolutely necessary; time was running out.

"How far is it to Charlotte?" Connie asked. "I need to find a bathroom."

"I'm not sure, but we just passed a gas station. Keep an eye open for a McDonald's. We'll stop there, grab something to eat and gas up."

Just east of Hamlet, Fanny's 1967 four door Buick pulled into a small roadside coffee shop.

"It's not McDonald's, but it will do," Fanny said.

"Okay, Fan. Would you like a cup of coffee?"

"No, I'm going to hit the john. After I fill the tank I'll get a cup of coffee and a table."

Connie entered the diner and was greeted by a young waitress with bronze skin, bright eyes, and a strong southern drawl.

"How ya'all doing this mornin'?" the girl asked.

Connie blushed from embarrassment; she had difficulty understanding the girl's simple greeting. "I need to use the ladies' room," Connie answered.

"It's out back," the girl drawled. "I'll need ta getcha da kay." The waitress reached under the counter and retrieved a key secured to a large round wooden piece of wood marked "toilet" and handed it to Connie.

Connie left the diner and approached Fanny who was standing next to the car. An elderly black man with baggy trousers and a straw hat was pumping gas.

Connie tugged on Fanny's arm and whispered, "They don't have an indoor bathroom, just one outside toilet for men and women."

Fanny shot a quick glimpse at the diner then muttered, "I don't care. I have to go before I have an accident."

When the man finished filling the tank he ambled over to Fanny. "Das seven dollas." The old man smiled showing a face full of worn teeth.

Fanny fumbled with a small change purse and withdrew a few folded bills. After counting out the money she reluctantly handed it to the man.

"How far is it to Charlotte?" she asked.

The man thought a moment, rolled his bloodshot eyes and replied, "Ain't but an hour or so. Jus stay own dis here road"

Both Dykson and Anders were obliged to use the noxious toilet facility with no lock on the door. Fanny was first to enter. What she saw was abhorrent. "God this is awfully dirty," she said.

Connie stood guard outside the toilet and anguished over the thought of following Fanny when her turn came. "Maybe I'll try to hold it," she mumbled.

An hour later the girls saw the sign: WELCOME TO NORTH CAROLINA. At a welcome booth they found an information brochure about Charlotte including a phone number for the Charlotte County School District. Fanny called the number and explained to the woman that answered that she was looking for a teaching job.

Before resuming their drive, both girls availed themselves of the clean women's room.

Connie Anders interviewed at two o'clock that afternoon at the Blueridge Road Middle School.

Fanny's interview was scheduled for three at the high school.

Connie's interview was with the school's principal. He was a man in his early forties as far as she could tell. He was of average height and build with a crew cut and glasses. The principal's overall appearance was droll, but flirtatious.

Hamilton Rowan the third was a graduate of Oswego State University in New York. When he learned that Connie was certified as a science teacher and she too graduated from Oswego, he decided to gobble her up before another school laid claim. Connie was offered a job teaching general science to students in the eighth grade. Rowan had a secondary reason for hiring Anders. He was a single man who had just been smitten by the girl from New York.

FANNY'S INTERVIEW WAS WITH A COMMITTEE of teachers. If she passed muster with the staff she would interview with the high school principal—Bubba Myers. It was a dilatory move to allow the principal time to make some calls.

"Good afternoon," said Myers, after Alison had introduced herself. "This is Bubba Myers calling from Charlotte North Carolina. I'd like to speak with your high school principal."

"One moment, Mr. Myers, I'll see if Mr. Rahin is in his office."

"Mr. Hatch," Myers shouted. "Not Mr. Rahin, I need to speak with the principal."

A perplexed Alison Block responded in a radiant voice, "I'm sorry Mr. Myers, but Mr. Rahin is the high school principal."

"Perhaps I'm confused," Myers replied. "Ms. Fanny Mae Dykson is applying for a job here in Charlotte County. I thought she said that her principal's name was Oliver Hatch."

"It's possible that she gave the wrong name by mistake," Alison answered. "I can connect you with Mr. Hatch's office. I believe that Mr. Rahin is there also."

"That'll be fine," Myers replied. "Perhaps I'll speak with both of them. Apparently we have two of your staff members here interviewing today."

Jim Rahin was the first to speak with Myers.

"Good afternoon," Jim said with a lilt in his voice. "I understand that you are interviewing a couple of my teachers."

"Yes," Myers concurred. "A Ms. Dykson is applying for a position in our physical education department and Constance Anders is interviewing for a teaching position in our middle school science department." Myers paused. "I'm a little confused though," he murmured. "I was sure that Ms. Dykson said that her principal was Oliver Hatch."

Jim started laughing. "I often get that here too. People get so nervous about interviewing that they often give the wrong name of their immediate supervisor. It really doesn't matter, I'm sure t both Mr. Hatch and I will give you a positive account of Ms. Dykson's teaching abilities."

"I met Ms. Dykson before she interviewed with our staff committee. I was less concerned with her teaching. She appears to be well qualified and I see where she had a tenure appointment. However, my first impression of the woman was that she was possessed of a dour personality." Myers paused. "How does she relate to staff, students and the community?"

Jim found the question formidable. He teetered on the right and wrong of the answer he was about to give. "Bubba, inasmuch as Fanny gave you Oliver's name, I'm going to let him speak to you about her overall personal attributes."

Oliver glared at Jim, and covered the mouthpiece on the phone. "Thanks a lot, pal. Hi Bubba, Oliver Hatch here. I guess the best way for me to characterize Ms. Dykson is to say that still water runs deep. Yeah, she comes off stiff and unyielding, but beneath that gloomy exterior is a warm breeze that blows an ingratiating personality." Oliver's conscience started to gnaw at him. "You know as well as I that you can't please everyone. Even Fanny has her detractors, but on balance, I think you will be pleased with her."

Jim and Oliver spent twenty minutes on the phone; in the end, Bubba Myers was satisfied. He informed Oliver that he intended to offer Fanny a job.

Oliver Hatch slapped Jim on the back, leaped for joy, and gasped, "It's over. She's gone." Oliver went to the phone. "I have to let the board know."

Jim placed his hand on Oliver's arm. "Hold on boss, there's still a little matter of the action against the school for its complicity."

Oliver paused. "Jim, you were right here when Mrs. Farintino said that she wanted Dykson gone. Well, she's gone."

Jim shook his head and waggled a finger at his boss. "You're forgetting something."

Oliver's ecstasy dissipated. "What are you driving at, Rahin?"

Jim started rubbing his finger and thumb together. "Money," he mused. "The lawyer fees and court costs are still out there. Remember?"

Oliver felt a slight shudder pass through him. "How much do you think they have incurred?"

"I don't know, but I can try to find out."

Jim drove his Chrysler Premier to the Farintino home. It was four in the afternoon. Sal Farintino was still at work, but Yolanda Farintino was sitting on the front porch. Melinda was seated to her mother's right reading a book. Mother and daughter spontaneously looked up as Jim started to ascend the steps leading to the porch.

"Good afternoon," Jim greeted. "I have some good news."

Yolanda Farintino set her knitting down and studied her guest.

Melinda marked her place in the book with a bookmark and went to greet Jim. "Mr. Rahin, it's always nice to see you. What's the good news?"

"Does it have to do with Ms. Dykson?" Mrs. Farintino asked.

"Yes it does," Jim replied. "She will no longer be teaching physical education at North Country."

Not taking time to savor the news, Yolanda asked tersely "Was she fired?"

Jim hesitated trying to couch his wording. "We were working on that when she left. She took a job down south—in the Carolinas."

Jim could read disappointment on Mrs. Farintino's brow.

"I wanted her to suffer just like my Melinda suffered."

Melinda went to her mother's side. "It's okay Mom. The important thing is that she's gone. No other student will have to put up with her bigotry."

"I have been asked to seek your word that now that Dykson is gone you will retract your suit against the district."

Mrs. Farintino retook her chair. "I don't think we can. We have bills. If we don't go through with the suit we'll be stuck with the lawyer's fee and other expenses. Sal knows more about that than I do."

"Mrs. Farintino, if you will let me know what your expenses are, I will try to convince the board to pay. You should not have to get stuck with that expense."

"I will talk to my husband," Yolanda said. "Whatever Sal decides to do will be okay with me."

Jim thanked Mrs. Farintino for her time and returned to the school.

Chapter 34

IN EARLY AUGUST THE NORTH COUNTRY Central Board of Education authorized the payment of three thousand dollars in satisfaction of legal fees incurred by the Farintinos. It was a small remuneration considering the alternative. Nevertheless, some board members blamed Jim. The prevailing opinion with the majority of the board was that Jim could have prevented the entire matter by asking that Fanny Dykson be suspended with pay pending a hearing before the board.

"I want to thank you, Jim, for not mentioning to the board that you had written Dykson up and that I threw the damn letter away. If I had placed the letter in her file I would have had grounds to suspend her and hold a hearing before the board." Oliver began to pace. "If I had had the guts to do that Fanny might have changed. The district wouldn't be out the money and the Farintinos would not have been put through the rigors of all that legal mumbo jumbo."

Jim sipped his coffee and replied in a sympathetic tone, "We all make mistakes, Ollie. Remember, at the time you were trying to build rapport with the Teachers' Association."

"Yeah, but that one was a no brainer. I should have known better. I was too lenient."

Jim set the cup he was holding on the top of Oliver's desk. "Ollie, now that the lawsuit is behind us, I want you to be the first to know that I'm being considered for the position as superintendent for Fort Craven Central School. It's a small school district southeast of Utica. Hope and I are going to have dinner with some board members this week. I guess that puts me on their short list. The board's decision has come down to me and an applicant from Long Island."

Oliver Hatch was caught off guard. "Geez, Jim, I knew you were looking, but I thought you were going to stay at least another year."

"Well I was, but this opportunity came up and with the climate here, with the board being what it is I thought it might be a good time for me to move on."

Oliver grumbled, "Does anyone else know?"

"No."

"If you get the job, will you stay long enough to bring Dean Bruce up to date on programs and such? I know you have lots of faith in his ability, but he's not you—if you know what I mean."

Jim smiled and went to the door. "I'll let you know how I make out." Halfway into the outer hall, Jim turned back. "Don't worry about Dean. Alison knows as much about running this high school as I do. She'll help him keep things on track."

In his office Jim contacted his secretary. "Alison, would you come in please. I have something very important to tell you."

Alison entered the room like a fresh, cool breeze on a stuffy autumn evening. Leaving her behind would be the most difficult thing Jim would have to endure. During the years as his secretary, Alison had been as close to him as his own wife. Her loyalty and invigorating work ethic had ingratiated her to him.

"Yes Mr. Rahin. What can I do for you?" Her smile, as always, was brilliant.

"Have a seat, Alison," said Jim. "I have something to say and it isn't going to be easy."

Alison's smile dimmed. "What have I done?" she gasped.

"Nothing, that's the problem, you have been the best secretary a man could hope for."

Alison panicked. "I'm being fired!"

Jim left his chair and went to her. "No, Alison, it's nothing like that. I may be leaving North Country. I just informed Mr.

Hatch and I thought it would be awful if you heard it from somebody other than me."

Alison's eyes glistened as emotion engulfed her. "I knew you had been looking, but somehow I never thought you would really leave."

"I'm pretty sure I will be offered a job as the district superintendent sometime this week."

Jim returned to his desk and sat quietly while Alison dabbed her eyes and forced a smile.

"Well, this is a moment for joy, not tears," Alison said. "Where is the lucky school?"

"If all goes well an announcement will be made by the end of the week. The school district is Fort Craven—it's near Utica.

"Hope is going to like that," Alison sniffled.

"Yeah, she's excited.

"Will we ever see you again?"

"I'm sure I'll be back this way from time to time. We are going to keep the cabin. Besides, our friendship doesn't have to end just because I'm taking another job."

"What about the house?"

"I'll put it on the market and hope it sells fast. If not, I'll try to rent it to an incoming staff member. Hope will also look for a job closer to the city."

Alison had almost recovered from the shock when there was a knock on the door. "Come in," Jim called.

Dean Bruce entered the office. "Jim, I'm sorry to intrude, but you need to look at this list of teacher assignments and see if you want to make any changes."

Jim winked at Alison. "Well, Mr. Bruce, if you were sitting in my chair what would you do?"

Dean grinned and raised his eyebrows. "Boy, if I were in your shoes, I'd move the…"

"Do it," Jim interrupted

Dean balked. "Yeah, but…"

"I said do it," Jim reiterated. "I'll support any decisions you make. In fact, I'm turning over the scheduling changes to you as of right now."

The broad grin on Dean's face returned. "Are you sure?"

Jim rose and went to the door. He placed his hand on Bruce's shoulder. "In fact, my friend, I'm going to let you work with Alison. She'll help you if I'm not here and you have a question..."

"Alison?" Dean blurted

"Yup—you will find that the school secretary is the heart and soul of this whole operation. A secretary can either make or break a principal. Treat her well. Now get out of here and let me finish what I was doing."

When Dean left the office Jim broke into laughter. "It's going to be his neck now. He will have to learn that the buck stops with him."

"You still should have told him," Alison giggled. "He may get himself into trouble."

A more serious Jim Rahin replied, "I'm relying on you to see that that doesn't happen."

ON FRIDAY JIM AND HOPE DROVE to Fort Craven Central School to meet with the school district's board of education. The trip took them east along the Mohawk River—just below the village of Herkimer.

When they arrived at the school they were greeted by the school board president and his wife. Caleb Pomroy was a large, imposing man of fifty some-odd years. He owned a small quick-stop on Route 5. He had three sons—one was still in school. Caleb had served on the board for fifteen years, the last five as its president.

Sylvia Pomroy reminded Jim of a painted beach ball; her arms and legs were too short for her body.

Jim exited the car and walked to the passenger's side to open the door for Hope.

"Oh, what a gentleman," Sylvia bubbled as her jowls danced. "I'm Mrs. Pomeroy—Caleb's wife." Mrs. Pomroy extended her hand in greeting.

If you are Mrs. Pomroy, you didn't have to say that you are Caleb's wife, Jim thought as he took her hand.

"Hi, Jim, it's good to see you again. Did you have an easy trip down from the north country?" Caleb interrupted.

"Yeah, it was a pretty drive." Gesturing toward Hope, Jim added "I'd like to introduce my wife Hope."

Sylvia waddled to Hope's side. "I'm so pleased to meet you my dear." She paused then after giving Hope the once over she continued. "My but you're a dainty little thing. We're going to have to fatten you up a little." Sylvia giggled her way back to where her husband was standing.

"Don't mind my wife," Caleb joked with a broad smile. "She thinks that every woman should have a great figure. To her, round is a great figure."

Sylvia laughed and joked, "Caleb just rolls me where he wants me to go."

Jim and Hope smiled politely.

"The rest of the board is waiting inside. Shall we join them?" Caleb asked.

Hope held Jim by the arm as they followed the Pomroys into the school.

The Fort Craven school building was built in 1935. It was old, but clean and well maintained. The halls and floors shined.

The foursome walked in silence until they reached the school's cafeteria. Upon entering the room they were greeted by the rest of the board.

The first to greet them was a former school teacher who was now a board member.

Julia Lanigan had taught sixth grade at Craven for thirty-five years. She retired two years earlier, ran for the vacant board seat, and won. Rumor had it that she was the reason the former superintendent left. Julia never married. Now as a board member, she conducted her day-to-day activities as if she were an assistant superintendent.

Jim knew as superintendent he would need to change that arrangement.

Rufus Upjohn, a local farmer, operated a dairy farm on the edge of town with his wife Matilda; Mrs. Upjohn didn't attend the dinner. Rufus was slight of build and short. Jim could tell from the hard, rough calluses on Rufus' hands that he led a hard life.

Easton Lynch, a tall, thin man of sixty fancied himself a poet. He claimed to have taught English poetry at Columbia, but there was little to verify his claim of employment. His wife, Gloria was a mousy little thing who could barely say hello. She dressed like a teenager. I wonder how she and Sylvia get along, Jim thought.

Roman Jervis was about Jim's age. He worked in the textile industry in nearby Mohawk. He was a graduate of Utica College and seemed down to earth. Roman and his wife Lee had two daughters in school. Roman had dark skin and brown eyes. His five-eight stature was fit; Lee Jervis was about Hope's size.

Following a round of introductions the spouses retired to the office conference room; the board members and Jim remained in the cafeteria.

"Mr. Rahims," Easton Lynch quipped after messaging the pencil-line mustache under his nose. "Fort Craven is a historic community with conservative values. We vote Republican and we expect our superintendent to reflect our values."

Jim's eyes narrowed as he starred at Lynch. "The Ra-HINs have always been a little old-fashioned." Jim emphasized the correct pronunciation of his name. He spoke in a soft yet sharp tone. "I don't necessarily vote the party line. I vote my conscience based on the candidate, his platform and how I feel about the individual."

Pausing, Jim looked at the other members of the board. "As far as upholding your values, I am a team player so long as the board's directives are legal and in the best interest of the students we serve."

There was an immediate undertone as board members mulled over Jim's comments.

Caleb Pomroy stepped forward. "Are we to understand, Mr. Rahin that you would not do a task ordered by the board if you felt that it was unreasonable?"

Jim shook his head. "No, I am here to serve at the pleasure of the board. But, please understand that I am also an officer of the State Education Department. I will not do something that I know to be illegal under education law or contrary to the best interest of children.

The undertone became louder.

"If what you seek for Fort Craven is a rubber stamp, a yes man, then I'm not the guy you want for the job."

Easton Lynch slammed his boney hand hard against the cafeteria table, pursed his chicken like lips and clucked, "What we don't want, Mr. Rahin, is a superintendent who is a loose cannon, who thinks he can ignore the wishes of this board and do as he damn well please."

"Yes," the spinster Julia Lanigan snapped, as she addressed Jim. "I spend a great deal of my time each day in the schools monitoring what is happening in the classrooms. When I ask that something be done, I expect your cooperation."

Jim shook his head and grinned. "Lady and gentlemen of the board, please understand that your authority lies in unity. You have no authority as an individual. If you are looking for change, you must ask for that while acting in concert with the other members of the board in open session. Changes must have the approval of the board as a whole. Jim turned to Julia. "Ms. Lanigan, if this board chooses to appoint me superintendent you will not be allowed to wander into schools and classrooms without the prior permission of the building principal and the classroom teacher."

Jim looked at the rest of the board members and lowered his voice. "As your superintendent there will be no micro-managing of the district's business. I will keep you informed on what is happening. If you, as a board, wish to make changes that's your prerogative. I will tell you where I stand on an issue. If we disagree and what you ask is not illegal it will be done your way. If it turns out to be a bad decision, you—not me, will have to answer to the public."

"That sounds more than fair to me," the small farmer said.

"I agree with Rufus," Roman Jervis echoed. "I, for one, don't want a yes man running the school." He looked at Julia Lanigan and pointed. "Julia I recall a time when you got pretty upset and came to a board meeting to complain because a parent entered your classroom without your knowledge. Well, all Mr. Rahin is saying is that he will not allow people to do what you had complained about."

Julia's face reddened and she stomped back to her spot at one of the cafeteria tables. "There is a difference," she scolded. "I'm a board member with over thirty years of teaching experience." She ran her hands over her hair and straightened her blouse. "That woman who barged into my classroom was an ignorant farm—"

"Not all farmers are ignorant," Rufus interrupted. "And not all teachers are smart." He grinned. "I remember you telling the board at a meeting not too long ago that in your judgment a certain teacher, with whom you had taught, was stupid."

There was an undertone of laughter as Lanigan slumped into a chair. "I didn't mean that farmers are stupid," she grumbled.

The interview went on for another thirty minutes until Angela Massatoni, the food service manager, appeared in the room and motioned to Pomroy. The conversation in the room stopped. Caleb nodded his head and the cafeteria manager disappeared into the kitchen.

"Mr. Rahin, we've bantered enough. If we don't know where you stand on education and the superintendency after three interviews, we shouldn't be on the selection committee. He looked at Lanigan. "Julia, will you inform the ladies that Mrs. Massatoni is ready to serve."

Without comment Julia left the room.

"Jim, we decided to have our cafeteria staff members prepare the dinner. I think you will be impressed with the quality of the meals served here at Fort Craven.

TWO HOURS LATER, JIM THANKED THE board for the opportunity to meet with them again. After shaking hands with the five members he was sure that at least two would not be voting in his favor. Lanigan and Lynch had all they could do to touch his hand and say goodbye.

Caleb walked Jim and Hope to the car. When Hope was seated in the passenger's seat, Caleb addressed Jim in a quiet whisper.

"You know, Jim, the board will make its final determination after tomorrow night. We will be meeting with the other finalist and his wife under the same format." Pomroy looked off into the darkness and gave a loud sigh. "Jim, you obviously are a very headstrong individual. I like that in a leader. You aren't afraid to speak your mind. I think you are an honest man." Caleb's mop of white hair bobbed as he shook his head and scowled.

"Unfortunately not everyone appreciates candor. You made a couple of enemies tonight."

Jim flashed a quick smile. "Better now than later after I'm appointed," he replied. "With me, what you see is what you get."

Jim walked to the driver's side of the car. "Mr. Pom—Caleb, I want to thank you for your support. If you ask anyone who knows me they will tell you that with me kids come first." He opened the door and entered. After rolling down the window he added, "Anyone who doesn't feel that way has no business being a teacher, administrator or board member."

As Jim drove away he noticed Caleb Pomroy standing in the dark shadow of the car's red tail lights. He's a good man, Jim thought.

On Monday morning Jim was preparing to drive to North Country. He was trying to build a little courage. How could he face Ollie and tell him that he didn't get the job? Jim thought about the disappointment Hope felt when he told her about the interview. She had called him a pigheaded ass.

"Why did you have to antagonize the board with your moral indignation?" she had said.

Jim finished his coffee and swallowed the last bit of burnt toast.

"Hope," he called. "I'm leaving. I'll see you sometime after four."

Jim was in the garage when Hope stuck her head out of the door and yelled, "Jim, phone."

Jim reentered the house and Jim took the phone. "Jim here."

"Congratulations," a voice on the other end of the line boomed.

It was Caleb Pomroy.

"Caleb!" Jim exclaimed. "I didn't expect to hear from you. I thought when I didn't hear from you on Saturday that the other guy won out."

"It was close. Lanigan and Lynch were holding out for the other candidate. When we couldn't reach a total agreement we decided to ask the women their opinion. Hope swung the deal. Everyone, including Julia, loved your wife."

There was a pause. When Caleb spoke again he was calmer. "Jim you will be officially appointed at the next meeting. We will expect you on the job by the first of September—sooner if possible."

Jim didn't know whether to shout for joy or cry. It had been a long journey. When he finished talking to Caleb Pomroy he hugged Hope and prepared for his last drive to North Country High as its high school principal.

Chapter 35

THE PARKING LOT AT THE SCHOOL was packed. That's strange, Jim thought. I don't remember having scheduled a meeting. Maybe Dean did. He really is taking to the job. Jim parked next to Dean Bruce's car and entered the building. There were black balloons hung everywhere. He poked his head into the custodian's office, but no one was there. Upon entering the high school office he bumped into more balloons.

Jim called to Alison. She was seated at her desk speaking to someone on the telephone. "Alison, what's going on? What's with the balloons?"

Alison motioned for Jim to wait. "Yes, that's true. We will try to put something together—yes, I'll let you know," she told the person on the line.

When she finished her call Alison spun in her chair and greeted Jim with a generous smile. "Hi, boss, how was the weekend."

Jim was consumed with the balloons and forgot to tell Alison about his appointment. "Oh, the weekend was fine. Why all the balloons?"

"The teachers are having a get-together in honor of Fanny Dykson and Connie Anders because they are leaving. I guess the girls came home to pack."

Jim grumbled, "I suppose I'll have to go in and congratulate them."

"That would be a nice gesture. Mr. Hatch is already in there."

Jim went to his office and took off his jacket. "Have you been over there yet?" he yelled.

"No, I'll go with you. This phone has been crazy all morning."

"I feel like a hypocrite," Jim snapped. "I don't like that woman and never did."

"What about Connie? She has never given you grief."

Jim shook his head. "Yeah, you're right. She's a good teacher. The kids will miss her."

Suddenly it struck Jim that Alison was so hung-up on the girls that she hadn't asked him about his interview. As they rounded the corner to the auditorium he thought, That's not like her.

Upon opening the auditorium door there was a cloud burst of cheers. The room was filled with banners and well-wishers.

Jim looked at Alison. She was applauding. He was immediately surrounded by staff members, all yelling, laughing, and talking at the same time.

Oliver Hatch took Jim's hand. "Congratulations, Jim, we all wish you the best."

"But—but how did you know? I just got the call this morning."

"On Saturday one of your board members from Craven, a former teacher there called Jerry Farmer to get the scoop on you. Apparently she found you overbearing, but after talking with Jerry her opinion changed."

Jim laughed. "Julia Lanigan. She taught sixth grade at Fort Craven for over thirty years. When she retired she became a board member. Julia is the micro-managing type." Jim waved to Joe Malone. "Anyway, Lanigan didn't like it when I told that her micro-managing days were over."

"How was the board as a whole?" Oliver asked.

"Not too bad. I'll have to gain the confidence of Julia and a guy by the name of Easton Lynch." Jim made a face. "He's a tall, thin drink of water from England—I think. He claims to have taught poetry at Columbia. The problem is that no one has been able to substantiate his claim. He can be a prissy bitch. He thinks that the superintendent should always do exactly what the board says and wants."

Oliver Hatch's eyes widened. "What did you say to that?"

A chant started, asking Jim to make a speech. "I'll fill you in on the meeting later—in your office."

It was close to noon when Jim left the auditorium. He returned to his office and approached his secretary.

"Alison, that's the first time you ever allowed me to be blindsided. I wondered why you didn't ask me about the job. You already knew."

"I'm sorry, Mr. R, but they made me promise." Alison rose from her desk and went to the counter where Jim was standing. "When Jerry called to tell me about the call he had received the word spread like wildfire. Mr. Hatch approved the balloons and the reception."

"Well I appreciate the support, but I'm not much on goodbye parties."

Alison grimaced. "Then I guess I better tell you so you aren't blindsided again."

Jim's eyes narrowed and he frowned. "Tell me what?"

"Mr. Hatch and the board are planning a surprise party for you this weekend."

"Like hell," Jim bellowed. "I won't go."

"I didn't have anything to do with it so you better see Mr. Hatch," Alison said. "Word has already gone out to the community. A bunch of people have already said they are coming."

In frustration Jim slammed his hand onto the counter. "Geez, I wish people wouldn't do that. I hate saying goodbye."

Twenty minutes later Jim was seated in front of Oliver's desk. "...so you see .Ollie. that in addition to having to listen to a bunch of people saying how sorry they are to see me go when they really were glad I was leaving is bullshit. I just hate saying goodbye. I will say farewell to those who I know are sincere."

"Okay, Jim, I'll see that the party is cancelled, but before the weather changes let's get out and play some golf."

"You got it. Maybe we can meet in Utica. Valley View is a great course. I think you'll like it.

"Do they have any good Italian restaurants down there?" Jim flashed a grin. "The best in New York State!"

ON SEPTEMBER FIRST OLIVER called Jim.

"Hey, Jim, are you ready for the start of the school year?"

"Hello Ollie, yeah, I think I'm ready. I have a good staff here. Most of the teachers graduated from the school or have lived in the immediate area. They have a vested interest in what happens here." Jim hesitated. "I still have the challenge of winning over two votes. It's going to be a challenge to get things I want. I have a majority, but I would like the full support of the board. What's up at your end?"

"Same old, same old. Bruce seems to have things under control and all the staffing is complete."

"That's great."

"Jim, I'm coming to Utica this weekend. How about getting together for some golf and dinner?"

"Sounds good to me. What time is good for you?"

"Late morning would be great. That would allow us time for dinner before I have to climb back over the mountain north."

ON SATURDAY MORNING Jim met Oliver, Dean Bruce and Joe Malone at ten forty-five. Joe and Dean took the opportunity to join the outing.

Joe Malone's first drive put the others on notice that he intended to win. The foursome had agreed on playing twenty-five cents a hole to the winner; double on birds. Two tie, all tie.

Oliver decided to drive with an iron rather than his driver. "I can't hit my driver to save my ass," he admitted

Dean was a novice. He had just recently started playing golf and continued to make all of the traditional mistakes of a first-time golfer.

Jim, loved to play golf, but he wasn't very good.

In the end Joe took most of the money, a whopping two dollars and twenty-five cents. Oliver won seventy-five cents, Jim a quarter, and Dean had to pay everyone. After putting the clubs away the men went to the lounge for a glass of beer and some laughter.

By five o'clock Jim was getting hungry. "Hey, Ollie, I thought you said something about having dinner after golf."

"I'm ready," said Oliver. "Where's a good Italian restaurant?"

"How about Cavallo's in New Hartford?" Jim asked. "They usually have a special and the prices are reasonable."

"I have never been to the Chesterfield Restaurant over on Bleecker Street. I heard their food is excellent," Dean said. "How about going there?"

"If you've never been to the Chesterfield, it's a must," Joe added. "I never had a bad meal."

"Then the Chesterfield it is," Oliver chimed.

The Chesterfield was located in east Utica just before Culver Avenue. Jim was familiar with the area. Many of his Italian relative' on his mother's side of the family lived in that part of the city.

Jim drove to Culver Avenue and then west on Bleecker Street. A few blocks later he reached the Chesterfield. To his chagrin the parking lot was full. He circled the block and parked on the street across from the restaurant. Jim exited the vehicle and waited for Oliver, but Oliver was nowhere to be found. I couldn't have lost him, he thought. Maybe they found a space to park in the lot and went in.

Jim crossed the street and waited a few minutes in front of the building. The smell of tomato sauce permeated the air enhancing his hunger. After waiting a minute or so Jim decided to go inside.

As he entered the restaurant his senses were overwhelmed with the full odor of an Italian kitchen, the chatter of men and women at the bar and bartenders clinking glasses as they poured the next round of drinks. Waiters and waitresses bustled about ordering drinks, carrying trays filled with picture perfect food and ringing up the bills of satisfied customers who had finished eating.

Jim scanned the faces around him in anticipation of spotting one of his buddies at the bar; they weren't there. He nudged his way through a family waiting to be seated and walked into the main dining area. There was music playing in the banquet room located behind a set of closed oak doors. There must be a wedding going on, he surmised.

Once again Jim did a visual search of the dining area hoping to catch a glimpse of his golf buddies.

There was a tap on his shoulder. He turned to face a young waitress wearing a toothy smile. "Are you Mr. Rahims?" she asked.

Jim groaned. "Close. I'm Mr. Rahin."

The girls faced showed a flicker of embarrassment before replying. "I'm sorry, Mr. Rahin. I was told to tell you that your friends are in the banquet hall." She stretched her smile. "This way please."

The waitress guided Jim along a narrow hall until they reached the solid oak door that had sealed off the music from the rest of the diners. When she opened the door Jim squinted. He had trouble seeing inside. The room was darker than the inside of an unlit closet.

Suddenly the lights went on and the room jumped alive with the cheers of a hundred well-wishers.

"Surprise!" people yelled time and again.

At the first table stood his golfing buddies, their wives, Hope, and Alison Block all applauding.

Jim smiled sheepishly and went to Hope's side. "Was this your idea?" he asked.

Hope shook her head. "No. I know better. I didn't know about this until after you had left the house this morning."

Jim scrunched up his mouth until his nose wrinkled. "Alison, is this your doing?"

"No," Alison replied. "I told you that I wouldn't be a party to blindsiding you again, but I think this is great."

"If you must blame someone, blame us," Oliver said as he was immediately joined by Dean and Joe. We weren't about to let you leave without a party."

Jim filled with pride and humility. He shook hands with his friends and said, "I started out wanting to become a superintendent of schools, but no accomplishment in my life will ever equal the reward of friendship that I feel here tonight, thank you all."